SIMPLY WICKED

D1004511

Books by Kate Pearce

SIMPLY SEXUAL

SIMPLY SINFUL

SIMPLY SHAMELESS

SIMPLY WICKED

SIMPLY INSATIABLE

SIMPLY FORBIDDEN

Published by Kensington Publishing Corp.

FOUNTAINDALE PUBLIC LIBRARY DISTRICT
300 West Briarcliff Road
Bolingbrook, IL 60440-2894
(630) 759-2102

SIMPLY WICKED

KATE PEARCE

APHRODISIA

KENSINGTON BOOKS
http://www.kensingtonbooks.com

APHRODISIA BOOKS are published by

Kensington Publishing Corp.
119 West 40th Street
New York, NY 10018

Copyright © 2009 by Kate Pearce

All rights reserved, No part of this book may be reproduced in any form or by any means without the prior written consent of the Publisher, excepting brief quotes used in reviews.

All Kensington Titles, Imprints, and Distributed Lines are available at special quantity discounts for bulk purchases for sales promotions, premiums, fund-raising, and educational or institutional use.

Special book excerpts or customized printings can also be created to fit specific needs. For details, write or phone the office of the Kensington special sales manager: Kensington Publishing Corp., 119 West 40th Street, New York, NY 10018, attn: Special Sales Department, Phone: 1-800-221-2647.

Aphrodisia and the A logo Reg. U.S. Pat & TM Off.

ISBN-13: 978-0-7582-3221-2
ISBN-10: 0-7582-3221-7

First Kensington Trade Paperback Printing: October 2009

10 9 8 7 6 5 4 3 2

Printed in the United States of America

This book is dedicated to my mother-in-law, Lolo, who didn't like to read the "naughty bits" but was always thrilled by my success anyway. Rest in peace.

1

London 1819

"Oh God, where am I?"

Anthony Sokorvsky opened one eye and swiftly closed it again. The birch floorboards he'd glimpsed and the black walls hung with instruments of pain and sexual gratification meant only one thing: he was still at Madame Helene's pleasure house. He licked his lips, tasting dried blood, brandy and the acrid tang of another man's cum.

With a groan he rolled onto his stomach, wincing as his morning erection scraped the rough wood. He was naked and still in the punishment corner. At least someone had had the decency to take the manacles from his wrists. Gingerly he sat up, fighting the urge to retch with every painful movement. What the hell had he done last night?

He stifled another groan. Nothing worse, he suspected, than he'd subjected himself to for the last few months. But something had changed. For the first time, the pain had far outweighed the pleasure. His wrists were bruised, his arse hurt and his back was torn from the lash of a whip. He buried his hands in his hair and closed his eyes.

God, what kind of man allowed himself to be used by other men for their sexual pleasure? At first, it had excited him. Now, it simply felt like he deserved it. He was almost twenty-six; surely it was time to move on?

A discreet cough sounded at the doorway. Blinking, Anthony forced himself to look up. Judd, Madame Helene's butler, bowed and held out a brown embroidered dressing gown.

"Good morning, my lord. I have a fresh set of clothes waiting for you downstairs in Madame's apartment and a bath if you would like."

Vaguely, Anthony looked around for his own clothes and couldn't see them. With a sigh, he held out his hand for the dressing gown.

"Thank you, Judd. I'll be along in a moment."

He couldn't bear to meet the older man's gaze. What must the butler think of him wallowing in a shameful pool of lust of his own making? His last conscious thought, before sexual pain and pleasure had converged to render him senseless, was of Lord Minshom bending over him—his laughter as Anthony came helplessly against the unforgiving floor.

Grimacing, Anthony stumbled to his feet and grabbed the mantelpiece for support. There must have been others. Faceless, nameless men he'd allowed to fuck and fondle him, hurt him if they liked. *God, what was wrong with him?*

Sunlight streamed through the windows on the lower levels as Madame's efficient servants brought the house back to perfection before the revelry began all over again. He felt his way down to the basement, where Madame kept her apartment, and breathed a sigh of relief when he found the bedroom empty, the bath beyond already filled and awaiting him.

With a groan, he sank into the perfumed depths. His flesh stung as he discovered new hurts inflicted upon him. Even his hair was filthy with other men's leavings. He slid down into the bath and allowed the water to close over his head. For a long moment he held his breath, thought about letting it out, of water filling his lungs, of peace . . .

"Anthony?"

He resurfaced with a start to find Madame Helene sitting beside the bath. She wore a plain blue gown that did little to dim her natural allure. She was easily the most beautiful woman Anthony had ever seen, and he had observed plenty at the pleasure house—Madame Helene made sure of that.

"Anthony, why are you still here?"

He blinked slowly at her, allowing the water droplets to run down his face.

"I'm not sure. I must've fallen asleep."

She sighed and leaned forward to pat his shoulder. He swallowed hard at the soft contact. After the harshness of the night, her touch was almost unbearable. His eyes began to sting.

"Anthony, *mon ami*, I am worried about you. We are all worried about you."

He sat up straighter to study her concerned face. "God, Valentin doesn't know what I do here, does he?"

She shrugged, the motion as fluid and elegant as a cat's. "I haven't told him, but Peter knows. I'm not sure if he would tell your brother or not."

Anthony continued to stare at her, his fingers gripping the edge of the bath until they hurt. "You won't ever tell Val, will you?"

"Why not? He of all men might understand why you allow these men to do what they want to you."

"Val wouldn't understand. After his experiences with Aliabad in Turkey he told me he hates being touched by men. What the hell is he going to say if he thinks I enjoy it?"

Her enigmatic smile was fleeting. "Your brother is a very complicated man. Perhaps you worry more that he still feels responsible for what happened to you." She stroked his wet skin. "We all feel responsible, Anthony—you were forced into an intolerable situation, drugged, raped and held hostage by a man who . . ."

"I do not want to talk about Aliabad. It happened years ago." He glared at her. "In truth, I will not discuss it, *ever*. It has nothing to do with my sexual tastes now."

Helene stood up, her smile disappearing. "Denial didn't work for your brother. Why should it work for you?"

Anthony let out his breath. "I'm sorry, madame. You have been nothing but kindness itself, but I cannot continue this ridiculous conversation. I've decided to change my ways. I no longer intend to avail myself of your punishment rooms."

Helene's skeptical expression didn't change. "I'm glad to hear it. Perhaps it is time for you to investigate the lighter side of love and romance."

He managed to nod. "Perhaps you are right."

She turned toward the door. "Do you wish me to send a message to the shipping office?"

He frowned and tried to look around for a clock.

"What time is it?"

"A little after ten."

"Then I'm already doomed, I had an appointment with Valentin at nine."

To the sound of Helene's soft laughter, Anthony sank back down into the bath until his head was under the water. Val was extraordinarily perceptive. One look at Anthony's face and he would not only demand an explanation for his lateness, but insist on examining his every action for the past week.

He sensed Helene didn't believe he meant to change. What did she see in him that made her doubt him? Did he somehow advertise his willingness to be abused on his very countenance? He resurfaced and reached for the cup of coffee Helene had set down for him beside the bath.

"Would you like me to scrub your back?"

Anthony's startled gaze flew to the doorway. Framed against the sunlight stood Christian Delornay, Helene's son. A permanent fixture for the last year at the pleasure house, seeing as he now lived there and worked for his mother. In the past, Anthony had never paid much attention to him, being far too busy with his own pursuit of sexual excess to worry about another man's.

"No, I thank you."

Christian shrugged, the gesture eloquent of his French upbringing as was his slightly accented English. From his prone position in the bath, Anthony took Christian's measure and reckoned they were of similar height, although as he understood it, Christian was only twenty.

"Are you sure?"

At Christian's amused tone, a now familiar burning rage churned in Anthony's gut.

"Absolutely, and you can get out as well."

"I am perfectly within my rights to be here. This is my mother's dressing room after all." Christian moved closer until Anthony was forced to look up at him.

"You often frequent your mother's bedroom, do you?"

Christian smiled. "Unworthy of you, Lord Anthony. Try again."

Anthony closed his eyes. "Get out."

"I will if you agree to have dinner with me and my sister tonight."

"Why would I want to do that?"

Christian skimmed his fingers along the rim of the bath. Anthony couldn't take his eyes away from the slow gliding motion.

"Because I asked? Because you wish me to go away so that you can finish your bath in peace?"

"All right."

"You will come?"

Anthony glared up at his smiling companion. "I said I would; now get out and shut the door behind you."

Christian bowed. "We will see you at seven then in the main salon."

As soon as Christian left, Anthony got out of the bath and dressed hurriedly in the plain brown coat, black breeches and matching waistcoat Judd had left for him. If he caught a cab down to the shipping office by the docks, he should still be able to meet Valentin. He paused to check his reflection in the mirror. His lips were a little bruised and swollen, but apart from that, he looked well enough. Lord Minshom was always very careful not to mark his lovers above the neck.

Anthony hurried up the steps of the Sokorvsky and Howard shipping company and cautiously opened the door to the main office. All seemed serene. He nodded at Taggart the office manager, who frowned and pointed at the clock. With an airy wave, Anthony continued down the hall to the narrow office he inhabited at the back of the two-story building.

He managed to open the shutters and sit down before his older brother strolled in through the open door.

"Good morning, Anthony, or should I say good afternoon?"

Anthony looked up from the quill pen he was pretending to sharpen and into his brother's face. People always exclaimed over Valentin's great beauty. Few seemed to notice the intelligence and ruthlessness concealed behind his less-than-amiable violet gaze.

"Good morning, Valentin. What can I do for you?"

"Be on time for your appointments?" Valentin took out his pocket watch and studied it. "We were supposed to meet at nine. It is now almost eleven. Where have you been?"

Anthony tried to look apologetic. "I overslept."

"You overslept." Valentin snapped the watch case shut and

began to pace the tattered strip of carpet. "That isn't good enough, Anthony. I run a business here, not a social club for bored aristocrats with nothing better to do with their time."

Heat rose on Anthony's cheeks. Trust his brother to come straight to the point. "That's unfair. I'm always punctual, and I do understand the nature of your business. Hell, I run it when you and Peter are out of town."

"Until recently I would've agreed with you, but in the last three months, you've become unreliable. You turn up late, you barely keep your mind on your work and you can't even re-member the names of our clients." Val stopped pacing and swung around to look at Anthony. "It's not good enough."

"This is the first time I've been late in over a month! Why are you making so much of it?"

"Because it is a symptom of the whole."

"What exactly are you trying to say, Val?"

"If you don't buck up your ideas, I'll be speaking to Peter about appointing a new deputy."

Anthony stared down at his clenched hands on the desk. "And what am I supposed to do instead?"

Val sighed. "For God's sake, Anthony, go back home and enjoy your life of privilege. You've worked here for four years and proved your independence to our father. Isn't it time for you to move on?"

Anthony got to his feet, his eyes level with his half brother. Yet another dismissal. Yet another man who thought him worthless. Anger streamed through him and threatened to sub-merge his usual common sense.

"Do you think I'm just playing at having a job?"

Val's eyebrows rose. "I beg your pardon?"

"Do you think you are the only one who can masquerade as a tradesman and yet still be in line for the position of marquis?"

"I don't want the title. You know that."

"Easy for you to say when it's yours, regardless."

"Do you want it?"

"No! It's just . . ." Anthony sighed in frustration.

A muscle twitched in Val's cheek. "Go on."

"I've worked hard for you and I've enjoyed every minute. Unlike many of my aristocratic friends, I still have my fortune intact, my health and my wits."

"I'm not sure about your wits."

Unease gnawed at Anthony's gut. "What?"

Valentin held his gaze. "You are late because you spend too much time whoring at Madame's pleasure house."

"And you never did that? Strange, I heard your reputation was legendary."

"I like to fuck, yes, but not like you do."

Anthony straightened. "And how do you know how I like to fuck?"

"I met Lord Minshom last night. In fact, he deliberately put himself in my way so that I had no choice but to speak to him."

"So?"

"He told me how much he enjoyed 'having' you last night."

"So?"

Val moved in close. "Dammit, Anthony, that man is a sexual predator of the worst kind. He likes to hurt, to punish and to humiliate."

"Perhaps he was lying."

"He wasn't. This isn't the first rumor that has reached me about your sexual tastes."

Anthony found he was trembling, a bone-deep tremor that he couldn't control. "Did Peter tell you what he saw me doing while you were 'having' him?"

Valentin's face tightened and his hand shot out. Anthony found himself flattened against the wall, Val's fingers at his throat. Every bruise on his body screamed a protest.

"Peter didn't tell me anything. And my relationship with him is my own business. This discussion is about you."

"I am perfectly capable of doing this job."

Val didn't release his punishing grip. "Really? Well you have the rest of this month to prove that to me and Peter before we ask you to leave."

He stepped back and rearranged the sleeve of his navy coat. "I have no wish to tell you how to live your life, but I cannot allow you to ruin my business."

Anthony cleared his throat. "Nice to see you have your priorities in order, Valentin. Business first, family second. You sound just like our father."

Valentin's mouth quirked up in the corner. "For our father, family *is* business." He let out his breath. "I have no right to tell you what to do. I can only offer you the benefit of my own experience."

Anthony stepped away from the wall and resumed his position at his desk. His fingers shook so badly he didn't dare pick up the pen knife in case he cut himself. He risked a smile at his brother.

"Please don't, Val. I've already had Madame Helene to deal with this morning, and no doubt I'll be hearing from Peter soon. I'm quite capable of resolving my own mistakes; in fact, I'd already decided to do so."

Valentin barked a laugh and turned to the door. "That's what I told myself, and look what a disaster that turned out to be."

"You have Sara, and a firstborn son. Doesn't that make you a lucky man?"

Val turned slowly around to stare at Anthony, his fine features for once softer and unguarded. "Yes it does, but I wasted many years denying my true self and what had been done to me."

"Then if you are at peace with your past, why can't you believe I will achieve that too?"

Anthony tensed at Valentin's suddenly shuttered expression. "I hope you do, brother. I truly hope you do. But allowing a man like Lord Minshom to own you, body and soul, scarcely seems the right way to achieve your aim."

"He does not own me."

Valentin's eyebrows rose. "Perhaps you should tell him that. He sounded remarkably proprietorial."

Anthony set his jaw and held his brother's gaze. "Damn you, *he does not own me.*"

Val bowed and headed for the door. "Then I wish you luck with your new path and hope you do not get led astray again."

"Thanks, Val. You have nothing to worry about, truly. I'll be a reformed man."

His brother's laugh echoed down the hall as he shut the door. Anthony barely restrained himself from running after him and planting him a facer. How dare his brother have so little faith in his ability to change? How dare he laugh?

Anthony took a deep breath and let it out. He'd prove everyone wrong. He'd become a model citizen, a business man of renown and a noted ladies' man—as soon as he'd found out what the Delornay twins wanted with him at dinner tonight. A thread of excitement wormed its way through his gloom.

2

Even at this early hour, the public rooms at the pleasure house were busy. At least forty people were gathered in the large salon, chattering and laughing, anticipating the delights Madame Helene had surely arranged for them. Anthony wondered how many of them frequented the top floor, the place where pain and pleasure blended and all pretenses were stripped away.

With a sense of wary anticipation, he spotted Christian at the buffet table and moved toward him.

"Good evening, Mr. Delornay."

"Good evening, my lord." Christian bowed and stepped back. "May I introduce my sister, Lisette?"

Anthony took the proffered hand and kissed it. Lisette Delornay was almost as tall as her brother, her fair hair not quite as blond, her eyes hazel. If the rumors were true, and Anthony had excellent sources, she looked more like her father, Lord Philip Knowles, than her twin did.

Despite her age, her smile was as sensual as her mother's, and Anthony couldn't help smiling back.

"It is a pleasure to meet you, my lord." Lisette gestured at the buffet. "If it pleases you, we will withdraw to our suite and eat privately."

He tucked her hand into the crook of his arm and patted it. "I'm happy to oblige, Miss Delornay. Please lead the way."

With Christian following along behind, Anthony soon found himself lost in the labyrinth of the big house as Lisette took him through to the more private areas.

"Here we are, my lord."

Anthony stepped through a doorway into a lavish suite of rooms decorated in pale silver and cream. A table stood in front of the fire laid for three, and an elderly woman rose from the couch to curtsey.

"Good evening, my lord. I'm Mrs. Smith-Porterhouse, Lisette's chaperone; I'll be in my room if anyone needs me."

Not an assignation then if Lisette's chaperone was nearby. Anthony wasn't sure if he was relieved or disappointed. Despite their age, the sexual antics of the Delornay twins were already legendary. Had he hoped to find an escape from Lord Minshom with them? He doubted they'd be able to stand up to the force of his lover's acerbic personality, but they were Helene's children after all.

"Lord Anthony?"

He bowed, aware that he'd been staring at Mrs. Smith-Porterhouse for far too long.

"My apologies, ma'am, I was woolgathering. It's a pleasure to meet you."

"And you too, sir." Mrs. Smith-Porterhouse nodded at Lisette. "I'll be back in a while to check on you, my dear."

Lisette looked resigned but not surprised. Anthony reckoned she still had a remarkable amount of freedom for an unmarried woman, but she wasn't exactly a young lady of the *ton*. As far as he understood it, her social position was far more ambiguous.

"Please, sit." Lisette headed for the table and Anthony moved to hold a chair out for her. "Thank you."

He waited until Christian sat too and then took his place between them. To his surprise, he was actually hungry, so he settled down to enjoy his dinner before entertaining any thoughts about what the twins wanted from him and what he was going to do about it. The Delornays were surprisingly cultured and amusing compared to his younger siblings, and he found himself enjoying their wicked gossip and banter.

By the time the remnants of the second course were removed and he nursed a large glass of brandy in his hands, he was feeling quite benign toward them. He waited until the last servant withdrew and fixed his gaze on Christian.

"Thank you for an excellent dinner. Now what exactly did you want to discuss with me?"

Christian exchanged a quick glance with Lisette. "We wish you to give us your word that anything we talk about goes no further, regardless of the outcome."

Anthony raised his eyebrows. "I'm not known as a tattletale. Of course, I'll keep your secrets."

"Good, then we wish you to help our sister, Marguerite."

Anthony put his glass down. "Your sister? I didn't even know you had a sister."

Lisette smiled. "She doesn't live with us and, in truth, she is only our half sister. She had a different father."

Were they referring to Lord Knowles's legitimate children? "An Englishman?"

"*Non*, we assume he was French. Marguerite is older than us. She is twenty-three."

"But your mother seems scarcely old enough to have given birth to you two, let alone another child."

Both of the twins glared at him, and he held up his hands. "I apologize. That is none of my business—I hold your mother in the highest regard."

Christian cleared his throat. "Anyway, Marguerite needs help, and we think you are the right man to provide it."

"Me?" Anthony laughed. "I doubt it. What exactly does she need? And please don't tell me she is looking for a husband."

"Marguerite is a widow. I doubt she'd want to marry you. That's why we want you to help her."

Intellectually, Anthony understood that no sane woman would want him in his present state, but it pained him to hear it spoken out loud. He struggled to keep his tone even. "I don't understand."

Christian smiled. "*She* doesn't want anything. She stays in her house and doesn't go out in case anyone starts gossiping about her."

"And what am I expected to do about that?"

Lisette sat forward, her hands clasped together on the table top. "We want you to squire her around town, take her to balls, picnics and concerts, and make her smile again."

Anthony stared at them. "Excuse my bluntness, but why in God's name would you think I'd do any of that? I'm not exactly known as a ladies' man."

"We know—why do you think we're asking for your help?"

"Now I'm completely at a loss."

"I overheard some of your conversation with my mother this morning," Christian said carefully. "You said that you wanted to change."

Anthony's smile disappeared. "I don't appreciate being spied on."

"I apologize, but it was unintentional. I wasn't expecting anyone except my mother or her lover to be in her boudoir at that time in the morning." Christian hesitated. "If you truly want to change, helping Marguerite might be beneficial to you. At least it might give you an opportunity to step away from a lifestyle which has obviously become abhorrent to you."

Anthony fought the temptation to smash his fist into Christian's calm face. But it was past time to face the truth, and Christian was repeating only what Anthony had realized for himself. However, it still stung to be judged by a mere youth.

"Your mother would not consider me a fit partner for Marguerite. I'm not sure that I do myself." He held Christian's gaze. "You know what I'm like; you know I'm usually involved with men."

"That's exactly why we think you'll be perfect for Marguerite. She's not ready to have a real sexual relationship with anyone. She's still 'in love' with her dead husband, but she does need to gain some experience with a man, and you will be perfect."

"But your mother will still object."

Lisette smiled. "Then we don't tell her."

"She knows everything that goes on here. I hardly think my gallivanting around with her daughter will escape her notice."

"But you won't be here, will you? You'll be escorting Marguerite to a different kind of place entirely. And don't you want to keep away from here, anyway?"

Anthony studied Lisette's face. Was it possible to change his life that easily?

"Excuse me for asking this, but if you two are not considered socially acceptable, how will your sister get away with it?"

Christian looked amused. "We *are* respectable. We just don't choose to embrace that particular environment. Marguerite has no choice. She married an English lord; therefore she is entitled and expected to enjoy the benefits of high society."

"Your sister is a titled lady?"

"*Oui*, Lady Justin Lockwood."

Anthony paused. "Wasn't there some scandal connected with her husband a few years ago?"

"He was involved in a duel with his best friend, Sir Harry Jones, and was fatally wounded."

"That's right. I remember it now. Weren't they both supposed to be in love with the same woman?"

Lisette glanced at Christian. "Something like that."

"Ah, that was your sister, Marguerite. Is that why she chooses to live in solitude?"

"Apparently so, although it seems ridiculous to me."

Anthony managed a smile. "Perhaps you have a stronger constitution than your sister."

Lisette met his gaze, and it was like looking straight into her mother's eyes. "That is possible. I'm hardly a shrinking violet."

"Hardly." Christian laughed and Lisette scowled at him. "Marguerite lives with a chaperone in a small house owned by the Lockwood family on Maddox Street. The Lockwoods don't particularly care for her, but they haven't dared to disassociate themselves because of her powerful supporters."

"I thought you said she had no family apart from you and her mother in England."

"She doesn't, but she has Viscount Harcourt DeVere and the Duke of Diable Delamere as godparents."

"Powerful allies indeed." Anthony studied his folded hands on the stained white damask tablecloth before looking up. "Have you spoken to your sister about this?"

"Not yet. We wanted to see if you were agreeable first." Christian looked inquiringly at Anthony.

Anthony allowed a silence to fall before he replied. "Why would she agree to this? What possible reason is there for her to want to change her life?"

Lisette held his gaze. "The same reasons you have. If she doesn't do something to save herself soon, she will become the kind of woman she has always despised."

"And what kind of woman is that?"

"One who is afraid." Christian said softly.

Anthony fought a shiver. Was it fear that held him back from trying a new path? Was he too afraid to step away from the familiar and find himself again?

He nodded abruptly. "I'll think about what you have said and give you an answer in the morning."

Anthony made his way back into the center of the pleasure house, his thoughts in chaos. Was it too late to go back, find the twins and tell them he wouldn't even consider the idea? He paused at the half-opened doorway to one of the more select second-floor rooms where some of Madame's patrons were enjoying a show. In the center of the room, two men attired in classical Grecian robes, laurel wreaths adorning their heads, were slowly undressing each other.

He moved closer to watch as the drapery fell away to reveal the oiled, muscled chest of one of the men. The second man kissed his way down the line of the fair-skinned man's sternum, tugging at the material that still covered his loins to reveal his erect cock.

A knot of tension settled low in Anthony's gut. Had he ever experienced such gentleness while having sex? Or had he just been fucked, his body a tool to be used by others for their enjoyment but never for his? He bit his lip. No, that wasn't fair. He'd enjoyed the roughness, craved it sometimes, and even begged for it.

"I'm surprised to see you here again tonight. You certainly are a glutton for punishment."

Anthony gently pulled the door shut. The bruises on his body seemed to throb in response to the softly drawled words spoken by the man behind him. He turned to face Lord Minshom, hands fisted at his sides. His nemesis wore an immaculately cut blue coat and black pantaloons, a diamond glittered in the white cravat at his throat.

"I'm not staying."

Lord Minshom's pale blue gaze flicked over Anthony's groin. "Why not? You're obviously aroused."

"Not by you."

"By that pathetic show in there? Two men acting like women?"

"Two men loving each other."

"Men don't *love* each other. They fuck to gain power, to win, to emerge as the winner."

"Not all of them."

Lord Minshom reached out and brushed his thumb over Anthony's lower lip. The subtle caress made all Anthony's senses come alive. He swallowed hard as Lord Minshom shoved his thumb into his mouth and moved it back and forth.

"I fuck to win."

Anthony jerked his head away and swiped his hand over his mouth. "I know. You've proved that to me many times."

"And you didn't like it? You didn't beg and plead for more?"

"I was a fool."

"You *are* a fool. You can't change your nature, Sokorvsky. You'll always be down on your knees begging for it."

Anthony closed his eyes as Lord Minshom's hand closed around his cock and squeezed hard. Like a lapdog, he was responding, his shaft growing and thickening at the other man's demands. He grabbed Lord Minshom's wrist and wrenched it away from his cock.

"No more. I'm done with you."

A slow smile illuminated the other man's face, drawing attention to the exquisite lines of his cheekbones and pale porcelain skin.

"Now that is amusing, Sokorvsky. You, having the nerve to tell me you've had enough. I didn't think you had the balls."

"Well, think again. I'm done."

"We'll see about that. Perhaps I was a little hard on you last night. When you're feeling better, you'll be back for more."

"Don't patronize me. I mean what I say."

Lord Minshom bowed, amusement clear in his narrowed eyes. "I'm sure you do—tonight. I'll see you in a couple of days, naked and bound in the punishment corner, eager to do my bidding as usual."

He nodded and walked away, leaving Anthony shaking. It seemed that no one believed he was capable of changing. He shoved away from the wall. Damn them all to hell, he'd take Marguerite Lockwood out and show them all how wrong they were.

3

"You did what?"

Marguerite Lockwood swung around to face her siblings who sat together on the small blue chaise longue in her shadowed drawing room.

"We asked Lord Anthony Sokorvsky to squire you around town." Lisette tried to look innocent. "Why are you so upset?"

"Because . . ." Marguerite spread her hands wide to express her inability to know where to start. "I don't need you interfering in my life."

"You do." Christian stood up and towered over her. "You've been holed up here like a fox avoiding the hounds for almost two years. Isn't it time you got on with your life?"

Marguerite narrowed her eyes and glared at them. The twins' self-composure continued to surprise and irritate her. Sometimes she felt as if she were the baby of the family.

"I am quite happy as I am. I enjoy every luxury. I don't have to worry about paying the rent . . ."

"You never go out."

Marguerite frowned at her brother. "Of course I go out. I haven't become a hermit!"

"All right, you never go out with a man."

"I'm a widow."

"Whose first marriage lasted barely a month."

Marguerite clenched her fists so hard her fingernails bit into her flesh. "Why are you being so cruel, Christian?"

He shrugged. "Because we've tried everything else and nothing has worked. You hardly ever even lose your temper anymore. We're all worried about you."

"A fine way to show you are worried by picking at me." Marguerite returned to her seat opposite the twins and glared at them.

Christian sighed as he too sat down. "I'm not trying to be cruel. I just want you to go out and enjoy yourself a bit more."

"With a man I've never met?"

"Anthony Sokorvsky is the second son of the Marquis of Stratham and a frequent guest at the pleasure house. He is perfectly respectable."

"And his presence at the pleasure house is supposed to recommend him to me?"

"Your husband visited *Maman's* establishment, and you liked him well enough."

Marguerite forced herself to ignore that unwelcome reminder and concentrate on the problem at hand. "And why would this Anthony Sokorvsky agree to escort me anyway? Is there something wrong with him?"

"Of course not. Like most young men, he is merely trying to avoid the matchmaking mothers. If he seems to be devoted to you, he hopes they will leave him alone."

Marguerite stared hard at Christian, aware that he wasn't quite telling her the truth, but as usual with her wily brother, she was unable to decipher exactly which part was the lie. She crossed her arms over her chest and sat back.

"I still don't want to go out."

"Marguerite . . ."

She scowled at them both. "I don't have to do anything you tell me to." Now she sounded like they were back in the nursery. "I'm an independent woman."

"Who never has any fun."

"I'll leave that to you two."

Lisette smiled and reached across to pat Marguerite's knee. "We just want you to be happy. Will you at least agree to meet him? If you hate him, I promise we'll stop bothering you."

Marguerite shrugged off Lisette's gentle touch. "All right, I'll meet him if it means you two will stop nagging me."

"Absolutely." Christian bowed and turned to help Lisette up. "We'll bring him for tea today at four."

Marguerite watched the twins leave, their satisfaction evident on their smiling faces. Silence descended over the house as the front door shut and she was alone again. She smoothed the folds of her lavender gown. Perhaps they were right. Perhaps it was time for her to stop hiding.

With an abrupt movement, she left the drawing room and hurried up the stairs to her bedroom. The miniature of Justin that his mother had reluctantly given her sat on a table beside her four-poster bed. She sat on the quilted cover and picked up the gold frame, scrutinized his ordinary features, the smile in his brown eyes and the subtle curve of his mouth. She touched the cold glass with a fingertip and then set the miniature on the pillow.

It was becoming harder to remember what Justin had really been like. His warmth, his beauty, the feel of him naked in her arms, moving over her, inside her. Marguerite shuddered as she contemplated her perfectly made bed. So cold now, so lonely after experiencing a man's love.

Maman had tactfully suggested Marguerite take advantage of the joys offered at the pleasure house. At first, she hadn't been able to bear the thought of another man touching her or even watching anyone else enjoy what she could not. Now ... she felt as empty as a dried-up lake. She stared at the frozen image of her husband. Would Justin understand that? Would he want her to be happy again?

She snatched up the portrait and kissed it, then she laughed at her own stupidity. Perhaps she was a little bored, but there was no need for such anxiety yet. She'd only agreed to meet Lord Anthony Sokorvsky, not go to bed with him. In a swirl of petticoats, she got up and hurried to find her bonnet and pelisse.

A long-overdue visit to her mama-in-law would remind her of where her true loyalties lay and seemed an excellent way to fill the time before she had to return for tea.

"Marguerite, my dear, do sit down."

To Marguerite's surprise, Lady Lockwood almost looked pleased to see her. She'd expected a scolding, or at least a show of indifference because of her recent neglect. She settled herself into a chair opposite her mama-in-law and mentally reviewed a list of excuses as to why she hadn't bothered to come and visit.

If she were honest, she'd admit that Lady Lockwood had never made her welcome, had, in truth, tried to deny that her marriage to Justin was legal. If it hadn't been for *Maman* and her powerful friends, Marguerite wouldn't have received even the reluctant recognition she had achieved or the financial compensation necessary to live like the widow of a wealthy husband.

"Have you come to celebrate with us?"

Marguerite smiled automatically as Lady Lockwood handed her a cup of tea. "Celebrate what?"

Color flooded Lady Lockwood's cheeks. "Oh, I do apologize. I thought you must have heard the news about Charles and Amelia."

"Your son, Charles?"

"Indeed." Lady Lockwood smiled even more brilliantly. "He and Amelia are expecting a child!"

Even as her stomach tightened, Marguerite schooled her features into an expression of delight. "That is wonderful news. You will have your first grandchild."

As Lady Lockwood continued to chatter, Marguerite struggled with a series of emotions she hadn't expected. Justin had been the oldest son, the one expected to inherit the title, to provide the heir, to take on the family responsibilities. And as his wife, those responsibilities would've been hers as well.

Did she want a child? Was she jealous? It seemed that she was. As she continued to listen to Lady Lockwood, Marguerite realized that not only was she losing sight of Justin, but that it seemed his family was as well. His younger brother would succeed to all his titles, give his parents their first grandchild and slowly but surely eclipse Justin until he was just a memory.

And it was all her fault.

After the obligatory twenty minutes, Marguerite stood up, kissed Lady Lockwood on the cheek and headed slowly down the wide staircase. Now she understood why her mama-in-law had treated her so kindly. She had become as unnecessary as her deceased husband, with no further part to play in the Lockwood dynastic ambitions. With a child on the way, it seemed that even the old resentments could be let go.

As she emerged from the grand mansion, a light drizzle caught at her face and made her blink. Did that make her obligation to remember and honor Justin less valid? No, she would never forget him. But perhaps it gave her the opportunity to move on without the oppressive weight of the Lockwood family's ruined expectations on her shoulders.

She nodded to the driver and stepped into the cab. Maybe

her meeting with Lord Anthony Sokorvsky would be more interesting than she'd thought.

By the time the dainty clock on her mantelpiece chimed four times, Marguerite's nerves had not only returned but multiplied. Why exactly had she let the twins tell her what to do again? She couldn't understand it. Somehow they seemed to undermine her defenses without even trying. She smoothed down the silk skirts of her favorite blue dress and walked back to the window.

A carriage had appeared outside. She recognized Christian's fair head as he removed his hat and stepped through the front door. Another unknown man followed him in. *Mon Dieu*. What on earth was she doing even contemplating going out into society again? She hurried to sit by the fire and picked up her embroidery.

The twins entered without ceremony, followed by a tall man fashionably attired in a chestnut brown coat, black breeches and shining top boots. His cravat was neither too modish nor too plain; his black hair was short and showed a tendency to curl at the ends.

"Good afternoon, Marguerite. Are you embroidering? I thought you hated sewing." Lisette gestured at the man beside her. "Look, we've brought him!"

Lisette's playful remark made Marguerite wince. She stuffed her embroidery down the side of her chair and looked up into the dark blue eyes of Lord Anthony Sokorvsky. She realized he was as embarrassed as she was. With a slight frown at Lisette, she got to her feet and held out her hand.

"Good afternoon, my lord."

He bowed, brought her hand to his lips and kissed it.

"Good afternoon, my lady. I hope you are having a pleasant day?"

His voice was low and held a hint of laughter. Was he amused by her? Was this whole thing a big joke? She motioned him to the seat opposite her and he sat down, stretching his long legs out toward the fire.

Lisette took a seat on the couch and then immediately jumped up.

"Shall I ring for some tea?"

"Why not? You treat this place as if it's your house anyway." Marguerite continued to smile through her teeth as Lisette laughed at her.

"Your siblings seem to have the ability to bamboozle us poor mortals into doing whatever they want."

Marguerite glanced across at Lord Anthony as he spoke.

"You've noticed that, have you?"

"Yes, I suspect that's the main reason I find myself here today."

Heat rose in Marguerite's cheeks. "There is no need for you to be here at all. You are quite free to leave."

He smiled and shook his head. "That's not what I meant. It is just entertaining to see the twins having the same effect on someone else as they do on me."

Goodness, he was attractive when he smiled: his generous mouth relaxed, and his blue eyes lit with humor and warmth. Why would a man who looked like that be willing to squire her around town?

Christian cleared his throat. "Lisette and I have to go. We have another appointment." He looked at Lord Anthony. "Will you be all right to get back to your home?"

"I'll be fine."

"Good." Christian bowed and took Lisette's hand. "We'll come and see you tomorrow, Marguerite!"

When the door slammed behind the twins, Marguerite sighed. As a widow, was it appropriate for her to entertain a single man alone? She suspected her mama-in-law would disapprove. Should she call her reluctant chaperone down from her room?

"Can I help you with something?"

Lord Anthony was staring at her, a quizzical smile on his lips. She subsided back into her chair.

"I was just wondering about the propriety of your visit. Are widows allowed to entertain unmarried men at home?"

"Allowed? I should imagine they are encouraged to do so."

She blinked at him. "Are you jesting, sir?"

"Of course I am." He sat forward, hands clasped together. "At least the twins' unconventional behavior has allowed us to move on from the dreary boundaries of polite conversation and actually get to know each other a little."

Marguerite gave a reluctant laugh. "I suppose that's true. They are annoying, aren't they?" She hesitated, forcing herself to meet his eyes. "You can leave if you want to. I won't be offended."

He smiled. "If I swear that I have no intention of leaping across the room and dishonoring you, may I stay for tea?"

"Why would you want to do that?"

"Because you intrigue me."

She shrugged. "I'm not worthy of such interest, sir."

"I think you are. Why would a woman as beautiful as you need an escort for the Season?"

"I don't need an escort."

He raised an eyebrow. "That's not what the twins told me, and you did agree to this meeting."

"I agreed to it to stop them bothering me, surely you can understand that."

He frowned. "Of course I can, but it doesn't explain why I've never met you before, why you don't go out into society."

"I doubt you frequent *ton* parties, my lord. Apparently you would be besieged by matchmaking mothers. How would you know if you'd met me?"

He held her gaze. "Because you are beautiful?"

"That is a ridiculous thing to say."

"Why? Because you don't think you are?" He smiled. "Surely beauty is in the eye of the beholder."

"Then you obviously need spectacles."

His smile widened. "My eyesight is considered superior, madame, and you are blushing."

Marguerite was saved from answering by the arrival of the tea tray. She busied herself setting things out, her mind awhirl. When had she last had such an improper and improbable conversation with a man? Never, was the answer. Lord Anthony was certainly different.

Anthony waited as Marguerite fussed over the tea cups and saucers. He didn't mind. It gave him the opportunity to observe her high cheekbones, huge dark eyes and cupid's bow mouth in profile. She was as classically beautiful as her mother, their coloring as different as the sun to the moon but breathtaking all the same.

She was petite too, her figure well suited to the higher-waisted gowns and long flowing lines of current fashion. He'd never really looked much at women before, but the purity of her beauty drew him in, made him want to kneel at her feet and worship her . . .

He shook his head to clear his thoughts as she presented him with a cup of tea.

"You do not want it?"

"Excuse me, ma'am, I was thinking about something else. The tea is most welcome."

He drank it fast, almost burning his tongue, eager to return to their conversation, surprised by how interested he was in finding out more about Marguerite.

"Are you willing to talk to me then?"

She stared at him, her expression dubious. "As long as you don't slobber over me."

He couldn't help smiling. "I did not slobber; I'm not a dog or a horse. I merely suggested I thought you beautiful."

"Then don't."

He set down his cup. "I'll stop if you agree to come out with me on Friday night."

"Why would I want to do that?"

"Because you are bored? Because you know you would enjoy my company?"

She half-smiled. "Not only blind but conceited as well."

He shrugged, surprised by how much he enjoyed her acerbic replies. It seemed all Helene's children had inherited their mother's unorthodox nature. He hoped to God that Marguerite was unique enough to understand and appreciate his requirements. He sighed.

"Can I be honest with you? I'm not just trying to avoid matchmaking mothers. I promised my brother I would turn over a new leaf, and that involves going out into society more and spending less time indulging in the excesses of the pleasure house. No offense intended to your mother, of course."

Marguerite nodded but didn't speak, her attention fixed on his face.

"We need each other. I want to reintroduce myself into polite society, and you need to enjoy yourself without feeling threatened by all the men who covet your beauty and wealth."

"You think that's why I don't go out?"

"Isn't it?"

She swallowed hard. "It's not as simple as that. After my husband died, there were many who blamed me for his death." She winced. "I can't believe I just told you that."

"He died in a duel, didn't he?"

"Yes, but . . ."

"He was an adult?"

"Yes . . ."

"Then he made a foolish decision and paid the price for it."

"But he wouldn't have fought the duel if he hadn't married me."

"If he was the kind of man who chose to settle his problems in such an archaic manner, then sooner or later he would probably have found some way to kill himself. You shouldn't hold yourself responsible for his stupidity."

Her chin went up. "Justin was not stupid!"

He inclined his head. "If you say so, but why allow a little gossip over something that happened so long ago affect your whole life? The *ton* has probably forgotten all about you."

"You are very rude."

"No, I'm just being honest." He smiled at her. "Isn't it refreshing?"

She glared at him for at least a minute before her face relaxed. "Yes, I suppose it is."

"May I call you Marguerite?"

"Why?"

"So that you can call me Anthony and we can be friends."

She put her cup down and stared at him. "I do not understand you at all."

"You should. I'm offering to be your friend—or do you have too many of them to care for another?"

Her cheeks flushed. "Everyone needs friends."

Anthony held out his hand. "Then good; let's agree to keep each other company for a while. We can brave the stares of the *ton* together and laugh at them behind their backs."

Marguerite took his hand and slowly shook it. "I will come out with you on Friday night."

He kissed her fingers. "Good, I'm looking forward to it already."

4

Anthony allowed his valet to help him into his tight navy blue coat and settle it on his shoulders. From Brody's muttered comments, he knew he looked well tonight and hoped Marguerite would think so too. It was strange to be dressing to go out on the town with a woman. When he wasn't at work or at Madame Helene's, he tended to pursue his pleasures with a group of gentlemen he'd known since his school days—younger sons of wealthy families and a few upstart cits who were happy to pay their way to be included in high society.

"You'll do, sir."

Anthony winked at Brody who scowled back at him.

"Thank you, I'm glad I meet with your approval."

Brody snorted. "Now don't come back with those fine clothes all ruined, sir."

"I promise I'll take care of them. I'm going to a ball at the Sutcliffs'. I doubt I'll get up to anything too dangerous there."

"You're going to a ball, sir? A real one?"

"Yes. Don't look so shocked."

Brody smiled and displayed several missing teeth. "Well I never. Are you sure it ain't at one of those ungodly places where men dress up as women?"

Anthony picked up his gloves and black cloak. "No, it is a real ball with real women."

"Well thank the lord for that. I thought the day would never come."

"Obviously your prayers have been answered; may I suggest you keep praying?"

Brody's amusement faded. "I will, sir, don't you ever doubt it."

Embarrassed by the gleam of devotion and real concern in Brody's brown eyes, Anthony turned away. That was the problem with servants who had known you since you were a child—nothing was sacred or secret. It seemed Helene was right and everyone was worried about him. He smiled. Perhaps tonight he would make Brody proud.

He came down the main staircase, his attention fixed on buttoning his gloves, and almost walked straight into his mother.

"Good evening, Mama, you look very nice." He bent to kiss her soft scented cheek. "Are you going out or coming in?"

She was dressed in pale green satin, with pearls at her throat and in the tiara in her hair. Her skin was so soft and unlined, it was hard to believe she was his mother. She had been only eighteen when Anthony was born, a bride of less than a year trying to deal with a household grieving for the loss of the first countess and kidnapping of the first-born son.

"I'm going to the Sutcliffs' ball." Her expression tightened. "I suppose you're off to Madame's."

There it was again, that note of apprehension beneath her tight smile. Had his behavior become so predictable and extreme that even his mother had noticed? He'd tried hard to conceal the worst of his excesses from her. He hastened to pat her hand.

"I'm not going to Madame's tonight; I have other plans. Perhaps I'll see you later?"

He felt her surprised expression follow him out of the house and into his waiting carriage.

By the time he walked up to Marguerite's narrow front door, it was already open. The butler who had admitted him and the twins on their previous visit bowed low.

"My lady is ready, my lord. She has been informed of your arrival."

Anthony stepped into the hallway and looked up toward the landing. Marguerite was in the process of descending the stairs, one hand grasped the skirt of her dark lilac gown. Diamonds glinted at her wrists, around her throat and in her hair. Behind her trailed an elderly rotund woman dressed in canary yellow which matched the color of her exceedingly obvious wig.

Anthony bowed as Marguerite reached him and held out his hand.

"You look . . ." he paused until she locked gazes with him. "I'm not allowed to say you're beautiful, am I? You look passable. Will that suffice?"

Her mouth twitched up at one corner. "Perfectly." She turned toward the older woman who had finally made it to the bottom of the stairs. "May I present Mrs. Lily Jones? She is one of Justin's great-aunts and my chaperone."

Anthony took the small pudgy hand held out to him and bowed. "Ma'am, it is a pleasure."

"I'm sure it isn't. You're probably wishing me to the devil." She scowled at Anthony. "I know what young men are like."

Anthony suppressed a grin and turned back to Marguerite. "Are you ready to go?"

She nodded and he took her hand and placed it on his sleeve. He bent closer. "Is she always so protective of you?"

"It's not that she's protective of me, she just hates men."

"All men? What about her husband?"

"Apparently, he was the worst."

He broke off the conversation to settle her into the carriage and return for Mrs. Jones. He took the seat opposite the ladies and smiled benignly even though Mrs. Jones continued to stare at him as if he were an insect that should be trodden underfoot. Luckily the journey to Grosvenor Square, where the Sutcliffs had their residence, was short, so he didn't have to endure the close scrutiny for long.

Anthony waited in the vast hallway for the ladies to reappear, absorbing the chattering crowds of people and the sense of excitement. He slowly inhaled the smell of over-perfumed bodies and, even worse, those who obviously didn't bathe at all. Why did people flock together like this? Was it really supposed to be fun?

He turned to find Marguerite at his elbow, her expression apprehensive, and smiled down at her. "Are you ready to brave the ballroom?"

She hesitated for so long that he almost repeated his question. "I suppose I am."

"That's the spirit, tallyho."

Anthony patted her hand as Mrs. Jones took up a position on his other side.

Marguerite looked up at him. "You sound as if you are encouraging your horse over a difficult fence."

He smiled. "I apologize; I was just trying to make you feel better. It seems I'll have to work on my social skills."

She squeezed his arm. "If I really hate it, we don't have to stay, do we?"

He paused at the top of the stairs to look down at her and saw the anxiety in her fine eyes.

"Of course not. I'll take you home whenever you wish as long as you allow me at least one dance with you first."

She tilted her head back, and he inhaled the scent of some sweet flower and her skin. So different from a man, so fragile and dainty, so unthreatening . . . He realized she was speaking and forced his unruly thoughts back to the present.

"You expect me to dance?"

"You know how, don't you?" He walked her straight into the ballroom, adroitly avoiding the receiving line and crush of guests waiting to be announced. No need to advertise their presence here; he was sure they'd be spotted soon enough. Mrs. Jones gave him another scathing look and rapped him on the arm with her closed fan.

"I'll be in the card room. Behave yourselves."

He bowed and watched her walk away, leaving him alone with Marguerite.

"It seems Mrs. Jones doesn't let her dislike of men interfere with her gambling."

Marguerite sighed. "She is already quite cross with me for making her come out at all. She was convinced her job as a chaperone was going to be easy because I liked to stay close to home. I can hardly insist she remain at my side. In truth, I'm glad to be free of her. I'm a widow, not a green girl."

"A fact for which I'm extremely grateful. I hate chaperones."

She sat in the gilded chair he pulled out for her and unfurled her fan. "Do you hate them because they stop you from misbehaving?"

He sat next to her, his knee touching hers, and leaned closer to be heard above the strains of the minuet being played.

"I just hate the whole hypocrisy of it. These women pretend to guard the innocent but take every opportunity to push the girls at men and wring a marriage proposal out of us before we've had time to even think."

"You sound as if you've had some experience with this."

He grimaced. "When I was younger and more foolish, perhaps. I've avoided places like these for the last couple of years."

"And taken yourself to the pleasure house instead."

He glanced sharply at her. "Do you disapprove of your mother's business?"

"Of course not. I admire my mother tremendously."

"But you don't use her facilities yourself."

She blushed. "I loved my husband, sir. I haven't ever felt the need to replace him."

Anthony studied her flushed cheeks. Had she just admitted she hadn't had sex since her husband died? His body stirred to life. How in God's name had she managed that? He'd done without sex for two days, and he was already getting randy.

Marguerite frowned at him. "From the expression on your face, you are about to ask me another of your embarrassing questions. Please don't."

"Why would you think that? I was just admiring your charming profile."

She sniffed her disbelief and closed her fan with a snap. "I'm not stupid, my lord."

"Anthony, call me Anthony, or Tony if you prefer." He couldn't help smiling down at her. She was so unlike most of the women of his acquaintance, so much more direct, so refreshing. The orchestra played a final chord and the dancers streamed off the floor, chattering and laughing. Anthony held out his hand. "Would you dance with me?"

She hesitated for less than a second. "I would like that."

He stood up and bowed, waited for her to place her hand in his and walked toward the dance floor. She curtsied gracefully and he inclined his head as the first strains of the old-fashioned country dance emerged. The dance was slow and stately and involved separating on every other measure. He wondered what it would feel like to have her fragile body in his arms, to swirl her around the floor held against him.

"My lord?"

"What?"

With a start he looked down into her eyes. What the hell was wrong with him, fantasizing about a woman?

"You are not attending to your steps. I've had to push you the right way twice now."

He circled her three times and then bowed, watched as she did the same. "I think I've forgotten the steps. Do you want to sit down?"

She gave him a frown. "*Non*, we would disrupt the set. Just concentrate."

He did his best, hid his amusement at her ordering him around as if he were her brother and managed to make it to the end of the dance.

"Next time we'll try something more lively."

He bore her off toward the refreshment room, ignoring the occasional startled glance from one of his old cronies.

"I didn't say I'd dance with you again."

"But you will. You enjoyed it, didn't you?"

His mother loved to dance and had patiently taught him the steps herself when he was a child. He glanced impatiently around the crowded room. Was she there yet?

"Anthony?"

He turned to find his older brother and Peter Howard at his elbow. Valentin looked very fine in black, and Peter wore blue and gray.

"Good evening."

Val continued to stare at him. "You're at a ball."

"I am."

"And yet, as far as I can tell, you're neither foxed nor insane."

Anthony scowled. "I'm also escorting a lady of my acquaintance, so please mind your manners." He touched Marguerite's arm. "Lady Justin Lockwood, may I present my older brother, the Earl of Landsdowne, and his business partner, Mr. Peter Howard?"

Valentin held out his hand, his smile pained, and kissed Marguerite's extended fingers. "Lord Valentin Sokorvsky will do perfectly well; you know I don't use that title, Anthony."

Peter Howard laughed. "And I have no title to speak of, so you'll probably remember me just fine."

"My brother and Peter run a shipping business together. I used to think I had a job there, but apparently I'm not up to scratch."

Val opened his mouth, but Peter got in first. "I wouldn't say that, although you have been a little distracted recently." He smiled at Marguerite. "It is, however, a pleasure to meet you, ma'am. You look familiar. Have we met before?"

"I doubt it," Anthony said. "The lady has only recently emerged from mourning her late husband."

"How did you meet her, then?" Valentin said.

Anthony winced as Marguerite pinched his arm and smiled up at him before answering for herself. "Through mutual friends. Lord Anthony was kind enough to offer to escort me to a few functions, so that I can find my feet again."

Val bowed. "And I'm sure he'll be the perfect gentleman, won't you?" He nodded cordially at Marguerite. "When I find my wife, I'll bring her over to meet you. I'm sure she'll be delighted to make your acquaintance."

"Thank you, my lord."

To Marguerite's amusement, Anthony continued to frown until Peter and his brother disappeared into the crowd. It seemed that Anthony's family was as good at speaking their minds as hers. She nudged his arm.

"You don't really have a 'job,' do you?"

Anthony looked down at her. "Why shouldn't I?"

"Because you have all this." She made a wide gesture of the room. "You are an aristocrat."

"So is Valentin, and he's the one who started a shipping company with Mr. Howard."

"Really? How fascinating."

He led her toward the buffet table and, without asking what she wanted, started loading food onto two plates.

"And you have worked there as well?"

He found a small table and plonked both of the plates down on it.

"For the last few years since I was sent down from Oxford. My father thought I was just going through a rebellious stage, but I've enjoyed every minute of it."

He glanced across at her, his blue eyes full of challenge. "Do I look too stupid to actually work for my living, like some overbred pedigree lap dog?"

She sensed the hurt behind his words and met his gaze without flinching. "Not at all. It is always refreshing to meet a man with a mind of his own, a man not content with living his life in a way that doesn't sit well with him."

His smile warmed her and he leaned closer. "That's exactly it. The job gave me a purpose when many of my contemporaries were too busy gambling, whoring and drinking away their allowances to think about their future. And I needed that steadying influence—" He abruptly stopped talking and stared into space. Marguerite held her breath, wondering what he would do next.

"Anyway, it seems I haven't been paying enough attention to my job recently, and Valentin thinks I should give it up and concentrate on being a man about town."

"What an unusual older brother you have."

Anthony's smile was guarded. "Indeed, much like the twins. Both of our families are trying to turn us into social butterflies when I suspect that, at heart, neither one of us truly wants to be here."

She reached across the table to touch his hand and felt his start of surprise before he enclosed her fingers in his.

"Actually, I am quite enjoying myself."

He squeezed her fingers. "I am too, but I suspect that is because I'm with you and not some simpering seventeen-year-old debutante."

Marguerite laughed and then looked up as a shadow fell across the table.

"Anthony, is that you? Valentin said I'd find you here, but I could scarcely believe it."

An older woman stared at her companion, both hands clasped to her breast. Anthony stood up, bringing Marguerite with him.

"Mama, may I present Lady Justin Lockwood?"

The woman stared at Marguerite as if she'd grown another head and then blushed. "Oh, a thousand apologies for my rudeness, I'm just so surprised to see Anthony here with you!"

Marguerite curtsied. "Your son has been very kind to me, ma'am."

"Oh, I'm sure he has. He can be quite charming when he wants to be."

"Mama . . ." Anthony sighed, and his mother patted his arm.

"I won't interrupt your evening any longer, my dears, but Lady Justin, please come and visit me at home one morning this week. I'd be delighted to see you again."

Marguerite sat back down and waited until Anthony had kissed his mother's cheek, submitted to a kiss in return and waved her off with a smile. When he sat, she studied him for a long moment.

"Why is your appearance here so startling that everyone we meet has to comment on it?"

He shifted restlessly in his seat. "Because I've avoided society like a plague for the last two years, and everyone's wondering what has coaxed me back."

Marguerite swallowed hard. "I hope they won't think it's me."

"Why ever not?"

"Because I'm trying to avoid becoming the subject of gossip, remember?" Marguerite rose clumsily to her feet. "Maybe this was a mistake. Will you take me home, please?"

Anthony followed her out of the ballroom and down the packed staircase to the equally crowded hall. He managed to catch her elbow and halt her flight, drawing her into the shadow of the stairwell near the servants' door.

"Don't go."

She looked up at him, her expression distraught. "I have to. I can't bear for people to look at me and whisper again; I simply can't."

"They won't, I can promise you that. Everyone will be too busy gossiping about me." He saw the doubt on her face and leaned in closer, rested one hand on the wall behind her head. "Please, Marguerite, we can do this. If we ignore the gossip, support each other and appear unaffected, it will soon die down, and we will both benefit from that."

She took a deep breath. "I'm not sure I'm ready."

He gave in to a strange desire to comfort her by kissing the top of her head. She smelled tantalizingly of violets and warm skin. Before his mind even registered his interest, his body was already reacting to her scent. At the touch of his lips, she went still and then raised her chin to look up at him.

He stared into her eyes, a dark blue similar to his own, wondered why it was suddenly so necessary to convince her to stay with him and why he would miss her if she changed her mind. She slowly licked her lips, and his cock hardened in a sudden aching rush.

"You didn't kill your husband, Marguerite, so why should you continue to suffer the consequences?"

She looked away from him then, and he almost regretted his words, but he needed to get his unruly thoughts and body under control. And what better way to do that than by mentioning her husband, the man she still claimed to love so much that she hadn't had sex since he died?

"It isn't that simple, Anthony."

"Nothing ever is, but you can't keep running away."

He took another breath, inhaling a hint of his own arousal along with the sweetness of her skin, and wondered if she was aware of his erect cock inches away from her stomach. Mentioning her husband hadn't destroyed his interest one bit.

"Are you all right, Anthony?"

He blinked as she gazed at him, the concern in her eyes an added balm to the side of himself he'd ruthlessly repressed for the last few years.

"I want to kiss you."

"Why?"

"I don't know." He watched her lips form a protest and edged closer so that his almost touched hers. "I just want to."

He lowered his mouth and closed that final crucial space, carefully licking along the line of her lips, sighed when they opened to admit his questing tongue. He shivered as she kissed him back, the flick of her tongue sending a spear of heat straight to his groin.

Someone bumped into him from behind, and he raised his head, aware that they were surrounded by hundreds of people. Marguerite deserved better than this. Dammit, she deserved more than he could ever give her. He stepped away from her and bowed.

"I'm sorry, that was damned impertinent of me."

She stared at him, her cheeks flushed, her eyes narrowed. Was she angry with him or aroused? It was hard to know with a woman.

"I'll go and get your cloak, find Mrs. Jones and summon the carriage."

She nodded but didn't speak, and he sped off on his errand. Even as his mind sent out its warnings, his body craved more. He hoped his erection would subside by the time he got back to Marguerite.

Marguerite remained against the wall, one hand pressed to her hot cheek. She'd let Anthony Sokorvsky kiss her. Not only that, but she'd kissed him back. So much for her protestations of love for Justin. Anthony must think her fickle now. She swallowed hard. If he'd kissed her again, she would've responded, slid her hand into his thick black hair and held him captive while he plundered her mouth and drew her tight against his body.

He'd been hard; she'd felt the hot press of his cock through the thin silk of her dress and had wanted to rub herself against him and try to recreate the amazing sensations Justin had first aroused in her. Would it be different with another man? Anthony was much taller and broader than Justin, and he'd tasted differently too, more of lemon and lavender than Justin's cigars and brandy.

God, what was she thinking? No wonder Anthony had backed away from her. He'd probably meant nothing by his kiss and here she was fantasizing about how he might perform in bed!

"Are you ready to leave, Marguerite? Mrs. Jones says she'll be back later."

Mentally berating her chaperone's lack of concern for her safety, Marguerite managed to hide her blushes as Anthony helped her into her cloak. To her relief, he seemed even less inclined to talk than she was. She could only pray that the carriage ride home would be equally silent and uneventful.

5

"I'm glad you agreed to go out with me again," Anthony said.

Marguerite bit her lip as he walked her back to their box after the interval. Mrs. Jones had decided to sit with one of her friends for the remainder of the performance, leaving her alone with Anthony in the Sokorvsky's box.

"I think I overreacted last time."

"It was, perhaps, understandable. No one likes to be gossiped about."

"That is true, but I can't continue to run away from everything, can I?"

He paused to open the door into the shared anteroom that connected the two adjoining boxes and looked down at her, his blue eyes glinting. "That's exactly what I told myself when I met you."

"That you should run away?"

His smile warmed her. "No, that I should take the unique opportunity you offered and make the best of it for both our sakes."

"Such a diplomat."

"A man in need of some honesty in his life could never succeed as a diplomat." He took her hand and led her into the ornate box. "I'm just delighted that you wanted to see me after the way I behaved."

She studied his expression, tried to guess whether her response to his kiss had repulsed or interested him. After almost a week of sleepless nights and vivid sexual dreams of Anthony, perhaps it was time to test the waters.

"Your behavior didn't offend me."

He paused before sitting in the chair beside her. "You didn't object to being kissed?"

Marguerite studied his cravat rather than risk a glance at his face. "I thought I would, but it was . . . nice."

"*Nice?*"

She looked up at him then, saw the male outrage on his face and fought a smile. "Yes."

He inclined his head a half inch. "I'm so glad I rate such expansive praise."

Marguerite sighed. "You only kissed me for a second. Would you prefer I lied and said it was earth-shattering?"

His mouth quirked up at one corner. "Of course I would."

She looked out over the theater, focused her attention on the thick red velvet and gold curtains across the front of the stage. Strange that she felt comfortable confiding such an intimate thing to a man she barely knew.

"It is difficult for me to admit even that. After my husband died, I thought I would never kiss a man again."

He didn't reply, and she continued to stare out over the rapidly filling theater. To a chorus of whistles and catcalls, the interior went dark and the curtains opened to reveal the archaic set for the second act. She jumped as he took her hand and squeezed.

"Nice is a perfectly acceptable word. And, to be honest, I

haven't kissed many women recently, so I might be out of practice."

Marguerite didn't believe that for a second. Any man who spent as much time at the pleasure house as Anthony did must be skilled indeed. His hand slid up her arm and over her shoulder, and he tilted up her chin.

"Perhaps we should try again."

She couldn't help but glance around. They sat in deep shadow and couldn't possibly be seen. She wanted him to kiss her with an intensity that surprised her.

"Marguerite?"

Anthony lowered his head until his mouth brushed hers. She closed her eyes as the tip of his tongue slid past her slightly open lips. She let him explore her mouth, touched her tongue to his and felt heat gather and settle low in her stomach. She couldn't believe how gentle and tentative he was being. In her limited experience, men took a woman's mouth like they took her sex, hard and fast. Not that that wasn't exciting in its own way, but this . . . this was simply enchanting.

Anthony drew back. "Well?"

"That was *very* nice."

He raised his eyebrows. "I progress. Perhaps one day I'll wring an excellent out of you."

She relaxed, content to sit beside him and watch the rest of the play unfold, her gloved hand held firmly within his. She'd imagined her intimate relationship with Justin was unique and couldn't be repeated. Perhaps she had inherited more of her mother's temperament than she realized and simply needed to be bedded regularly. The revolutionary thought both alarmed and intrigued her.

Her mother insisted that women were perfectly entitled to enjoy sex as much as men, and that there was no shame in it. Marguerite licked her lips and tasted Anthony. Was she bold enough to ask for more, and more important, would Anthony be willing?

Anthony stood up and stretched as the curtains parted yet again to reveal the grinning and bowing actors. A stir of movement in the box opposite him caught his eye, and he recognized Lord Minshom with his latest mistress and usual crowd of obnoxious cronies. God, he hoped Minshom hadn't seen him. He touched Marguerite's shoulder.

"I'll go and fetch our cloaks and order the carriage. Don't worry if I take a while; it can be a terrible scrum out there."

"There's no rush. I'm happy to wait here and see if Mrs. Jones returns or if she has made other arrangements to get home."

"That woman is an appalling chaperone, you know."

"I know. Aren't you glad?"

He grinned at her, left the box and headed down the main staircase to find someone to call his carriage. Caught up in the teeming masses of people exiting, he found himself outside, fighting to re-enter the theater.

"Sokorvsky."

He half-turned to find Lord Minshom in front of him. He tried to avoid him but was ruthlessly pushed back against the wall of the ornate stone building and then shoved into a narrow passage to the side. His shoulder hit the wall, and he lost his balance and fell to his knees.

"Aren't you pleased to see me?" Minshom murmured. He wore black and white, and his teeth gleamed in the darkness.

"No." Anthony flinched as Minshom kept him down on his knees in the filth of the gutter.

"Already half erect, I see. I didn't know you were capable of getting it up for a woman."

"That is none of your damned business." Anthony tried to rise, but Minshom tightened his hand in his hair and shoved Anthony's face against his groin.

"My, you are eager tonight. Is that because you've been denying your true nature, playing the gentleman, bestowing nothing more than a chaste kiss on the lips of your beloved?"

His grip tightened. Between the combined scent of Minshom's arousal and the hard press of the man's cock against his tightly closed lips, Anthony couldn't breathe.

"Don't you want to suck me off?"

Anthony used all his strength to pull away and stand upright. He rubbed his hand over his mouth before looking at Minshom.

"I don't . . . want this."

"You want it all right. You're primed and ready to go." Minshom flicked Anthony's pantaloons and then dragged his nails over the taut white satin, plucked at the wetness already seeping through. "You'll be coming before you know it, pleading with me to give you more."

"No."

"No?" Minshom brought his fingers to his mouth and licked them, brushed them across Anthony's tightly compressed lips. "This doesn't taste like no."

Anthony swallowed hard against a desire to sink to his knees and take what the other man offered and have done with it. He readjusted his cock with shaking fingers and forced his erection to conform to the tight-fitting garment. Why was he trying to pretend he could ever have a successful relationship with a woman with his perverted sexual needs?

"I want to change. This doesn't help."

Surprise flickered in Minshom's cold gaze. "Why should I help you? I want you right where you belong, servicing me."

"I don't believe that's where I belong."

"You think you'll do better in a woman's bed?"

Anthony forced himself to meet Lord Minshom's hard blue eyes. "Surely I need to find that out for myself?"

He winced as Minshom grabbed the back of his head and drew him close, kissed him hard on the mouth.

"I'm not giving you up. And when you do crawl back to me, I'll make you pay for your disobedience."

A shiver of anticipation coiled through Anthony's gut, and he pushed it away, hoping Minshom hadn't seen the flare of excitement in his eyes.

Laughing softly, Minshom stepped back. "You can't hide your true nature, Sokorvsky. You need the pain to find the pleasure. That's just the way you are made. Have a good evening."

Anthony leaned against the wall until Minshom disappeared and then found his way back into the theater. God, his legs were shaking and his cock throbbed with every labored breath he took. He'd seen men who couldn't do without alcohol or opium continue to feed their cravings even though they knew it would kill them. Was he doomed to crave sexual domination for the rest of his life?

He paused at the bottom of the stairs. How the hell could he go back to Marguerite in this state? He licked his lips and tasted a hint of his own pre-cum and Lord Minshom's spicy cologne. He couldn't help but contrast it to the softness of Marguerite's response to him, the warm welcome of her mouth.

He remembered to check that Mrs. Jones had departed, tip the footman stationed in the anteroom and retrieve their cloaks before he had to face Marguerite. To his relief, she sat patiently in her chair, her elbow propped on the edge of the box, hand under her chin. Her smile was full of welcome and made him feel even worse.

"Are you all right, my lord?" Her gaze fell to his legs. "Did you fall? Your pantaloons are dirty."

He managed a nod as he handed her into her cloak. "In my eagerness to get back to you, I slipped on the steps."

"You didn't need to worry. I knew you'd come back." She

chuckled. "I hardly think you're the kind of man who would leave a lady stranded."

God, he couldn't even smile at that. He'd been so close to following Lord Minshom farther into the shadows behind the theater and giving him what he'd wanted.

Marguerite's amusement faded, and she touched his arm. "Are you sure you're all right?"

"I'm sure." He kept his cloak draped over his arm, hoping it concealed the bulge of his still-hard cock, and offered her his hand. "Shall we go? The carriage should be there by now."

He opened the door and led her into the anteroom just as the large party from the box beside them decided to exit too. Overwhelmed by their numbers, he was pushed back against Marguerite, his large body pressing her into the wall. He almost came as his shaft jerked against her stomach and pulled away as quickly as he could. He didn't dare apologize in case she hadn't noticed, and he hardly wanted to draw attention to his cock.

She was quiet on the way down the stairs, even quieter as he settled her in the carriage. He glanced at her closed expression. Damnation, had he offended her? And how on earth was he going to explain such a lapse of good manners?

The carriage moved off, and he braced himself against the side, keeping his cloak draped over the lower half of his body, although it might well be too late for such modesty.

Marguerite met his gaze, her blue eyes clear. "It's all right. I have been married, you know."

"I beg your pardon?"

She flicked a gaze down at his groin. "I understand how men can become inconveniently aroused."

"You do?"

"And as I caused this, when we kissed, perhaps I should be the one to do something about it."

Anthony sat forward just as she sank to her knees in front of him. "Marguerite, you didn't . . . God, what are you doing?"

Her hands worked at the straining buttons of his pantaloons until his cock was revealed in all its thick, heated glory. She looked up at him, the slight color on her cheeks the only sign of any lack of composure.

"I'm going to suck your cock."

"*What?*"

"Surely you've had that done to you before?"

"Yes, but . . ." *not by a woman.*

"My husband showed me how to do it. He assured me that most men like it. Is that not true?"

"Yes, but . . ." Her hand slid lower and cupped his balls and the base of his shaft. His cock jerked as if seeking her mouth. "God . . ."

She leaned closer, her breath warm on his flesh, and her tongue flicked out to catch a drop of pre-cum. He groaned and angled his hips toward her. She licked him again, the whole juicy wet purple crown this time, and he sighed.

"You do like it, then."

He opened his eyes to stare down at her. "Yes."

"No 'but' this time?"

"No."

"Then I'll keep going."

She opened her mouth and allowed the first four or five inches of his cock inside her. The sensitive head caught at the back of her throat, and he tried to pull back, but her grip was too strong. He groaned again as she took him even deeper, sucking him while her fingers stroked and shaped his balls.

"Harder."

He couldn't stop the harsh command, needed more, needed something to stop him from worrying about how fast he was going to come down her throat. He brought his hand down to cradle the back of her head, to hold her exactly where he wanted her, not that she seemed to want to stop or leave him unsatisfied.

Pressure built in his balls and at the base of his spine. His hips rolled with each tug on his flesh, pushing his shaft deeper, fucking her mouth with an eagerness he couldn't believe.

He managed to mutter, "If you don't want my cum in your mouth, I'll pull out." But she didn't ease up, just kept her lips tightly around him and sucked hard. He began to groan with every stroke, tried to shove himself deeper with every grind of his hips until he finally exploded, leaving him breathless and frozen on the edge of the seat, his shaft still buried in her throat.

Anthony carefully pulled out and tucked his now limp cock back into his underclothes, buttoning his placket. While he adjusted his clothing, Marguerite wiped her mouth and resumed her seat opposite him.

"Marguerite . . ."

"*Oui?*"

"That was . . . very nice."

"I'm glad you enjoyed it."

To his annoyance the carriage stopped and his driver knocked on the door.

"My lord, we're at my lady's house."

Marguerite stood and smoothed down her skirts. "Don't worry about getting out. Dawson can escort me to the door. Thank you for a lovely evening. Good night."

She descended from the carriage so fast that Anthony had barely registered her request before the door was shut in his face. He stared down at his groin. A woman had just sucked him off and he'd enjoyed every damned agonizing second of it.

Marguerite ran up the front steps and then the stairs to her bedroom as if pursued by the furies. She allowed her maid to loosen her gown and corset and then dismissed her. Finally alone, she sat at her dressing table, pulled out the pins from her hair and stared at her wild reflection. Touching Anthony had aroused her, had made her want a man inside her again. Shocked by the eagerness in her eyes, she covered her face with her hands and took several long breaths.

Despite his initial surprise, Anthony had liked her sucking him. And she had enjoyed it too, had almost wished that he'd picked her up and shoved his cock deep inside her until she shuddered and shook along with him. Heat pooled low in her belly, and she was aware that her breasts ached.

She slipped her arms out of her dress and studied her breasts, sliding her fingers inside her corset to squeeze and pinch her already hard nipples. Would Anthony be gentle with her? His kiss had been more self-assured this evening, and his demands for her to suck him harder indicated that he wasn't averse to a little rough play.

With a silent curse, Marguerite stood up and let her dress and loosened corset fall to the floor. How was she ever going to sleep, her body waking from its long slumber of sexual deprivation, her blood warm and flowing wantonly? And how was she ever going to survive in a society that expected her to deny her needs and wait on a man's lust or interest?

She took off her shift and crawled into bed naked, enjoyed the coolness of the satin cover and the rougher caress of the linen sheets. Under the covers, she allowed one hand to fondle her breasts while the other slid down over her stomach to touch her already wet and ready sex.

Would Anthony like her body? Would he enjoy placing his mouth over her sex, licking at her swollen clit and sliding his fingers and tongue inside her? She moaned as she worked her clit with her thumb until she was gasping and sobbing and . . . God, wanting so badly her climax made her cry.

Would Anthony enjoy that too? Marguerite rolled over onto her stomach and opened her eyes. She was probably far too inexperienced to interest him anyway. Just because he liked her touching him didn't mean he wanted to touch her back. Men were often selfish. And did she truly want to court such scandal by sleeping with him? He was hardly the conventional man she had imagined, the man she would eventually marry and live with in peaceful harmony for the rest of her life.

She smiled into the darkness. But she wasn't planning on finding that particular man for years. She simply needed to restore her confidence and slake that part of her nature that missed the physical side of marriage. There were ways to remedy her lack of experience, and she had entrée into the most unique pleasure house in England. If she truly decided to follow her body's desires and enjoy sex, she was determined to be good at it.

Her gaze caught Justin's portrait, and she suddenly felt guilty. Here she was, plotting to seduce another man without a thought for her dead husband. Would he hate her? Or would he be generous enough to forgive her for all her sins? At least this time, she was going into the relationship with her eyes open, with no uncomfortable emotions such as love to consider. This was not about marriage—it was about rediscovering her sexual self. Surely Justin of all people would approve of that?

"Brody. Now you've assured yourself that I have returned without harm, go away. I'm quite capable of putting myself to bed."

"All right, sir, good night."

Anthony waited until the door shut with a definite bang behind his offended valet and then sank down onto the side of the bed. Marguerite had sucked his cock, and he'd simply sat there like an idiot and let her . . . He groaned as his shaft jerked and began to fill out again.

He'd wanted to pull her onto his lap, open her legs and fill her with his cock until she screamed. Yet he'd done nothing but take what she'd offered and given nothing in return. He stripped off his clothes and blew out all the candles except the one next to his bed.

But what could he give her? What did a woman like Marguerite want? He palmed his shaft, felt it thicken and lengthen, and sighed. One release was never enough, and, as returning to the pleasure house and Lord Minshom was not an option, his hand and his assortment of toys would have to suffice.

He rummaged in the drawer next to his bed and pulled out a thick leather cock ring, which had three circles to slide over his cock and balls with buckles to draw the straps tight until he achieved the satisfaction he needed. He was deliberately rough with himself as he encircled his balls with the leather and pulled the straps as tight as he could.

He was even rougher with his cock, sliding the thick leather strap home through the buckle until his shaft throbbed along with his heartbeat and pre-cum coated his fingers. The blood trapped in his shaft made the crown of his cock exquisitely sensitive. Groaning, he reached into the drawer again, found a flower-shaped pin with a short silver-wired stem and coiled it around the tip of his cock. As he worked his cock between his hands, the flower wedged against the wet opening and slid in and out, adding to the exquisite sensitivity.

He worked his shaft harder, kneeling on the bed and rested his forehead against the headboard so he could watch his flesh strain against the leather. He caught the glint of the silver pin and coiled wire gripping his crown, the heavy weight of his constrained balls aching and screaming with the need to defy the tight bindings and come. An image of Marguerite sucking his bound cock while Lord Minshom fucked his arse blazed through his brain, and he climaxed, forcing the thick jets of seed through the pain and into blessed release.

He fell forward, panting as if he'd run a mile, his cock still twitching and coming into the smooth white sheets. With a groan he rolled onto his back and carefully unbuckled the leather ties and removed the silver pin. His heartbeat was so loud he couldn't hear the ticking clock.

Marguerite had sucked his cock, and yet he had no idea how to please her. Anthony stared up at the embroidered brown bed hangings. Devil take it. He'd have to ask for help.

6

"Is that you, Miss Marguerite? Are you looking for your mother?"

"Good evening, Judd."

Marguerite smiled at her mother's butler as he gestured for her to come farther into the warm homely kitchen of the pleasure house. In truth, her mother was the last person she wanted to see. Helene had a gift for knowing exactly what Marguerite most wanted to hide, and she had plenty to conceal at the moment.

"Madame is away at her other house tonight. Do you want me to send her a message?"

"No, don't disturb her. I just came to see my sister."

Her mother rarely left her business to spend time at the townhouse with her husband, Lord Philip Knowles, the twins' father. The last thing Marguerite wanted to do was interrupt their evening together. Although Philip was involved in the establishment, she knew he was often frustrated by Helene's insistence that they keep their marriage secret. And if she sent a message, Marguerite knew her mother would always come.

"Miss Lisette was in the main salon with Captain David Gray. Do you wish to go up to the pleasure house or shall I ask your sister to come down to the kitchen?"

Marguerite swallowed hard. "No, I'll go and find her." She hesitated by the door. "I don't suppose you have a mask I could borrow, do you?"

"Of course, my lady. I'll go and find you one. Do you have any preference as to color?"

By the time Marguerite was masked and following Judd up the stairs, her heart was pounding. One never quite knew what one might encounter at the pleasure house, and she had become such a prude. To her relief, the main salon seemed relatively quiet, the guests more inclined to relax and eat than partake in an orgy.

She saw Lisette's blond head at one of the tables and headed in her direction. Her sister wore an impeccably cut cream satin gown that emphasized her slenderness and displayed her bosom to advantage. The man sitting next to Lisette immediately rose to his feet and bowed. Marguerite gave him a distracted smile and wondered why Lisette was spending her valuable time with him. He seemed far too ordinary to warrant her sister's capricious attention, and rather old. She judged him to be in his early thirties, if not more.

"Lisette."

"Marguerite, what on earth are you doing here?"

Marguerite frowned and glanced pointedly at her male companion. Lisette shrugged. "It's all right. This is my friend, Captain David Gray. He's known *Maman* forever and is completely trustworthy."

"Ma'am." Captain Gray bowed and then turned to Lisette. "Perhaps I should go and mingle for a while."

"All right, but don't forget to come back and talk to me later."

"Of course, Miss Delornay."

Marguerite watched him walk away and then turned to Lisette who was still smiling. "He seems like a nice man."

"He is. Why do you make it sound like a criticism?"

Marguerite sat opposite Lisette in the chair David had vacated. "He just seems a little old for you."

"Old for me to what?"

"You know what I mean."

Lisette wrinkled her nose. "Marguerite you are such a prude. David is my friend, not my lover. I think he prefers men actually, but it is difficult to say." She touched Marguerite's hand. "What are you doing here, anyway?"

"I wanted to ask your advice."

"Mine? Are you feeling quite the thing?"

Marguerite scowled and lowered her voice. "If you are going to laugh at me, I'll go."

Lisette made a presentable attempt to straighten her face. "No, I promise I'll listen. How can I help?"

"I need to see how a woman pleasures a man."

Lisette's mouth dropped open. "I beg your pardon?"

"Lisette!" Marguerite hissed. "I need you to show me a room where I can watch a woman making love to a man, and you mustn't breathe a word of this to *Maman*."

"As if I would." Lisette frowned. "Are you sure about this?"

"Of course I am. You and Christian were the ones who told me to get out more!"

"Yes, but . . . you seem to have progressed rather more quickly than we anticipated." Lisette elbowed Marguerite in the ribs. "Anthony Sokorvsky must be some kind of fertility god."

"Oh, be quiet. Can you help me or not?"

"Of course I can." Lisette got to her feet, bringing Marguerite with her. "I know the perfect room. Come on."

Anthony slipped into the main salon of the pleasure house and looked cautiously around. To his relief there was no sign of

Madame Helene, Lord Minshom or his brother. At least he might be able to conduct his business with a modicum of decorum. If such a thing was possible. He groaned inwardly.

"Anthony?"

He turned and found Peter Howard smiling at him.

"Good evening, Peter." Anthony gestured to the quietest corner of the room. "Thank you for coming."

Peter settled himself in a chair and studied Anthony for a long moment. "You sound very formal. Is something wrong?"

Anthony stared at his brother's best friend, a man he respected immensely. A man who had suffered the worst life could throw at him, and yet had not only survived, but found love.

"I need your help."

Peter's blue eyes narrowed. "Of course, anything."

Anthony looked desperately around the crowded room. "Is there somewhere else we can talk?"

Peter got instantly to his feet. "Let's go upstairs."

He led Anthony into one of the more private rooms on the second level and shut the door.

"Now what is it? Are you in trouble?"

Anthony leaned back against the door. "Not the kind of trouble you might think, but I do need some advice."

Peter's charming smile reappeared. "And before you ask, I promise I won't tell Val anything."

"Or Madame Helene."

"Really? Why is that?"

"Just promise."

Peter shrugged. "Of course. Now how can I help?"

As he struggled to find the right words, Anthony started to pace the room. "I want to seduce a woman."

"So?"

"I want to do it properly."

Peter looked puzzled. "Then find an experienced woman here at the pleasure house and perfect your skills."

"It's not as simple as that."

"What do you mean?"

Anthony stopped walking, his back to Peter, and closed his eyes. "I've never bedded a woman."

"I beg your pardon?"

Anthony swung around to glare at Peter. "I've never had sex with a woman. How the hell am I supposed to make sure she enjoys it, when I have absolutely no idea what I'm doing?"

Peter's stunned expression made Anthony want to run and hide.

"But you're twenty-five."

"And I was raped by a man when I was barely twenty."

"God, Anthony . . ."

He tried to smile, to laugh it off. "I've fucked a lot of men though, or should I say, they've fucked me, so I do have some experience."

"Excuse me for asking this, but is there a particular reason for your sudden desire for a woman?"

Anthony scowled. "My reasons are my own, but why shouldn't I have sex with anyone I want to?"

Peter hesitated, his calm gaze on Anthony's. "You know there is no shame in admitting you prefer men. You don't have to bed a woman to prove something to Val, your family or, most important, to yourself."

"Why does everyone assume I prefer men? When have I *ever* expressed a preference?"

Peter examined his fingernails. "People assume things, and the fact that you've never been seen with a woman perhaps explains it." He looked up. "And the fact that you're twenty-five and have only fucked men."

Anthony stared helplessly at Peter, his hands fisted at his sides, his heart racing along with his thoughts. How much could he reveal about the change in his feelings, about his doubts about everything he'd once believed true about himself?

"Recently I realized that I no longer enjoyed being sexually humiliated."

"By Minshom?"

"By anyone. I realized that I wanted to try to find out what *I* want, not what I am told I should like or forced to participate in."

"There's nothing wrong in that."

"Thank you. It's taken me long enough to work that out. But I have now, and I intend to try to find out for myself."

"You do know you might not like what you discover?"

Anthony looked up, saw the understanding on Peter's face and shrugged. "You mean I might realize that I do need pain to enjoy sex and really prefer men?"

"That is a distinct possibility. Some might say that your choices so far have actually been the right ones and that you are simply fighting your true nature."

"Would you say that?"

"No, I'd tell you to go out and experiment, to find out what you truly desire and embrace it, whatever it may be."

Anthony swallowed hard. "Thank you, Peter."

Peter nodded slowly, his face once more calm and thoughtful. "Then we need to find you an experienced and discreet woman."

"Yes, that would be helpful."

Peter got up. "Will you stay here while I go and inquire if the lady I'm thinking about is available this evening?"

"Of course."

After Peter left, Anthony sank into a chair and buried his face in his hands. That had been one of the hardest things he'd ever had to do. He hadn't told Peter that he tended to avoid women, afraid that they'd laugh at his inexperience or, worse, that he'd somehow hurt them with his perverted lusts. Marguerite was different somehow. Her gentleness combined with her acerbic French pragmatism intrigued him.

He wanted to touch her intimately, to see her body convulse in the throes of passion, to strip away the artifice and understand what made a woman's love different from a man's. His cock stirred at the thought, and he glanced at the door, wondering whether Peter would actually come back after all or just leave him to stew.

The door opened and he shot to his feet, smoothed back his disordered hair. Peter was smiling.

"I've found the perfect woman. She'll make you wear some kind of leather mask to conceal your identity." He shrugged. "She doesn't like to know whom she's fucking, and she loves to play the dominant role. I didn't think that would bother you at all."

Peter's matter-of-fact explanation made Anthony want to groan. Apparently his sexual tastes were known to more people than he realized.

"That sounds perfectly acceptable, Peter. Thanks for your help." He swallowed hard. "Shall we go?"

"Stop crowding me!"

"I'm not."

Marguerite glared at Lisette, who walked ahead of her in the narrow viewing passageway between the rooms on the second floor.

"Why couldn't we just go into one of the public rooms off the main salon and sit down? Why does it have to be here?"

Lisette turned to face Marguerite. "Because what you need to see is far more intimate than that, and there is a woman on this floor who specializes in training men to perform at their sexual peak."

Marguerite sighed and followed her sister to the next viewing station. She had to assume Lisette knew what she was doing, but she still felt apprehensive.

"Of course," Lisette whispered, "if you want to try it for yourself, I'm sure I could persuade David to lie down and let you crawl all over him. It might be fun."

"No, this is fine, thank you."

Lisette nudged her. "Coward."

Of course she was a coward; who could doubt it?

Marguerite leaned against the wall and peered through the small mirror right into the room. A woman dressed in a black lace corset, stockings and high polished riding boots paced the room. She carried a thin whip that she constantly slapped against her thigh. Although not in her first bloom of youth, she was a magnificent creature. Auburn hair piled high on her head, milk-white skin and a lush bosom to drive men wild.

Marguerite looked down at her own average breasts. Not only was the woman beautiful, but she radiated confidence, something Marguerite had lost and desperately needed to rediscover if she wanted to get anywhere with Anthony. And she did want Anthony—his lack of aggression and innate honesty appealed to her. He offered her a chance to make up for the mistakes of the past, to rediscover the sexual being she was meant to be after the distortion of her marriage.

"Look," Lisette whispered. "Here he comes . . ."

Rather like horse blinkers, the leather headgear which covered the top half of Anthony's face and his hair also constricted his side vision. Anthony focused on the woman in front of him, which wasn't a hardship since she was a vision of formidable female beauty. A lush redhead clad in leather and lace, a whip in her hand and a frown on her face.

She pointed the whip at him. "You may call me mistress. Strip off and don't speak unless I tell you to."

Anthony nodded and slowly removed his clothes, aware of her circling him as he undressed, her gaze flicking over his

body as if she were judging horseflesh. To his surprise, she reminded him of many of the men he'd been with—supremely
confident, supremely dominant and quite capable of making
him do whatever she wanted him to. Peter had chosen well.
He'd almost found a female version of Lord Minshom. Somehow the thought calmed Anthony's nerves.

"Hurry up."

The whip grazed his buttock and he jumped. When he was
naked, he straightened and faced her again. She nodded slowly.

"Very nice. Now get down on your knees."

Anthony obliged and waited as she came to stand close to
him.

"The first thing you need to learn is that women have needs,
they are not simply to be fucked for breeding purposes. They
are to be made love to." She used the whip to raise his chin.
"You are going to learn to put your selfish desires aside and
please your woman."

She walked back toward an ornate gilt chair and sat down.
"Come here."

Anthony wasn't sure if he was supposed to crawl or get up
and walk. He decided to stand, aware that every time she barked
out a command, his cock hardened even more. She didn't look
pleased at his decision, but allowed him to kneel back in front
of her without comment or applying the whip.

"Put your hands behind your back and keep them there.
Now pay attention."

She opened her legs to display her shaved sex, and Anthony
inhaled the scent of her arousal. He shivered as she rubbed the
tip of the whip over a small knot of protruding flesh right at the
top of the curved mouthlike interior.

"This is my love bud, my hard nub, my pearl, my clit—you
may call it what you will, but you will learn to pay it the same
amount of obsessive attention that you pay your cock. Think

of it as a minicock, the source of extreme pleasure and ultimate bliss for a woman, and for you, if you tend to it carefully."

She took the whip away. "I want you to lick it, suck it, play with it until I tell you to stop."

Anthony forced himself not to close his eyes as he leaned forward between her widespread white thighs. Her hand encircled the back of his leather-clad head and pushed him closer.

"Do it."

He obliged, his tongue sliding over the surprisingly slippery flesh until it met the harder knot of nerves and he was able to explore. His curiosity grew as she pressed closer, urging him on as he sucked and licked and used his teeth on the increasingly swollen bud. He forgot about time, about breathing, about anything other than pleasuring that small piece of her that seemed to bring so much joy.

His body joined the rhythm, his erect shaft bumping against the wood and brocade of the chair until he wanted to groan. He jerked as she slid the whip between his legs and tapped his cock.

"Move back; this is not for you. Slide your mouth downward, lick my folds and use your tongue like a cock to slide inside me."

Anthony gulped in some much needed air and moved lower, fascinated by the plump mounds of her flesh, the softer lips within and the wet warm hole at her very center. He pointed his tongue and pushed inside her, felt her muscles contract around him and repeated the action until his jaw began to ache.

Her hand tightened on his head, holding him still, his tongue deep inside her.

"Give me your hand."

He blindly raised his arm, and she gripped his wrist, settling his fingers over the swell of her breast and the lace of her corset.

"Touch my breast, squeeze my nipple, make me come."

God, he was on fire, so eager to please her, so consumed by her enjoyment that he would've done anything she told him to at that point.

"That's nice, keep it up, slide your fingers inside me alongside your tongue."

He managed to get two fingers in with his working mouth, pumped them back and forth like a real cock as she pressed down on him. Would Marguerite like this dual penetration of tongue and fingers? Would she call his name as she came?

"Ah . . ." Her cry set off a series of clenching and tightening of her internal muscles. He was amazed at how strong the grip on his fingers became before she released him with a flood of cream. He turned his face into her thigh and fought to breathe, his cock so hard now he could feel every pulse of his heartbeat in his aroused flesh.

"Very good. Now get up and come over to the bed."

He waited until she positioned herself on the red silk covers and then climbed up beside her. Her smile wasn't pleasant.

"You haven't finished yet. Unlike men, women can come more than once. Remember that." She patted her stomach. "Straddle me but be careful not to crush me."

Anthony was also careful not to allow his cock to brush against her hip as he swung one leg over her body and settled over her, his weight balanced on his hands and knees. His balls rested against the scratchy black lace of her corset and his shaft rose like some hideous purple stalk against his belly.

"Kiss my breasts."

He leaned forward and did as he was told, enjoyed the softness of her skin against his mouth, the hard thrust of her nipple between his teeth. As he moved over her, his trapped cock grew exquisitely sensitive, but his training by Lord Minshom stood him in good stead, and he was able to stave off the craving to come.

Her hands drifted over his body, caressed his buttocks, the

underside of his balls, his back, in an endless stream of sensation. He continued to suckle her until she was moaning with every tug of his mouth on her tight nipple.

"Stop now and sit up."

He drew back, stared down at her, his breathing as hectic as her own. She touched his dripping shaft with one finger.

"I'm impressed that you haven't come yet."

He managed a shaky smile, remembering just in time not to speak.

"Perhaps I should reward you." She considered him, her finger making torturous patterns on his throbbing wet cock. "Turn around."

Anthony stared at her until she made an impatient noise. "Turn around until your head is over my sex and your arse is near my face. Now make me come again."

He obliged, dipped his head and tasted her, used his tongue and teeth and fingers to make her slick and wet again. He almost choked as he felt her swallow his shaft and start to suck, matched his rhythm to hers, forgot about everything but the instinctive need to make her come before he did.

She bucked against his fingers, raised her hips to shove against his face. No finesse now, only the play of body on body in a race for completion and a release he wanted more than anything. She spasmed against his three thrusting fingers, and he couldn't hold on any longer, letting his cum spill down her throat in hot urgent pulses.

When she released his cock, he rolled away onto his back and stared up at the white-painted ceiling. Interesting that in the final throes of passion, women acted much like men, so greedy for completion that it all became about the pursuit of the purely physical.

"You did well, young man. You have excellent stamina. Any woman should be glad to have you in her bed."

Anthony opened his eyes and regarded the redheaded woman.

His lips twitched at the thought of her giving him a certificate of approval for him to display on his bedroom wall to impress his future wife.

"Thank you. I enjoyed it."

Her smile was warmer now.

"I'm delighted to hear it." She waved her fingers at him. "Now off you go, I have another man to train in half an hour."

Marguerite pressed her fingers to her lips as she watched the man pleasure the red-haired woman with his mouth and fingers. Would she have the courage to demand such delicious things from a man? More to the point, would Anthony let her tell him what to do like that?

Lisette elbowed her in the ribs. "He's rather nice, isn't he? I wonder what his name is."

"Ssh."

Marguerite was curious herself, but she had no intention of letting Lisette know that. The man's body was muscled, his buttocks tight and high, his chest lightly furred. And his cock . . . She refused to think about how big and hard he looked, how wet and ready to slip inside a woman's most secret place and give her what she needed.

She licked her lips as the woman lay back on the bed and invited the man to straddle her. In the candlelight, she noticed thin diagonal white lines marred the smooth surface of the man's back. At the base of his spine it looked as if someone had tried to carve their initials into his skin. Even through her arousal, her stomach tightened. Who could've done that to this man?

"Lisette?" she whispered. "He appears to be scarred."

Lisette shrugged. "A lot of Englishmen look like that; it's a legacy of their public school education." She patted Marguerite's arm. "I promised to meet David; come and find me when you've finished watching."

Marguerite waved a distracted good-bye and returned her

attention to the room. How barbaric the English upper class were, sending their boys away from home at such a young age and leaving them to the tender mercies of men who often didn't have their best interests at heart.

She watched the man suckle the woman's breasts, wondered how he managed to stay so erect for so long. In her limited experience, men came far too quickly. A deep longing stirred inside her, and her womb clenched, releasing its own cream as the man reversed his position and settled to lick and finger the woman's sex again.

She wanted that feeling so badly. With a furtive look up and down the narrow passageway, she slipped her hand through the pocket opening of her dress, pushed her petticoat out of the way and settled her fingers over her mound. Oh, God, she was so wet, so ready to be taken . . . Her body easily yielded to allow two of her fingers inside.

Could she treat Anthony like this? Tell him what she wanted, make him go down to his knees and service her? The last time she'd tried to be sexually adventurous had proved a disaster. Memories of Justin and his friend Sir Harry Jones assailed her, the terrible complexities of unrequited love. Was she brave enough to try again?

The red-haired woman started to come, her cries filling the room. Marguerite climaxed too, closing her eyes against the ecstasy in the woman's face as she sucked the man's cock to completion. There was power in this for a woman, but was she prepared to wield it again?

When she found the courage to look back into the room again, the man had gone, leaving the woman on the bed. Her satisfied smile made Marguerite jealous. Trying to pretend that her intimate life had died with Justin hadn't worked at all. She had to come to terms with her needs and find what she wanted.

Marguerite brought her fingers to her lips and inhaled her own scent. She wanted to make a man beg for her, but she wanted to be made to beg even more. The salacious thought shocked her to the core. Was she more like her mother than she had ever imagined? Did she still crave the forbidden, the sinful, the unknown?

With a moan, Marguerite ripped off her mask and stumbled along the passageway, her hand on the wall to aid her flight. She pushed open the door that led back into the main hallway and collided with a hard male body.

"I beg your pardon, sir."

"Marguerite?"

She looked up into Anthony's surprised face and wanted to cry. Of all the people to meet at this embarrassing moment of self-revelation, why did it have to be him?

7

———————

"I was looking for my sister."

Marguerite blurted the words out as Anthony stared down at her. Her cheeks were flushed, and she looked on the verge of tears. Her slender body shook in his arms. A silver mask fell from her fingers, and she made no move to pick it up. He glanced back at the door she'd exited from.

"In there?"

She pulled out of his grasp and ineffectually patted her hair. "I just took a shortcut to avoid walking along the main corridor alone. I'm not really supposed to be here tonight."

"Neither am I."

She started back along the hallway, almost running in her eagerness to get away from him, but he kept after her, his gaze fixed on the back of her head.

"Marguerite, will you slow down?"

She came to an abrupt halt and turned on him.

"Why? Do you want to tell me what you are doing here? Didn't you say you wanted to keep away from this place?"

Unaccustomed resentment filled him. *Dammit, he'd come here for her.*

"*You* said you never came here at all."

She walked off again, reached the main staircase and started down to the main salons. He followed her, catching her arm at the bottom of the stairs.

"Marguerite, are you angry because I am here or because I found you here?"

She glared up at him. "Both."

Well at least she was being honest. He drew her away from the staircase toward the servants' door.

"I'm sure you have a key to the private areas of the house. Let's go through here."

He followed her onto the darkened landing beyond the green-baize-covered door and waited for his eyes to adjust to the dim lighting. The starkness of his new surroundings was a huge contrast to the lavishness of the salons.

"Men are such deceivers."

"Not all men, and who says I was deceiving you?"

Her eyes flashed a challenge at him. "You've had sex. I can smell it on you."

"I didn't, really, I was just . . ."

Hell, his explanation sounded weak even to his own ears. He could hardly tell her he'd been improving his technique for her benefit. Marguerite took three steps away from him, her shoulders rigid, and her arms hugging her waist.

"Why didn't you have sex with me?"

He struggled not to gawp at her. "What on earth is that supposed to mean?"

"It means that I have turned into a figure of fun. A lonely widow who can't do without a man in her bed. A woman reduced to arguing with a man about why he won't have sex with her."

"I don't quite follow you."

She swung around to face him. "Of course you don't; you're a man."

He spread his hands wide. "What do you want me to say, Marguerite? I'm sorry that I'm a man, I'm sorry that I didn't immediately put you over my shoulder, climb the stairs and ravish you on our first meeting?"

"Now you are being absurd."

"Then help me understand."

She slowly raised her head. In the dim light, tears glinted in the corners of her fine eyes. "I told you I loved my husband so much that I couldn't contemplate bedding another man."

"Yes, I remember."

"And yet the first time you kissed me, I kissed you back."

He inclined his head. "You did."

"And then . . . then I sucked your cock."

He leaned back against the wall, tried to appear relaxed even as his body responded to that intimate memory. "Yes."

"I lied to myself because I was afraid to admit I liked being bedded far more than a lady should." She grimaced. "I want to be a chaste and pure widow, but I can't seem to stop wanting."

"I'm sure your mother would say that a woman is entitled to just as much enjoyment in bed as a man."

She went still. "And do you agree with her?"

He shrugged. "Of course."

"But it feels wrong to have such brazen thoughts, to want something so . . . basic."

"Why?"

She looked at him and then away. "Because sex is such a powerful thing. Strong emotions can ruin people's lives."

"Are you thinking about your husband again?"

"No, about myself and my mother. The passion she and Philip shared almost destroyed her."

"But she found love with him, didn't she, so wasn't it all worth it?"

"For her, perhaps. For her children, it meant a lifetime of separation, of not knowing." She sighed. "Please don't misunderstand me, I have nothing but admiration for my mother, but I swore to myself that I would live a more conventional life and avoid grand passions if I could."

Silence fell between them as he contemplated her. "Do you think your needs will shock me?"

"I don't know."

"Marguerite, nothing shocks me."

She tried to smile. "I doubt it."

"And what, if you were to be completely honest at this particular moment, would you want from me?"

She shivered. "Your hands on me, your mouth . . ."

His pulse quickened. "And if I offered you those things, in the spirit of honesty between us, would you be shocked by my behavior?"

"No, as I said, you are a man."

"But if, as your mother insists, we are sexual equals, why shouldn't you get what you desire?"

She didn't speak, but her body angled away from him, poised for flight. He held out his hand.

"Marguerite . . ."

She turned slowly, and he pulled her hard against him. In truth, he hadn't expected to be exercising his newfound skills quite so quickly, but he wasn't about to let Marguerite down again. He sought her mouth, kissing her lips until she opened to him. Her hand curved around the base of his skull, keeping him close.

She moaned against his mouth, the plaintive sound enough to make him hard and encourage his hands to roam her body at will.

"Please . . ."

He kissed her throat, her ear, the line of her jaw.

"What do you want, Marguerite?"

She grabbed his right hand and settled it over her breast. He ran his fingers along the edge of her bodice and the silk whispered back. Sliding the tip of his index finger below the fabric, he found her nipple already hard and ready for him. God, he wanted to taste her there.

He drew her back over his arm and bent his head, shoved aside as much of her bodice and corset as he could and settled his mouth over her breast. Her fingers tightened in his hair, urging him on even as his hand slid over her hip and rucked up her skirts and petticoat. He cupped her mound in his palm and held still.

"Do you want me here?"

"Yes, oh please, yes."

He thumbed her swollen bud, felt her shiver in his arms and slid one finger through her slick wet heat, his heart pounding, his breathing as uneven as hers. This meant so much more with Marguerite; his desire to please her knew no boundaries. He began to move his finger in and out, wondered how his cock would feel doing the same, wanted to come at the very thought of it.

"More, give me more."

He smiled as she arched against him, her sex pressing into his trapped hand, so demanding for such a petite woman, so sure of what she needed from him. She shuddered as he added two more fingers and pumped harder. Her whole body shook as she climaxed and clung to him as if he offered her everything a man could give her. For a glorious moment, he felt as if he could even be that man.

After she finished clenching and writhing against his fingers, he simply held her balanced on his palm, her whole body relaxed against him, as languid and satisfied as a kitten. Her curls tickled his face and he bent his head to nuzzle her neck.

"Better?"

She shifted in his arms. He reluctantly raised his head as she pushed him away.

"What did I do now?"

Her lips were swollen from his kisses, her hair disordered, her skirt creased, and yet she looked more beautiful to him than she ever had before. He found himself grinning at her like a fool and realized she wasn't smiling back.

"You gave me what I asked for."

"And that was wrong?"

She raised her chin to look him in the eyes. "No, it was . . . wonderful."

"Then why aren't you happy?"

"Because you proved to me how much I want to be bedded."

Anthony sighed. God, why were women so complicated? At least a man took his pleasure and walked away without having to analyze every second of it.

"I'll bed you if you want."

She briefly closed her eyes. "Don't say that."

"Why not? It's the truth."

She moved suddenly toward the stairs, pausing to look over her shoulder at him. "Now I'll be dreaming about you all night."

"And that is a bad thing? I'll be dreaming about you too." He held out his hand again. "If you really want me, come back inside and we'll find a room."

"I can't do that."

"Why not?"

"Because . . . I can't."

Anthony let his hand fall back to his side. "I'm not good enough for you now?"

"That's not what I said!"

He bowed, aware of an ache in his cock and, ridiculously, his heart. "Perhaps you'd prefer to experiment with someone else?"

Marguerite sighed. "You are being stupid, and I am in no state to argue with you anymore. Come and see me tomorrow, and we'll discuss this in a reasonable manner."

"But I don't feel reasonable."

"I can see that."

He watched as she sped down the stairs, skirts flying, and her kid slippers barely making a sound. Part of him wanted to follow her, push her against the wall and bury his thick shaft deep inside her until she screamed her release. He slammed his hand into the wall, enjoying the pain that shot up his arm.

But what if she really was done with him? He pressed his forehead into the cold unforgiving brick. God, he hated this self-doubt. Minshom had done this to him, and he needed to stop believing it. At the thought of his tormentor, Anthony's frustrated cock started to throb in anticipation. Was that what he really needed now? To go up to the third floor, kneel in front of Minshom and repent for his stupid fantasy that he could connect sexually with a woman?

A sound below him made him straighten up and spin around. Was Marguerite coming back? His shaft responded with enthusiasm. But it wasn't a woman's light tread on the stairs. It was a man's heavier footfall.

Anthony leaned back against the wall as Captain David Gray appeared on the landing, hat in hand, blue coat unfastened as if he'd just arrived. He hesitated when he saw Anthony, but his smile was warm.

"What are you doing here?"

Anthony simply stared at him. He'd known David for years, knew that his friend had no illusions about what he was or what he wanted.

"I'm hiding, I suppose."

"From what?"

"From myself."

David nodded as if Anthony made perfect sense. "I haven't seen you on the third floor for a while. Is that what you're trying to avoid?"

"Yes."

"I can understand that. I try to avoid it myself." He gestured at the stairs. "I was just about to leave; would you care to walk out with me?"

"I don't know if I can."

"Because you think you can't survive the night without Lord Minshom's attentions?"

Anthony's eyes snapped to David's. "How the hell did you know that?"

"Because a few years ago I felt the same." David's smile disappeared. "But I broke free of him, so it is possible."

"Perhaps you are simply a stronger man than I am."

"No, I'm not. I just learned to value myself more."

Anthony dropped his gaze. "At this moment I crave his 'attention' more than I want to breathe."

"He has that effect on people, but there are many other ways to achieve sexual satisfaction without submitting to that bastard." He paused. "What if I offered you one alternative to Lord Minshom and the third floor?"

Anthony straightened and ran an unsteady hand through his already disordered hair. "You have an alternative?"

David's smile was calm. "At my lodgings, if you care to join me."

Dark excitement threaded through Anthony's body. He was hard and ready to fuck. If he couldn't have Marguerite—and why should she want him inside her after all—he needed someone, and if Lord Minshom was out of the question, David would definitely do.

Marguerite stepped into the kitchen, her face flushed, her whole body still trembling from Anthony's caresses.

"Marguerite, are you all right?"

She jumped and turned to face her mother, who sat in the shadows beside the hearth. Despite the lateness of the hour, her mother still looked beautiful as she rocked back and forth in the old pine chair, her dainty feet swinging with every motion.

"I thought you were staying with Philip tonight."

Helene made a dismissive gesture. "We made magnificent love and then he had to spoil it by insisting we make plans to spend more time together. Men are so annoying."

Marguerite stayed where she was and leaned back against the door. She hoped her mother couldn't see her too well.

"I can understand Philip's frustration, *Maman*. You are a very busy woman."

"He knew that when we married. That is no excuse."

Marguerite knew it was pointless to argue. She'd never understood the inner workings of her mother's tempestuous marriage with Philip. They, however, seemed to thrive on it.

"And what are you doing here, Marguerite, so flushed and unlike yourself?"

Silently Marguerite groaned. Her mother was notorious for her ability to sniff out romantic discord, the beginnings of an affair or the ending of a marriage.

"I came to see Lisette."

"And?"

"And she was upstairs in the pleasure house with a Captain Gray, so I went to find her."

"That must have been a while ago, as Lisette was just here talking to me."

"I know, I just saw Captain Gray on the stairs. He told me Lisette was here."

Helene stopped rocking. "Marguerite, come and sit where I can see you, and tell me what is going on."

When her mother used that voice, it was very hard to disobey. Marguerite came closer, trying to decide which pieces of the story she could share and which not.

"*Bon*," her mother said. "Now tell me why you lingered in the salons."

"Because Lisette called me a coward and dared me to look around while I was up there."

"That sounds like your sister. But why did you agree?"

"Because I was curious?"

"Finally!" Helene clapped her hands together. "I knew you were too young to bury yourself in your husband's grave."

"*Maman . . .*" Marguerite hunched one shoulder.

"Now what advice can I give you about starting again?" Helene sat forward, her expression purposeful. "The most important thing, I believe, is how to avoid a pregnancy, *oui*?"

Marguerite stared helplessly at her mother. Perhaps it would be better to simply keep quiet and listen. She might pick up some useful advice without having to betray herself.

"Yes, *Maman*."

"I've spoken about this with many women over the years, and I have a few ideas about when is the best time to conceive or, in your case, to avoid making love." She frowned at Marguerite. "And before you suggest that any real gentleman would pull out before his seed emptied into your womb, then think again. In the throes of passion, many men forget this most basic thing, or would secretly like you to be pregnant in the first place."

"I'm not sure . . ."

Helene kept talking, her slim fingers ticking off each point as she made it. "It is the middle of your moon cycle that you must avoid. I think a woman is most fertile then. I'm not sure why, but that seems to be the case. It's easy to work that out, my dear, just note the day you start to bleed and count on from there until the day you bleed again."

"*Maman . . .*"

Helene stood up and patted Marguerite's shoulder. "I know—it's a lot to take in. Come and see me tomorrow and I'll show you how to use a sea sponge dipped in vinegar as well."

What on earth did vinegar have to do with anything? Marguerite dredged up a smile. "I'll do that, and thank you."

Marguerite got up too and gathered her belongings. Her mother's businesslike attitude toward sex never ceased to amaze her. At least it had stopped her inquiring too deeply about exactly what was wrong. Perhaps she should be grateful for her mother's incessant chatter. Marguerite clutched her bonnet to her chest. And perhaps her mother knew her better than she realized and had achieved what she intended all along.

"Here we are."

David opened the door to his lodging and led Anthony inside, shutting the door behind him. Anthony looked around the Spartan apartment in surprise.

"It's very clean."

David shrugged as he took off his hat and gloves. "When you've lived in a tiny cabin on a ship for months, you learn to stow your belongings carefully so that they don't all descend on you in a storm."

"I hadn't thought of that."

Anthony continued to walk around the room, touching the mahogany desk in the corner, the pair of leather wing chairs by the welcoming fire.

"Do you live alone?"

"Yes, I have a man who comes in every morning to help with the essentials, and a woman who cooks for me when I'm here. I've never cared to have live-in help. I find it a little suffocating."

"I agree, but as I still live at home, there's nothing I can do about it."

"Would your family object if you had your own suite of rooms?"

Anthony stroked the worn brown leather of the chair. "It's complicated. My father almost lost one of his sons, and he's determined not to lose the other."

"That must be something of a burden for you."

"I suppose it is. I've never really thought about it before."

"Perhaps you should. My father was glad to see the back of me." David's smile didn't reach his eyes. "He insisted that as the fourth son of an impoverished earl I was a damned inconvenience. I was expected to make my own way in the world." David picked up a candelabrum and headed down a dark hallway. "Bring the brandy."

Anthony picked up the bottle and two glasses and followed the source of the light. He drew in an unsteady breath as he realized he was in David's bedroom. Again, the room was stark—a narrow bed with dark red coverings and two other pieces of furniture that looked distinctly foreign.

David indicated a large black lacquered chair that sat in front of a mirror.

"I bought this in *Heung Gong* harbor a couple of years ago." His fingers trailed over the high ladder back and down to the red silk cushion on the high seat. "It is exactly the right height for *shibari*."

"What is that?"

David smiled. "Literally it means beautiful bondage, or so I was told. It's an ancient erotic art from the land of the rising sun. The exact translation proved elusive and, to be honest, the pleasure was so extreme that I didn't really care to inquire any further. I was too busy enjoying it."

Anthony licked his lips as his excitement grew. "Will I enjoy it too?"

"I hope so. Will you take off your clothes?"

8

"What exactly are you going to do to me?"

Anthony stripped and watched as David took off his coat, cravat and waistcoat and then opened one of the drawers in the red lacquered oriental cabinet beside the bed. As David turned back to him he couldn't suppress a tremor of excitement.

"I'm going to tie you up, but I want to take care of your arse first."

He opened a flat box to reveal a collection of jade and ivory phalluses and a selection of perfumed oils.

"Do you have a preference?"

Anthony swallowed hard. "You're not going to fuck me?"

"Perhaps later. There are more interesting things I wish to try first." David hesitated, his fingers wrapped around one of the carved ivory shafts. "Unless you have changed your mind."

"No, I haven't. It's just that Minshom . . ."

"Always fucked you first? But I'm not Minshom, and remember, I'm trying to show you that there are other ways to achieve the levels of pleasure you crave."

Anthony mustered a smile. He had to stop expecting the worst and trust his companion. "Then go ahead, choose for me and I'll be content."

"I hope you'll be more than content." David stroked one long finger along the length of Anthony's already erect cock. "I want to hear you scream."

He drew his hand away from Anthony's shaft, over his hip and cupped his buttock. Anthony sighed and tried to relax. He was so eager to fuck that the slightest touch made his cock twitch and his balls tighten with need. David moved behind him, his fingers stroking and caressing Anthony's flesh until he wanted to groan.

"I'll use sandalwood oil. It's my personal favorite and nothing like that acrid flowery stuff Minshom prefers."

Anthony gasped as David slid one oiled finger inside his arse and then another. His mouth trailed along Anthony's shoulder, paused to nip, lick and nibble his skin. Anthony arched his back, asking for more, and sighed when David replaced his fingers with the hardness of the thick ivory phallus.

"Don't come yet," David murmured and then bit down hard on Anthony's ear lobe. "We've hardly begun."

"I won't."

"Excellent. Then come and sit in the chair."

Anthony moved carefully toward the cushioned seat and sat down. There were no armrests, so he anchored his hands on the edge of the seat. His cock throbbed, setting off a vibration through the embedded phallus that made it difficult for him to breathe, let alone think.

David took a black silk bag out of the chest and brought it across to Anthony. He slowly untied the silk cords and tipped the contents into his hand.

"This is *shibari* rope. It can be made of hemp or jute, or in this case, fine linen." David stroked the carefully tied skein. "I had it dyed red because I like the contrast against white skin. Each rope is about twenty-three feet long. That's the traditional length, I'm not sure why."

Anthony stared at the thin red linen, imagined it wrapped around his body and licked his lips.

David smiled. "The aim, I'm told, is not to use any knots. Unfortunately I'm not an expert, so I might need to use one or two. Are you ready?"

The sudden question made Anthony look up from his fascinated contemplation of the rope into David's calm blue eyes. He swallowed hard.

"Yes."

"Good. Will you put your hands behind the back of the chair?"

Anthony almost wanted to close his eyes as David knelt in front of him and brought both ends of the rope from under the seat. He positioned Anthony's knees and ankles against the cold wood of the chair legs and wrapped the linen around his knees, holding them in place. With a practiced motion, he brought the ropes over Anthony's knees and started cross-binding his thighs to the seat.

Anthony flexed his thigh muscles and realized the linen wasn't tight at all. David touched his hip.

"Think of it as a corset. You have to be completely laced up before you tighten the strings."

"Ah, that helps," Anthony muttered. "I've always wondered what it felt like to wear a corset."

"Really? That is, of course, another avenue you could explore at Madame's if you chose to. I believe Tuesdays and Thursdays are the most popular nights for the mollies."

David's quiet chuckle made Anthony smile even as his breath hitched when the cords were crossed behind the chair and then back under his balls. David paused as if to admire the effect and then added another twist of the linen to separate Anthony's balls and bring them high and close to the root of his shaft.

Anthony couldn't take his gaze away from David's deft fingers as he arranged his balls to his liking, drew the cords back through the slats of the chair and away from his groin. For the first time, Anthony felt the tug of the rope as David wrapped it around his wrists and secured them to the back of the chair.

"And now for your cock."

Anthony craned to look as David brought the rope forward again and wrapped it twice around the base of his shaft, across his hips and back behind the chair. As the rope extended over his body and secured him tightly in place, Anthony wondered if he should struggle like a fly in a spider's web or simply give in and wait to be eaten alive.

"Your cock looks magnificent," David said quietly.

"It does?"

Anthony groaned as David bent and kissed the straining tip. The linen had drawn his cock away from his stomach in an aching curve of hot, trembling, swollen flesh.

"Almost done."

David stood and continued winding the linen around Anthony's torso until he was bound tightly to the chair. He could feel each individual wooden slat against his skin, the softness of the silk cushion, the hardness of the phallus. When David reached his neck, he laid the cords loosely around Anthony's throat. He moved closer, kissed his way down the path of the rope that framed Anthony's nipples, and sucked one into his mouth.

"Christ . . ."

Anthony would've jumped, but as his body was held immobile there was nothing he could do to stop David sucking anything he wanted to. The thought should've frightened him, but it didn't. He liked this, this lack of control, the inability to pretend he didn't want what he was being offered.

His cock jerked as David's breeches brushed against it, and wetness slid down his shaft. He tried not to moan as David kissed his way down his body, past his hips, his thighs, avoided his cock and ended up back at Anthony's knees. With one last lingering kiss, David stepped behind the chair.

Anthony almost flinched as he saw his shadowed outline in the long mirror on the wall. As David had said, the red linen looked stark against his white skin. He stared at his bound body and felt no shame, only a sense of heightened anticipation.

"You look beautiful tied up for me."

Anthony raised his eyes and met David's gaze in the mirror. He didn't say anything. He hoped David saw his acceptance in his face. David nodded.

"Are you ready to come for me now?"

David picked up the two ends of rope and began to pull. It was if he had set light to a line of gunpowder. Anthony gasped as the cloth bit deeper into his chest and stomach, binding him to the unforgiving frame of the chair. He groaned as the sensation moved lower until it reached his balls and cock, his thighs . . . tightened and tightened until he couldn't stand it anymore and he came, his seed exploding from the tip of his shaft, soaking the cloth.

Anthony closed his eyes as the incredible sensations finally ebbed. David released the ends of the rope and reduced the tension, but not enough for Anthony to move freely.

"That was . . . interesting," he croaked.

David came around and crouched between Anthony's legs. "I'm glad you enjoyed it. We haven't finished yet." He leaned forward and licked at the wet pool of cum on Anthony's stomach. After he'd cleaned it all off him, he focused his attention on Anthony's balls until Anthony was half erect again and eager for more.

"What now?"

David unbuttoned his breeches and pulled his shirt over his head. "Now we enjoy this together."

Anthony watched carefully as David stripped off his breeches to reveal his already erect cock. His own shaft twitched in response. In the pleasure house, David rarely shed his clothes, so he'd forgotten how big David was. He seemed to prefer to keep his sexual encounters to the minimum. Not for the first time, Anthony wondered why. "Did Minshom put you off fucking altogether?"

David ran a leisurely hand over his shaft. "No, why?"

"Because you seem to be happier giving sexual favors than receiving them."

"Minshom didn't do that to me. By the time I met him, I was already damaged and so was he." His smile was wry. "I admit he took me to a new low, but I clawed my way out from under him eventually."

"How?"

"It was quite simple. I was replaced." He sought Anthony's gaze. "He met you."

"I didn't know that. You were always very pleasant to me."

"Of course I was. I was too busy trying to beg my way back into Minshom's bed to upset his new toy." He shrugged. "And eventually I realized I was glad it was you rather than me."

Anthony grimaced. "I wish he'd find someone else."

"Perhaps he will."

"At the moment, he's so angry I've walked away from him that he's determined to have me back."

David straddled Anthony's lap, his feet taking his weight on either side of the chair. "He'll get over it. He's a grown man and no fool."

"God, I hope so."

David unwound the ends of the red cords from around Anthony's neck, leaving him still bound to the chair, and brought them between their bodies. Anthony held his breath as David wound the linen around both cocks, binding them intricately together. He could now feel the pulse of David's shaft as intimately as his own.

He shuddered as David drew the cord around both their necks and tightened the coiled rope. His cock tried to fill out, met the resistance of the linen and David's flesh, and began to burn and throb. David slid a hand into his hair and drew Anthony closer. He could no longer look down and see their cocks, only feel the erotic vise pulling tight as David rocked into him.

"God . . ."

David moved faster, jerking Anthony's cock, pressing him down into the silk pillow and onto the base of the phallus until he saw nothing but need, wanted nothing but the red tide of desire that scorched and consumed him. He came as David came, shouted the other man's name as he climaxed, his hot cum bursting through the tightly wrapped linen to mingle with David's.

This time it took longer for him to recover, and it took David a while to lift himself away and unwrap their cocks.

"Did you like that?"

Anthony let out a slow breath. "Yes."

"Good."

David cupped Anthony's balls and used his thumbnail to draw a line on the underside of his cock.

"Devil take it, David, I'm not sure if I can . . ."

"You can. I'll make sure of it."

Anthony licked his lips. "Will you fuck me while you make me hard?"

"Haven't you been fucked enough?"

"What do you mean?"

David bent to lick the swollen crown of Anthony's cock, insinuated his tongue in the slit, making Anthony strain against his bonds. He swallowed hard. "Fuck me, please."

"I'd rather you fucked me."

"I'm tied to a chair, how do you expect me to do that?"

"We'll manage." David's slow smile was a sinful invitation as he straddled Anthony's lap and grasped Anthony's cock around the linen that still bound it. He knelt up, guided Anthony's wet shaft toward his arse and slowly lowered himself down.

"Ah . . . that's good."

Anthony held his gaze. "You'll have to do all the work. It hardly seems fair." He groaned as David started to move on him hard and fast. "Fuck me, please."

"Not until you come for me."

David groaned as he got into his rhythm, his eyes closed, his cock sliding against Anthony's belly and the linen rope as he worked. Anthony's cum tightened his trapped balls, making him moan. He had no way of slowing or stopping David, no control at all. He knew he'd have to come when the other man demanded it.

At that thought, he climaxed deep inside David, heard the other man's growl of satisfaction at his complete surrender. Abruptly, David lifted himself off, leaving Anthony's cock feeling cold and bereft.

"I'll fuck you now."

David moved behind the chair, removed the thick phallus from Anthony's arse and shoved himself deep. His fingers brushed Anthony's throat as he sought the ends of the rope and tightened the bonds making Anthony gasp for air.

"David . . ."

Anthony's cock responded to David's presence and started to fill out again. The soreness and suddenness of the rough penetration caused another erotic surge through his overwrought senses and made him want to scream. David reached around and took control of Anthony's cock, rubbing him hard in time to his thrusts.

"I'm coming." David's hoarse words in Anthony's ear and the sting of teeth settling on his shoulder jerked him into another release. It was almost painful this time, each spurt of seed, so hot and raw that he did scream.

When he opened his eyes, he was free of the rope and David sat cross-legged on the floor in front of him. His sea blue gaze was contemplative; some of his blond hair had escaped its ribbon and curled around his face. His muscled skin gleamed with the sweat of his exertions as he slowly breathed in and out. Anthony licked his lips, tasted his own blood. David's gaze followed the slight motion, and he smiled.

"I don't usually fuck anyone these days."

"Neither do I," Anthony replied. "But perhaps I should try it more often."

"I heard a rumor that you were looking for a wife."

Anthony stiffened at the abrupt change of subject. "I'm not."

"Then why are you escorting Lisette's sister around town?"

Cautiously, Anthony sat forward and fixed his gaze on David. "Lisette shouldn't have told you that."

David shrugged. "I won't repeat it. I was just interested to hear your reasons."

"I told you, I'm trying to get away from the third floor. Marguerite offers me an opportunity."

"Does she know what you are really like?"

"She knows enough not to judge me." Anthony got up, aware of his body aching and shaking as it came down from its sexual high.

"I'm not judging you, Anthony," David said gently. "And it might interest you to know that women often enjoy the art of *shibari* as well."

"I have to get home."

Anthony gathered his clothes and thrust one leg into his pantaloons. He tried to imagine Marguerite's body adorned with the red linen cord and saw it so vividly that his well-used body whispered a protest.

David pulled on his shirt and breeches and leaned up against the wall, arms crossed as he watched Anthony dress.

"I didn't mean to spoil our evening."

"You didn't."

"I hate to contradict you, but I obviously did."

Anthony tucked his shirt into his pantaloons and looked for his cravat. David brought it over and helped him fold the linen into something resembling a decent knot and deftly pinned it in place at his throat.

"There, you look almost respectable now."

"But I'm not, am I?" Anthony met David's gaze. "I'm not the sort of man who should be sniffing around a woman's skirts."

David gripped his shoulders. "You don't know that. Some men are able to satisfy both sexes. Perhaps you are one of them."

"But, you're right; I'm not being completely honest with Marguerite, am I? And I told her I would be."

"With all due respect, she is Madame Helene's daughter. Maybe she will understand you better than you think?"

Anthony tried to smile. "Unlikely when I don't even understand myself."

David handed him his waistcoat and held out his coat. "My opinion is worth little, but having struggled to survive Lord Minshom's attentions myself, I understand what you are going through. The man is like an addiction, isn't he? Even now I sometimes find myself wanting to go to him and beg him to take me on again."

Anthony let out his breath. "But perhaps in my selfish attempts to escape him, I might involve someone I've started to care about."

David leaned in and kissed his cheek. "If Marguerite is anything like her mother, she'll survive."

"God, I hope so."

David bowed and gestured at the door. "You'll be fine, my friend. Now go home and get some sleep, and if you want your own set of *shibari* ropes, let me know."

Anthony paused at the door, held out his hand. "I don't know what to say. You not only stopped me from debasing myself in front of Minshom tonight, but gave me one of the best sexual experiences of my life."

"Good."

"If there is anything I can ever do for you in return, just let me know."

David's smile was wry as he shook Anthony's proffered hand. "Well, if you ever see me going anywhere near Minshom again, stop me."

"I'll do that, and thank you again."

"Good luck and good night."

Anthony went through to the main door of the house and put on his hat and cloak. He had no idea what the time was but knew it must be late. He hoped to God that by the time he got home, his mother would have gone to bed. She'd developed an unsettling habit of waiting up for him, which simply exacerbated his guilt and his desire not to tell her anything about his life at all.

Perhaps David had a point and it was time for him to move out . . . He started to walk toward the main thoroughfare, checking for potential hazards in the shadows as he progressed. He wasn't sure if he had the guts to live alone. At least at his parents' house he had to maintain some standards. If he were alone, there would be no one to stop him but himself. He stopped walking, allowed the biting wind to swirl around him and breathed in the bitter cold air.

David had been kind to him, far kinder than any of his other lovers. His life would be much easier if he could be with a man like David. But David hadn't asked for that kind of relationship, had he? Anthony winced. Did he realize that Anthony was too damaged to reciprocate properly? Or did he understand Anthony's need to reach out to Marguerite? Hell, he didn't know anymore.

He glimpsed an approaching hackney cab and increased his pace. Telling Marguerite the truth about his sexual cravings was the honest thing to do, but dammit, she *liked* him. She wanted to be with him. Could he keep up the facade that everything was perfect in his life for much longer? Marguerite was no fool, and part of him longed to confide in her, to see if she would still want him despite his failings.

"Damnation," Anthony cursed under his breath.

He was far too tired to contemplate his future tonight. He sighed. David had certainly worn him out. Tomorrow was quite soon enough to reflect on what he'd learned and to try to make some sense of how he should go on.

9

————————

Marguerite hurried out of the anonymous back entrance of the pleasure house on Barrington Square and headed for the park. Tucked discreetly in her bag were a selection of small sponges and some tansy oil, courtesy of her mother. Her cheeks still felt hot after Helene's frank explanations, but Marguerite was grateful nonetheless.

To her continued surprise, her mother hadn't asked for any details as to why Marguerite was suddenly willing to listen to a lecture about how to avoid pregnancy. Marguerite suspected Helene was just glad her daughter was contemplating making love to anyone and had held back from questioning her for fear of alienating Marguerite completely. It was not like Helene at all, but Marguerite was grateful for the reprieve.

The clock on the church tower at the corner of the busy square struck eleven, and Marguerite increased her pace. She was due at the Lockwoods' to celebrate Charles Lockwood's birthday. In truth, she had no inclination to attend, but her mama-in-law had insisted, and she had reluctantly promised to make an appearance. The Lockwoods en masse were never very pleased to see her, but she'd always liked Justin's younger brother Charles, and she was willing to brave the others for his sake.

Spots of rain darkened the flagstones ahead of her, and clouds covered the brightness of the sun. It was usually far quicker to cross through the gardens of the adjoining squares than to go around the busy streets in her carriage. She hadn't reckoned on the rain. Marguerite picked up her pale green muslin skirts and ran toward the imposing white steps of Lockwood House. With her head lowered, she wasn't completely surprised when she ran into another person also ascending the steps.

"I beg your pardon, sir," she gasped as he steadied her elbow and prevented her falling. "I couldn't see where I was going."

"I noticed that."

The man's smile was pained as if she had somehow injured him in her precipitous flight. Marguerite pulled out of his grasp, straightened her bonnet and bobbed him a small curtsey.

"As I said, I apologize. Did I hurt you?"

He kept staring, his pale face inscrutable, and his light blue eyes fixed on hers. What she could see of his hair was crow black, making her guess he was in his early thirties. He wore a simply cut dark blue coat, black breeches and well-polished boots, which gleamed despite the gloom.

"Not at all, ma'am." He offered her his arm. "Shall we go in?"

Marguerite hesitated, but he didn't move on. He wasn't a member of the Lockwood family she'd met before, but that didn't mean he didn't have a perfect right to be at the party. She reluctantly placed her fingers on his pristine sleeve and headed inside. He took off his hat, waited as she gave her pelisse to the footman and ascended the stairs to the drawing room at her side. She couldn't fault his manners, but there was something in his thorough appraisal that made her uneasy.

"Marguerite?"

She looked up as Lady Lockwood came toward her. "Good morning, ma'am."

Lady Lockwood brushed her lips against Marguerite's cheek and then turned to her companion. "I didn't know you were acquainted with my daughter-in-law, Lord Minshom. Did Justin introduce you?"

Marguerite stepped slightly away from her silent companion. "We haven't been formally introduced. We simply arrived on the steps together, and Lord Minshom was kind enough to escort me in."

"It was a pleasure, my lady."

"Minshom is a distant connection on my father's side. His mother and I met as debutantes and were married in the same year." Lady Lockwood's smile was fond and far warmer than the one she'd offered Marguerite. "I believe I am one of your godparents."

Lord Minshom bowed to them both, his smile dazzling, his pale eyes cold. "I believe you are, although you scarcely look old enough."

Lady Lockwood laughed and tapped his sleeve with her fan. "You are an incorrigible flirt. Now pray don't forget to give your good wishes to Charles in person. He is over by the window with dear sweet Amelia." She nodded and walked back into the chattering throng, leaving Marguerite stranded with her silent companion.

He bowed slightly. "My condolences on your husband's death. Despite the disparity in our ages, I considered Justin a friend."

Marguerite inclined her head. "Thank you, my lord. It was a terrible tragedy."

"Indeed. Did the authorities ever prosecute anyone over the duel?"

"I don't believe so, sir," Marguerite said carefully. "As far as I understand it, the man fled the country."

Lord Minshom smiled and showed perfect white teeth. "You sound almost disappointed. Did you want to dispense justice on him yourself?"

Marguerite met his amused gaze. "I would've liked to hear his side of the story. The reports I received about the cause of the duel were very garbled."

He shrugged. "I believe that is often the case when men are in their cups. They say and do things that are contrary to their true natures."

"Having known both men, I still find it difficult to understand exactly why they decided to fight to the death."

"You met Sir Harry?"

"Indeed I did; in fact, he accompanied us on our honeymoon in Europe."

"Did he really? How amusing."

Marguerite raised her chin. "I would hardly consider it amusing, sir, seeing as my husband died at his hand."

"Touché, my lady." He met her gaze, his eyes as hard as her own. "Men are animals at heart, Lady Justin, don't forget that." He gestured at the window where Charles stood surrounded by friends. "Shall we go and pay our respects?"

He took her hand again and led her forward before she had a chance to escape him. And why would she wish to do so? His frank discourse had not only alarmed her but surprised her. At least he was honest. He was probably the only person present who would bother to speak to her about Justin. Everyone else avoided the subject at all costs.

Marguerite hesitated and patted her reticule.

"Please go ahead. I have a present for Charles. I need to find it before I meet with him."

She turned toward a small table close to the wall and dumped her reticule on the surface. After untying the knots, she opened the bag wide and rummaged inside for the small package.

"May I help you, ma'am?"

She jumped as she realized Lord Minshom had remained at her side and was now looking over her shoulder at the exposed contents of her bag. She felt her cheeks redden. Perhaps he wouldn't notice the sponges and oils. It was unlikely that a man in his position would care or even know how a woman might protect herself. Thankfully, she grabbed the small wrapped present and drew the strings of her reticule tight.

"Thank you, sir, but I've found what I was looking for."

To her relief, he said nothing and simply followed her over toward Charles.

"Marguerite, how nice to see you!"

"It's wonderful to see you too, Charles, and may I wish you a happy birthday?" She kissed his cheek, drawing back quickly as Amelia, his wife, cleared her throat.

Charles's warm greeting wasn't replicated on Amelia's face. Marguerite wasn't quite sure why, but Amelia had always seen her as a competitor. In an effort to diffuse any potential awkwardness, Marguerite smiled. "Good morning, Amelia, and congratulations on your exciting news."

Amelia placed her hand on her rounded stomach and smiled smugly. "Thank you. I'm thrilled to be carrying the heir to such an ancient and esteemed title."

"Amelia . . ." Charles's urgent whisper made Marguerite smile even harder.

She allowed Amelia her moment of victory, determined not to spoil the young couple's joy. It was yet another small way to remain loyal to Justin and his family, even if they didn't appreciate it.

"I have a gift for you, Charles."

She handed Charles the small package, waiting anxiously as

he opened it to reveal the miniature portrait of Amelia she'd labored over.

"It is beautiful." Charles looked up, admiration clear in his eyes. "Is this your own work?"

Marguerite shrugged. "It is nothing."

"May I?" Lord Minshom took the frame and held it up to his eyeglass.

"It is exquisite. You are obviously a woman of many talents, Lady Justin." He handed it back to Charles. "I think you have just been given something your family will cherish for generations."

Amelia rolled her eyes, but Charles nodded. "I agree. Thank you, Marguerite; I shall carry this with me always."

Marguerite glanced around the others in the group and saw some of the faces were still hostile. And who could blame them? She'd let the family down in so many ways. It was definitely time to beat a retreat.

"It was a pleasure to see you both again, but unfortunately, I have to leave. Mrs. Jones is sick, and I promised to return to her side as soon as I could."

In truth, Mrs. Jones was sleeping off the effects of overindulging at dinner the night before, but the Lockwoods didn't need to know that. Marguerite's incompetent chaperone suited her perfectly, and she had no wish for her to be replaced.

Charles sighed. "I'm sorry to see you go, Marguerite. We'll have to invite you around for dinner when Amelia is feeling more the thing."

"That would be delightful." Marguerite met Amelia's eye and knew the invitation would never be issued, but she smiled nonetheless. "Now I must go and say good-bye to your mother."

Charles drew her into a hug and took the opportunity to whisper in her ear. "I always think of Justin on days like this. I miss him like hell, don't you Marguerite?"

"*Oui*," she whispered. "But I think he would be very proud of you."

He released her with another smile, and she went to find Lady Lockwood, ready to repeat her story about Mrs. Jones and make her escape. With a small prayer of thanks, she headed down the stairs and waited in the cold marble hall for the footman to fetch her things. A portrait of the Lockwood children above the fireplace caught her attention, and she wandered over to study Justin's innocent face.

After he'd died, she'd tried to paint a portrait of him but had been unable to catch his essence. Her memories of him were too painful to allow her gift to surface. Would he have put on weight by now like Charles? Or would he still be as tall and elegant as the mysteriously blunt Lord Minshom?

"Lady Justin?"

As if conjured from her imagination, Marguerite turned to find Lord Minshom at the bottom of the stairs. He took her coat from the footman and held it out.

"I notice you arrived on foot. Would you permit me to escort you home?"

Marguerite thrust an arm into the coat sleeve he held out for her. The clean flowery scent of his body surrounded her as he enveloped her in the thick fabric.

"I would hate to take you out of your way, sir." She glanced doubtfully out of the door, which the footman now held open, and viewed the steady rain.

"It would be a pleasure, my lady. I only intended to stay for a few moments, so we can be off immediately. I instructed my coachman to walk the horses rather than stable them."

He took her arm and guided her down the slippery steps into his luxurious coach. Marguerite settled herself on the seat and waited as he took the place opposite her. She gave him a tentative smile.

"I haven't told you where I live."

He shrugged. "I asked Lady Lockwood. My coachman already has your direction."

"You were so sure I would accompany you then?"

"In this weather? You would've been a fool not to. And you do not strike me as a foolish woman." He shifted in the seat, placing his arm along the back to brace himself against the motion of the carriage. "And, I have always wanted to meet you."

"Why?"

"Because I heard a lot about you from Justin and Sir Harry." His gaze was keen. "They both found you beautiful and irresistible."

Marguerite managed a tight smile even as her throat dried up. Earlier Lord Minshom had seemed surprised that she'd even known Sir Harry. Despite his benign appearance, this man was sharp as a needle and, as a friend of Justin, not necessarily inclined to like her.

"I don't claim to be a beauty, sir."

He considered her for a long moment, his head angled to one side. "You don't need to claim anything. You are beautiful." He frowned. "You remind me of somebody, but I can't quite put my finger on it."

Her heart accelerated and thumped in her chest. Was he one of her mother's clients? He had the look of a man who could afford the high fees of the pleasure house and had the appetite to enjoy them.

"Ah, perhaps that's it." He clicked his fingers making her jump. "I believe I saw you at the theater the other night with an acquaintance of mine, Lord Anthony Sokorvsky."

"I was at the theater, sir. It was most enjoyable."

"I'm sure it was. And Sokorvsky can be good company when he chooses." Lord Minshom's dismissive smile flashed out. There was an unmistakable edge to his voice when he mentioned Anthony. Desperately, Marguerite wondered how to change the subject.

"Do you live near the Lockwoods, Lord Minshom?"

"Actually I have a house on Hanover Square. It isn't that far from where you live on Maddox Street." He crossed one long leg over the other. "I seem to remember visiting that house when I was a child and meeting an elderly female relative of Justin's who had lots of cats."

"That's correct, sir. The Lockwoods offered me the house after Miss Priscilla's death. It was very kind of them."

Lord Minshom raised his dark eyebrows. "Hardly. As the widow of their eldest son, one might expect a lot more—a place in their home and their affection, perhaps?"

How interesting that he'd picked up on the lack of welcome for her at the Lockwoods' and had the nerve to mention it. "And what if 'one' did not wish to live with the Lockwoods?"

He stared at her and then nodded. "I can see how they might make you feel unwelcome."

She raised her chin. "I am not complaining, sir. The family has been more than generous."

"Indeed."

Marguerite stared out the window as they rounded a corner and a familiar row of terraced townhouses appeared. She began to gather her things and retied the ribbons of her bonnet.

"Thank you for bringing me home, Lord Minshom."

He smiled as the carriage drew to a halt. "It was my pleasure." He shifted along the seat toward the door his coachman was already opening. "As I said, I've always looked forward to meeting you."

Marguerite ducked her head to exit the carriage and stilled as Lord Minshom's hard fingers closed around her upper arm.

"At least allow me to escort you to your door."

She sighed as he exited the carriage ahead of her and waited until he helped her down. The rain had almost stopped, although black clouds continued to boil and churn overhead.

Lord Minshom kissed her gloved hand, his expression once more impossible to read.

"Good-bye, Lady Justin. I hope we'll meet again soon."

I hope we don't. Marguerite bobbed a curtsey and managed to smile back before hurrying to her door. Lord Minshom had unsettled her; his intimate knowledge of both the Lockwood family and her deceased husband made her nervous. Exactly how close a friend had he been to Justin?

Even worse, if he was a patron of the pleasure house, he might know exactly where Justin's sexual tastes lay and how he'd chosen to enjoy them. He might even know her mother. Behind that bland smile, did Lord Minshom harbor a grudge against the woman who had caused Justin's death, and if so, what did he intend to do about it?

10

"Anthony, are you still here? I was about to lock up."

Anthony looked up from the document he was squinting at. His office was so dark he could barely see Peter's silhouette in the doorway. With a groan, he dropped his quill pen and flexed his fingers.

"I didn't realize it was so late."

Peter leaned against the door jamb and crossed his arms. "I know Val and I asked you to work harder, but we don't expect you to kill yourself."

"I won't. I just wanted to finish this."

"And have you finished?"

Anthony sighed. "I suppose it will have to do." He glanced at the clock and shot to his feet. "Damnation! I was invited for dinner at eight."

Peter's quiet chuckle filled the room. "You'd better hurry, then. Ladies don't like it when you are late."

Anthony stopped buttoning his coat. "How did you know it was a lady who'd asked me to dinner, and is that really true?"

Peter grinned. "I've never seen you move that quickly before, so I assumed you weren't going home. And, in truth, all the ladies I've known haven't taken to being ignored well."

Anthony grabbed his hat and gloves and hesitated by the door. "Do you think a man should always tell a lady the truth about himself?"

"About why he's late for dinner, or are you speaking in more general terms?"

"More generally."

Peter considered him. "I think it depends on the type of relationship you have. For example, Abigail knows everything about me and my less-than-perfect past, yet she still loves me." His slight smile died. "Unfortunately, not all women are so accepting."

Anthony fiddled with his hat. "I don't know how much I should reveal about my sexual tastes."

"Do you trust her?"

Anthony thought about that, pictured Marguerite's blue eyes and serious face. "Yes."

"Then tell her."

"And if she turns away from me in disgust?"

"Then she wasn't the right woman for you, was she?"

Anthony sighed and walked toward the main office, which for once was quiet and deserted. "You're not being much help."

"I know." Peter clapped Anthony on the back. "Tell her some of it, then, but for God's sake, don't lie."

Anthony bade him good night, took a cautious look around the desolate, grimy streets and decided to walk back to the main thoroughfare to find a hackney cab. Despite attending to his work, he'd spent most of the day wondering what he should tell Marguerite and how she would react.

One thing was clear. He couldn't allow her to see him as a perfect gentleman; he wasn't comfortable with that pretense at all. He genuinely liked her and wanted her respect. But what could he say that wouldn't shock her?

Nothing.

His whole life was a series of humiliations. Why the devil would she ever want to be associated with him anyway? On that glum note, he hailed a cab and headed for Marguerite's house on Maddox Street.

Marguerite stuck her spoon in the bowl of gooseberry fool in front of her and slowly sucked the tart fruit from the silverware. Perhaps she was indeed a fool. Mrs. Jones had gone to bed, leaving Marguerite still waiting at the dining table for dear, dear Anthony to appear. In anticipation of his visit, she'd put on her favorite gown, allowed her maid to curl her hair into a cascade of ringlets and left off all but one of her petticoats.

And he hadn't arrived. Marguerite took another swig of her red wine and savored the acidic taste. She wanted to squirm in her seat, to pace the room, to do something to get rid of the frustrated desire that lurked under her skin. She felt like the female cat in the convent kitchen that yowled and scratched to be let out whenever the males gathered to serenade her in the gardens.

So much for being ready to take a chance on another man . . . Marguerite's fingers curled around the glass bowl. If Anthony appeared at this moment, he might find himself covered in green goopy pudding.

There was a knock on the door and her butler appeared. "My lady, there is a gentleman here to see you. It is rather late. Do you want me to turn him away?"

Her butler's offended expression said that she should do just that, but Marguerite realized she wanted to see Anthony far too much to care about propriety.

"It's all right, Jarvis. Ask him in and then you can retire."

"Of course, my lady."

Marguerite sat back in her chair as Anthony strode into the

room. His dark hair was disordered, his cheeks flushed as if he had been running. She pointed at the clock on the mantelpiece.

"You are late."

He bowed low. "I know. Will you accept my profound apologies?"

"It depends on what you have been doing instead of honoring your obligation to me."

His smile was wary. "I was at work and I forgot the time."

"Your work was more important than me?"

He sighed and sat on the delicate gilt chair next to hers. "Of course not. It's just that with my job in jeopardy, I sometimes try too hard to prove my worthiness."

"Why is your job at risk?"

He shrugged. "Because it was only supposed to be temporary, and now my father and Val want me to give it up and live like a true gentleman."

"They want you to be idle?"

"Apparently so."

"That is ridiculous."

He glanced up at her then, his vivid blue eyes full of laughter, and took her hands. "I can't help but agree with you."

She snatched her hands away, not quite ready to forgive him yet, her courage bolstered by the two glasses of red wine she'd already drunk. "Have you eaten?"

He surveyed the array of dishes on the table and swallowed hard. "Unfortunately not."

She waved a hand at him. "Then help yourself."

She waited as he gathered himself a large plate of cold food, poured him a glass of the rich red wine and then sat back to finish her dessert.

"May I say you look beautiful tonight?"

Marguerite frowned down at her favorite blue gown and then at him. "Didn't we agree that you wouldn't use that word?"

"Why does it offend you so much?"

Marguerite shrugged. "My mother is beautiful."

"She is, but does that mean you can't be beautiful as well? Do you think she would resent it?"

"No, of course not. It's just that I hate to be judged on my appearance."

"But how else is a man to judge you? It's not as if any of us can see what's inside a person on a first meeting."

Marguerite swallowed hard. "Justin said he fell in love with my face on our first meeting."

"Ah, now I understand." Anthony put down his fork.

"Because you are so beautiful yourself?"

He grimaced. "Not *that*, but I've heard myself described as a handsome man."

"You are."

"Thank you." His smile dimmed. "But I also get fed up with being characterized as a charming addle-pated idiot."

"I don't think you are an idiot, but I do wonder why a man with all your attributes isn't married yet."

"I'm only twenty-five!"

"But you are also the son of a marquis."

"The second son. And, as my half brother has already been obliging enough to provide my father with a grandson, I have no reason to marry at all."

Marguerite regarded Anthony. "It must have been difficult for you when Valentin returned from the dead."

He glanced up, his expression hardening. "Are you trying to suggest I'm jealous of my brother?"

"Are you?"

"Not at all. In truth, I was relieved when he turned up. It took my father's often obsessive attention away from me."

"Then, if not jealousy, what do you conceal behind that handsome face that has made you avoid your social obligations for all these years?"

"Why should you assume I conceal anything?"

She opened her eyes wide at him. "You were the one who suggested there was more to you than a pretty face."

He stared at her, his mouth a thin line. "Are you trying to start a fight with me because I was late?"

"Not *just* because of that."

He drained his wine glass and placed it back on the table with a thump. "I've apologized, what more can I do?"

"Honor your promise to me?"

"What promise?"

"To be honest."

He sighed, "God, Marguerite, sometimes you remind me of your mother."

"I'll take that as a compliment. Now tell me what lies beneath your charm and good looks."

He refilled her glass and then his own; his hand shook, spilling red wine on the white damask tablecloth. His smile had gone and there was a bleakness in his eyes that made him seem the stranger he claimed to be.

He inhaled slowly. "I like to have sex with men as well as women." He looked straight at her. "Is that honest enough for you?"

Marguerite's chest tightened, and she fought an absurd desire to laugh. What was it about her that attracted such men? And was that why Christian had introduced her to Anthony? She took another sip of her wine and kept staring at him.

Anthony shrugged. "Well?"

"Well, what?"

"Have I disgusted you? I've certainly rendered you almost speechless."

She licked her lips, tasted the sharpness of the grapes. "I'm not disgusted."

"Why not?" His mouth twisted. "Sometimes I disgust myself."

"That is understandable when such liaisons can result in severe penalties under the law." Now she sounded as prim and proper as a governess, but it was hard to frame her replies when her heart was beating so wildly. Was she being given a second chance to understand the complexity of her sexual nature? Would she be able to help Anthony as she hadn't been able to help Justin?

She met his gaze, observing the brittle tension in his. "It hasn't stopped me wanting you—if that is what you are worrying about."

He let out his breath. "Are you sure?"

"Of course I am."

He stood up so fast that his chair tipped over, and pulled her into his arms. "Thank God."

She struggled to free her hand and curved it around his neck, bringing his face down to hers. His lips brushed her mouth and she shivered.

"Marguerite, I want to take you to bed. Will you let me?"

She nodded, and he took her hand and dragged her toward the door. The hallway was deserted, the house quiet. She directed him up the stairs and into her bedroom at the back of the house. A single candle burned by the bed, and the banked fire glowed in the hearth. She caught the scent of her own perfume, the powder she used on her face, the burned smell of the curling tongs.

Anthony shut the door and leaned against it, his expression in shadow, the tension in his body palpable.

"Do you really want me, Marguerite?"

"*Oui.*"

She reached up to draw the pins from her hair, watched him take an unsteady step toward her and knew that everything would be all right.

* * *

Anthony watched Marguerite's dark hair fall around her face and shoulders and swallowed hard. What the hell was he supposed to do now? Pick her up, throw her on the bed and ravish her? His cock was already hard and eager for anything, but his mind . . . His meager experience with women rose to mock him, to make him incapable of speech or action.

Marguerite came closer, and he inhaled the sweet scent of violets. She turned her back on him.

"Will you help me out of this gown, please?"

She sounded almost as scared as he felt. He stared at the small pearl buttons and wondered if his big blunt fingers would be able to manipulate them without shaking too much. He attempted the first one, breathed a little easier as it obligingly slipped free. Her bodice gaped forward, giving him an excellent view not only of the creamy slopes of her shoulders but of the tops of her breasts.

He wanted to taste her skin. With a groan, he dipped his head and touched his lips to her throat. She sighed and leaned back into him, his fingers crushed between them, his heart racing.

"Unlace my corset too."

He studied the spiral bindings until he worked out how to release her and set to work coaxing the long strings through the holes. His mouth was dry, his breathing uneven. It was one thing to sexually service an unknown woman at the pleasure house, but making love to Marguerite, a woman he desired and liked, was a completely different equation. Would she detect his lack of expertise?

She turned in his arms, allowed her gown and corset to fall to the thick carpet. She was covered by only a thin muslin shift now, her nipples and the dark shadow between her legs visible through the sheer material. She tugged at his cravat.

"May I help you undress?"

He nodded and stood still as she eased him out of his tight-fitting coat and waistcoat and unpinned his cravat. Her smile was beautiful as she touched him, and he yearned for her hands on other parts of his body, especially his cock. To be handled with such gentleness almost brought tears to his eyes. So different from Minshom and the other men, so humbling . . .

He cupped her cheek, drew her mouth toward his and kissed her soft, willing lips. Her hand slid between them and worked on the button of his pantaloons. He gasped as she wrapped her hand around the base of his shaft and squeezed hard.

"Anthony, you know you said I couldn't shock you?"

He dragged his attention from his aching cock to her face. To his surprise, she looked almost as worried as he felt.

"You can do anything you want to me, Marguerite."

She leaned in and bit down on his lower lip. "Would you mind if I had my way with you first? It's been a long time since I've been with a man, and I'm a little concerned about being at your mercy."

He blinked at her as her fingers continued to caress his cock and balls. Had she heard that he liked it rough? Was she really afraid that he might harm her? He forced himself to respond. "I'd never hurt you."

She patted his cheek. "I know that. It's just that you are a big man, and I'd like to be in control of how you take me . . ." She stopped talking and stared up at him, biting her lip.

Suddenly he understood her all too well and was more than willing to oblige her. "I'd be delighted."

Her laugh was low and full of relief. "Then take off your shoes and pantaloons and get on the bed."

He stripped everything off and went to lie on the white sheets of the pristine bed. His cock rose, seeking relief, seeking a release he knew only Marguerite could give him tonight. He settled back against the headboard and waited for her to join him. The mattress barely dipped as she climbed onto the high bed and crawled toward him.

For one awful moment, he wanted to hide himself from her unabashed stare. Would she like what she saw? Would she somehow sense how unworthy he was of her regard and tell him to leave? He flinched as she straddled his hips, fisting his hands by his sides in an effort not to touch her. Her breasts danced in front of his eyes, their red tips already tight and ready for his mouth.

"Anthony, are you all right?"

He blinked and found her staring at him quizzically. Her face was as beautiful and delicate as the rest of her. He felt the wet heat from her sex on his balls, the way his cock brushed against the skin of her stomach as he tried to breathe normally.

She sighed. "I know I said I wanted to be in charge this first time, but I didn't mean to stop you enjoying it."

"I am enjoying it. Can't you tell?"

"I've heard that some men don't like a woman to be too aggressive in bed. Is that true?"

"I wouldn't know. I'm quite happy lying here, waiting for you to take me."

She finally smiled at him. "Are you sure?"

He glanced down at his eager cock, rolled his hips toward her body. "God, yes."

She knelt up and grasped his shaft around the base, drawing the tip back toward her. He groaned as he brushed against her core and was guided inside her. Instinctively, he tried to thrust upward but was met by a tightness that held him at bay.

Marguerite licked her lips. "Perhaps you are too big."

"Perhaps you should be wetter."

Anthony gritted his teeth and wrapped his fingers over hers on his cock. He knew too well how painful a forced penetration could be, and he wasn't going to allow that to happen to Marguerite. The lessons he'd been given about arousing a woman resonated in his head.

"Let me help you."

He sat up straighter, drew one of her breasts into his mouth and began to suckle. She sighed deep in her throat and rocked toward him with every pull of his mouth. He withdrew his cock from the tight hole and instead rubbed the wet crown against the bundle of nerves at the front of her sex.

Strange that he could aid her, even stranger that she was obviously enjoying what he was trying to do. He transferred his attention to her other breast and used his left hand to caress her soft buttocks, to slide his fingers lower and penetrate her sex from behind—wet now and wider, easing his way, opening to his touch like a flower.

"Anthony . . ."

She moaned his name, kissed the top of his head, his ear, anything she could reach, her nails digging into his shoulder as she moved with him. He couldn't believe how natural it felt to have her like this, her cream coating his fingers, the crown of his sensitive cock rubbing her clitoris.

He closed his eyes and repositioned his cock against her now slick entrance, encouraged her to guide him inside. This time he slid in at least three inches, the whole thick purple crown inside her. He felt her flesh give and yet not give, encase him in a lush cave that shifted and changed the deeper he penetrated her.

"Take more, Marguerite."

He leaned back to watch the glorious sight of her body poised over his, his shaft disappearing inside her, and almost came. This was nothing like taking a man. Her sheath undulated and pulsed around his shaft, drawing him deeper even through the threat he'd be trapped forever, making him want to stay inside her more than breathe.

"God . . ."

He grasped her hips, encouraged her to shimmy lower, and groaned as she finally took him all. She looked at him, her smile tentative, her eyes huge in the shadowed darkness.

"You are even bigger than I thought you'd be."

He held still, let her body settle around him and enjoyed the tight grip of a woman's passage on his cock for the first time.

"You thought about having me like this?"

She stroked his chest, her thumbs feathering over his nipples making him shiver. "Of course."

"Then perhaps you should continue to play out your fantasy and make me come for you." He hesitated. "Unless you wish me to pull out . . ."

She shook her head. "That isn't necessary."

Anthony tightened his grip on her hips. "Then will you have mercy and ride me to completion?"

She started to move on him, her sex sliding up and down his shaft, squeezing and releasing him with a fierceness he would not have dreamed possible but that he was experiencing it first-hand. So tight now he could feel his cum being forced up his shaft by the demands of Marguerite's body.

"Don't stop," he managed to groan, as she continued to move on him. He remembered to find her clit, thumbed her in time to their combined thrusts, felt the moment when she climaxed like a punch in the gut as his cock was squeezed to extremes and began to spurt seed deep inside her. The spasm seemed endless as he rocked and writhed beneath her, heard her answering moan of completion.

She collapsed over his chest and he held her there, one hand splayed over her buttocks, his cock still throbbing inside her. She threaded her fingers into his hair and cuddled deeper, her body shaking with little aftershocks as she curled up against him.

He kissed the top of her head, inhaled her beguiling scent. She'd trusted him to make it good for her, trusted him enough to let him inside her, for God's sake. He smoothed his hand over her hair and felt her move closer. He'd never felt like this before in his life—so complete, so sexually sated, so happy. His eyes flew open.

How the hell had she done that to him? And what the hell was he going to do now?

Marguerite squeezed her eyes tightly shut as tears continued to seep from them. She hadn't realized how difficult it would be, had naively thought the sexual act would remain the same, even with a different man. But it hadn't been like that all. Anthony was completely different from Justin; his smell, the texture of his skin, the way he moved beneath her—all different and infinitely strange.

Anthony sighed and kissed the top of her head, drew her closer into the curve of his warm muscular body. She managed to stop crying, terrified the tears would touch his skin and wake him up. She didn't regret what she had done in the slightest, yet somehow it felt like the ultimate betrayal of Justin, another area of her life where he had been supplanted, another new experience to eradicate his memory.

She turned her face into Anthony's shoulder and inhaled his particular scent. There was no way back now. She could only hope she would be able to live with the consequences and not allow her guilt to destroy the fragile beginnings of something she hoped would be precious.

11

Marguerite woke up slowly with a sense that something was different. The thud of another heartbeat under her cheek and the feel of a warm masculine body sprawled beneath her made her open her eyes wide.

"Anthony?"

"Hmm . . . ?" He touched her face, trailed his finger down to her throat. It was still dark, and although no light penetrated the thick blue velvet curtains, the birds had started singing into the stillness.

"You should go home."

"Hmm . . ."

His hand moved lower, slid down her back to cup her buttocks and squeezed hard. She squirmed against him, felt his erect cock jerk against her stomach.

"Anthony . . ."

"I need to be inside you." He rolled her onto her back and kneed her legs apart, slid his shaft deep inside her and started to thrust. Marguerite could do nothing but grab his wide shoulders and hang on, answer his kisses with her own, demand answers and replenish needs she'd almost forgotten existed. She lifted her hips to meet each hard stroke, gloried in the sensation of him moving over her, taking her, fucking her.

He groaned and rocked harder, ground himself against her sex until she wanted to scream and writhe, bite and scratch. Her climax caught her by surprise, forced him to stiffen too and come inside her. He sank down, his body covering hers completely.

She lay still and let his weight settle over her like a heavy living blanket. He suddenly rolled off her.

"Did I hurt you?"

His quiet question made her turn her head to look at him. "*Non.*"

"Are you sure?"

"Why would you even think that?"

He stared at her, his face a pale outline in the darkness. "Because I'm more used to being with men, and they aren't quite as delicate as you are."

He moved to the side of the bed, groaned as his feet thumped onto the wooden floorboards. Marguerite rose up on one elbow to watch him gather his clothes and put them on, his movements jerky and unsure in the dim light.

"Anthony, are you all right?"

"Of course I am. You told me it was time to go, and I'm leaving."

Marguerite gathered the sheets tightly around her breasts. Although he sounded quite amiable, he was hardly exhibiting the loverlike behavior she had unconsciously expected. She bit down on her lip.

"Is this how you treat your male lovers?"

He paused, his hands at his throat as he wrapped his cravat around his shirt collar. "What?"

She waved her fingers toward the door. "You just get out of bed and walk away without a word?"

"Usually, yes."

"Oh." She lay back down and pulled the covers up to her chin. "Good-bye, then."

He came back to the bed and sat on the edge, reaching out to touch her hunched shoulder. "Marguerite?"

"Go away."

She refused to look at him; obviously the experience they had just shared meant nothing more to him than any of his other, no doubt varied, sexual conquests.

"Marguerite . . . there is something I want to say to you, but I refuse to talk to a pillow."

She opened her eyes and stared into his face. His smile was so tender it made her want to cry. "*What?*"

"You are right: men don't make polite bedfellows, but you . . ." He swallowed hard, traced the line of her cheekbone with his fingertip. "I'm not sure I even have the right words. You honor me by accepting me into your bed." He kissed her nose. "Over you, inside you . . ."

Now she felt foolish for having snapped at him. She turned her head and kissed his finger. "All right. You can go now."

"Are you sure?" He slid his thumb along her lower lip, and she tasted herself, him and something metallic. She sighed as he bent to kiss her.

"May I take you out tonight?"

"If you promise not to be late again."

His quiet chuckle made her feel both treasured and appreciated. "If I'm late, don't let me in. I don't deserve to be forgiven twice and in such an intimate and, quite frankly, such an encouraging manner."

"Go away, Anthony."

He retreated to the door, kissed his fingers to her and left. Her body felt different; muscles she'd forgotten she owned pulled at her and made her ache. She slid her hand down to her belly and then lower, to where she was still wet and open from his lovemaking. She must remember to take the sponge out . . .

With a contented smile she turned onto her side and closed her eyes. There was plenty of time for the practicalities of life. For the moment, she just wanted to luxuriate in the fascinating physical effects of being bedded by a man.

Anthony was still smiling as he walked quietly across the marble floor of his father's grand house and toward the servants' stairs. It appeared his mother had gone to bed, so he had nothing to fear from her. And it was unlikely that even the servants would be up at four in the morning.

Making love to Marguerite had been a revelation. Her fierce natural response to him was as arousing as any of the calculated beatings or sexual toys Minshom used. He shuddered as he remembered how powerful he'd felt when he put Marguerite on her back and shoved his cock deep . . .

Alerted by the flickering glow of a candle, he paused by his father's half-open study door. Had someone forgotten to snuff out the lights? He pushed at the door, squinting into the sudden glare.

"Anthony?"

He stiffened as he realized his father sat behind his ornate mahogany desk, a quill pen in his hand, his spectacles perched on the end of his nose. For some reason, the harshness of the setting made him look older, more careworn and infinitely more human.

"Father." Anthony tried to appear relaxed, feeling like his ten-year-old self caught in some mischief. "What are you doing up so late?"

"I might ask the same of you."

Anthony shrugged. "I thought I was expected to behave like a young man about town. Isn't this what you wanted? Me staggering home late and in my cups?"

His father's expression tightened. "Come in and shut the door."

"Actually, Father, I'm rather tired. I was heading for bed."

"*I said* come in and sit down."

Anthony straightened and did what he was told. The grim set of his father's mouth made it impossible to refuse. "What can I do for you, sir?"

"You can stop working at Valentin's place of business, for one."

Anthony gripped the arms of the chair. "We've already had this discussion. You'd prefer me to racket about town like a fool rather than seek honest employment. I don't agree."

"I didn't say that."

"You might not have used those exact words, but that is what you implied."

"There are other ways to be employed rather than in trade."

Anthony laughed. "You make it sound like I'm whoring down at the docks rather than working in a respectable shipping company."

The marquis whipped off his spectacles. "I'm glad you mentioned whoring. I've heard you like to play with the mollies and the sadists on the top floor at Madame Helene's."

Anthony hoped his shock didn't show on his face. "What the devil is that supposed to mean?"

"I'm not dead, Anthony—I do venture out into society, and I hear the gossip about you in the clubs."

"And you believe it?"

"You wouldn't be the first of my sons to make a name for himself as a libertine."

"A libertine is a far cry from calling me a male prostitute, sir."

The marquis fixed him with a hard stare, which reminded Anthony forcibly of Valentin. "If you allow others to use you as they will, what else should I call you?"

"A man who likes sex?"

"Not the kind of sex a man should be proud of."

Anthony raised his eyebrows. "And who made you the judge of what is acceptable? If I was out fucking ten different women a night like Val used to, would that make it better?"

"Of course it wouldn't, but it would be better than the choices you make now."

Anthony bit back his next answer and forced himself to relax in his chair. He would not allow his father to ruin his evening with Marguerite with insinuations about his past.

"The rumors about me are no longer correct, sir. Recently I have seen the error of my ways." Ruthlessly, Anthony buried the erotic memory of his evening with David Gray and stared right into his father's eyes. "So you have nothing to worry about." He half-rose from his chair. "If there is nothing else you wish to say to me, I'll go to bed."

His father's fist thumped onto the desk. "Anthony, will you please listen to me? Why do you think I'm sitting here at this time in the morning?"

"Because you wanted to talk to me about my lack of morals and responsibility?"

"I did want to talk to you, but I'm also trying to run an estate that includes five dwellings, two farms, three villages and approximately two thousand tenants."

Anthony sat back down. "But you have staff to do that for you."

"It is a foolish man who allows his servants to run his business completely for him. I like to oversee the details. It stops sloppiness, deceit and incompetence."

"Well, that's highly commendable, but I don't see what it has to do with me."

"There's no need to be sarcastic, Anthony."

Anthony sighed. "I apologize, but I really don't know what you are getting at."

"I need help."

"To run the estates? Then why not hire more people?"

"I need more involvement from my family, dammit, not strangers." The marquis slammed the book in front of him shut and glared at Anthony. "I need you."

A coldness settled low in Anthony's gut as he stared at his father. "Valentin is your heir."

"I know that, but you are his brother. You are perfectly capable of running the estates if you choose to."

Anger threaded through the ice in his veins, and Anthony sat forward. "And why aren't you having this conversation with Valentin? He's the eldest son; surely he is the one who should take care of his own damned inheritance?"

"Valentin is . . . difficult."

Anthony realized he was standing, shoved back his chair. "He certainly is 'difficult.' And you won't ask him to do anything he doesn't care to, will you? Are you worried he'll disappear on you again? That's why you're asking me to step into his shoes."

"My relationship with Valentin is no concern of yours."

"Isn't it? How strange, it seems like it has everything to do with me. Val gets to do what he likes because he's the prodigal son, and I . . ." Anthony stopped talking, realized what he'd said and simply glared at his father. "I'm supposed to roll over, take whatever the pair of you decide to hand out to me and be grateful."

The marquis stood too, his still-handsome face cold. "I didn't realize how jealous you were of your brother—considering all he suffered, how can you be so cruel?"

"Why shouldn't I be? When he came back, he took everything from me."

God, had he really said that out loud—had he really felt that? He ran a hand through his hair, trying to collect his scattered emotions. "I'm sorry, sir, I didn't mean that. I'm obviously overtired."

His father stared at him. "Anthony . . . Valentin could never . . ."

"It's all right, sir. I understand." He managed to dredge up a smile and a bow. "I'll certainly think about what you have suggested, although I'm not sure how Valentin will react to the idea of losing me."

The marquis dropped his gaze to the papers on his desk and shuffled them around. Anthony let out his breath. "Valentin's already agreed, hasn't he?"

"Actually, he was the one who suggested it."

"Of course he did. What a masterful piece of manipulation. He not only gets me out of his business, but ensures I'm stuck serving his needs in another capacity for as long as I live. And he doesn't even have to pay me any more."

"As to that, I would, of course, increase your allowance to cover all your additional costs."

"I expect you'd both like me to rusticate in the countryside far from temptation as well, wouldn't you? So much for me prostituting myself for trade or for sex; you'll allow it only if I keep it in the family!"

"For God's sake, Anthony, whatever is the matter with you? I'm only asking you to display some loyalty. This isn't like you at all." The marquis strode to the window and pulled open the drapes. Thin dawn light filtered through the grimy window panes. "Perhaps we'll have this discussion again when you are sober."

"I'm completely sober, Father." Anthony walked across to the door and grabbed the handle. "And don't worry: I'll certainly think about what you've said."

"Where the devil did you say you were tonight?" The marquis's harsh question made Anthony turn back.

"I didn't."

"From the state of you, I'd assume you were at Madame's." His mouth twisted. "So much for changing your ways."

"I haven't been to Madame's."

"Then why is there blood all over your pantaloons and on your hand?"

Anthony glanced down at his white satin pantaloons, saw the splashes of red seeping through the fabric and went cold. God, he had hurt Marguerite, and she'd denied it. Hell and damnation! She must have been too afraid to tell him. He flung open the door as his stomach threatened to rebel.

"Anthony . . ."

He couldn't bear to speak to his father, not now, not when he knew what he'd done. With a curse he hurried upstairs to his room, stripped off his clothes and quickly splashed himself with cold water. He had to get back to Marguerite, to see if she was all right and to promise her that he'd never touch her again.

Marguerite opened her eyes. Something was preventing her from going back to sleep, and it wasn't the noisy sparrows congregating on the roof of the mews below her window. Idly, she allowed her mind to float, hoped whatever it was that was worrying her would surface and become clear. Her hand drifted down to her stomach again and she winced. Anthony had been extremely careful with her, so there was no reason for her to feel so . . .

She sat up so quickly she felt dizzy. Now she knew what that strange pressure meant. She carefully pulled back the covers, saw the faint red stain on the sheets and between her thighs and let out her breath. Her courses had begun, that's why she felt so peculiar.

She carefully moved to the edge of the high bed and felt for the floor with her toes. Shivering in the cold, she managed to fumble across to her dressing table and find the rags and bindings she needed. There was just enough water left in the jug to wash with. Then she returned to bed and cuddled back into the warmth she and Anthony had created.

She wrapped her arms around her aching stomach and curled up into a tight ball. If her mother's information was correct, there would be no child to mar the perfection of her night with Anthony. Another thought prevented Marguerite from falling back to sleep. Had Anthony noticed her courses had begun? And if so, was he offended? Maybe that was why he had left so abruptly. Justin had been horrified at her even mentioning she bled and had refused to share the same bed. Perhaps her French pragmatism about such things was not appreciated in England by any man.

Marguerite smiled into the half darkness. Hopefully Anthony was made of sterner stuff and had gone home to rest without a care in the world.

"You don't understand, I need to see her."

"I'm sorry, my lord, but my lady isn't receiving visitors at this hour of the morning."

Anthony glared into the unresponsive face of Marguerite's butler. True, it was barely light and he'd had to bang on the kitchen door for at least ten minutes to get anyone to pay attention to him over the morning clatter, but he had to see if Marguerite was all right.

"Is my lady's maid here?"

"She is, sir, but . . ."

Anthony took a guinea out of his pocket and pressed it into the butler's unresisting hand. "Perhaps she might be able to check on her mistress and ask if she wants to see me. Tell her it is extremely important."

The butler pocketed the coin and turned back into the kitchen. "Mary, come here."

A pretty black-haired young woman dressed in crisp pink

muslin and an apron rushed over, her expression full of curiosity.

"Yes, Mr. Jarvis?"

"Go and see if her ladyship is awake, and ask her when it would be convenient for her to see Lord Anthony, here."

"Yes, sir!"

Mary bobbed a curtsey and hurried off, looking thrilled to be involved in such early morning drama. Anthony shivered as the wind came up and buttoned the neck of his coat.

"Can I at least come inside and keep warm?"

The butler grudgingly stepped back. "All right, my lord, but don't try any funny business. I'll have you know, her ladyship is a respectable woman."

"I know. I'm the last person in the world who'd argue with that."

"Then you just sit here and wait quietly, sir."

Anthony sat at the big oak table and stretched his hands toward the fire. It appeared that every older male he encountered today was intent on making him feel like an inadequate boy.

"Here you go, sir."

The cook set an earthenware mug in front of him and poured some weak tea from a pot into it. He smiled his thanks. He was too cold to care about the quality of the beverage, just grateful to have something warm inside him after his hasty flight out of his parents' house and back into the streets.

He looked over his shoulder as the kitchen door opened to reveal a smiling Mary.

"Her ladyship says she'll see you, sir."

Anthony got up, aware of the disapproval emanating from the kitchen staff around him. It seemed they all cared for their mistress, which he supposed was a good thing. He bowed at the cook and the butler.

"Thank you for your help. I promise I won't keep her long."

He ran up the stairs two at a time and found his way back to her bedroom, hesitated outside the door long enough for Mary to catch up with him.

"She's still in bed, sir, and not feeling quite the thing, so please be quiet."

Anthony let himself into the shadowed room and stopped several feet from the bed. Marguerite lay back against a mound of pillows, her face a pale shadow against the darkness of her unbound hair. He swallowed hard.

"Are you all right?"

"I'm a little tired, but that is to be expected." She frowned. "Why did you come back? Did you forget something?"

He ignored her questions, concentrated on her face. "Are you angry with me?"

"Why would I be angry?"

He glanced behind him, made sure that Mary had left them alone and advanced on the bed. "As I said, I'm used to bedding men." He took her hand and squeezed it. "I only hope you can forgive me and I assure you I will never trouble you again."

"Anthony, what are you talking about?"

"I'm here to apologize for . . . injuring you."

"You didn't . . ."

"I beg to disagree, I hurt you. I saw the blood."

Her hand flew to her mouth, "*Mon Dieu.* I didn't think about that."

He sat on the side of the bed, still holding her hand, watched her concern change to something more difficult to interpret. He swallowed hard, tried to find the right words to comfort her. "I should never have touched you. I'm obviously not capable of bedding a woman." An even more appalling thought crossed his mind. "Unless, I was your first . . . unless Justin didn't, couldn't . . ."

"Justin could and he did. You didn't take my virginity, Anthony, I'm quite certain of that." Marguerite let go of his hand.

"Did you really come back because you thought you'd injured me with your lovemaking?"

He managed to nod. To his astonishment she started to blush.

"I thought, perhaps you wanted to . . . chastise me."

"For what?"

She held his gaze, her blue eyes full of unexpected awkwardness. "For allowing you into my bed when I was expecting my monthly courses."

Anthony stared at her. *What the hell did that mean?* He vaguely recollected some feminine conversations between his mother and sisters that always stopped the moment they realized he was in the room. He felt a blush creep up his cheeks.

"Oh, that . . ."

"Yes, that . . ." She grimaced. "Justin felt the same way. He refused to come near me when I bled. I forget that the English can be a little more fastidious about these things than the French."

Anthony stared at her clenched hands, taking them back into his. "I didn't realize. I thought I'd hurt you."

"But you didn't."

He leaned in toward her until their foreheads touched. "I can't tell you how relieved I am. I thought . . ."

"Ssh." She pushed a lock of his hair back from his face. "You would never hurt me. You should know by now that women are a lot stronger than they look."

"I know that," he whispered. "But, God . . ." He closed his eyes, allowed her sweet scent to surround him, to heal his ragged nerves. After a long moment, he took a deep breath and kissed her nose. "I should go."

"Yes, you should. My staff will be gossiping about this for days. Let's just hope my mama-in-law doesn't get to hear about it."

He moved off the bed and looked back at her. "Stay well, Marguerite."

"I will." She blew him a kiss. "Now go, or you will be late for work."

Anthony bowed and headed for the door. At her mention of his current employment, the tension returned to his gut. At least he'd settled the most important problem. Now he just had to find the nerve to face Valentin.

12

Anthony pushed open the front door of the shipping office and shut it quickly behind him to keep out the rising wind. The main office was half empty, but Taggart, the manager, was at his desk. He looked up when Anthony reached him, and took off his spectacles.

"You're in early this morning, sir."

Anthony removed his hat and gloves. "Miracles do happen, Mr. Taggart, although in truth, I haven't actually been to bed yet. Is my brother in?"

Taggart polished his spectacles on his handkerchief and nodded. "Yes, indeed he is, sir. Always an early riser, our Lord Valentin."

"And let's not forget all his other Godlike qualities either, shall we?" Anthony muttered as he set off past Taggart to his brother's office, his heart hammering in his chest, his mouth dry. He knocked on the door, heard Val's muted voice bidding him enter.

His brother sat at his desk, pen in hand, attention fixed on one of the accounting books. Despite the chill in the oak-paneled room, his black coat hung over the back of his chair. He glanced up, irritation clear on his fine-featured face and in his violet eyes.

"What is it, Taggart? Oh, it's you Anthony."

"Good morning, Valentin."

Anthony ignored his brother's gesture for him to be seated and instead found a spot to plant his booted feet right in front of Val's desk. Eventually Val looked up at him again.

"Is something the matter?"

"You could say that. I had the misfortune to be cornered by our father last night."

"Did you?" Val put down his pen and sat back, his expression guarded. "And what did he have to say for himself?"

Anthony set his jaw. "You should know. You bloody well orchestrated it."

"What are you implying?"

"You told him I would make the perfect estate manager for you."

"I *told* him that you had an excellent head for business and that if he needed any help with the books then he should have no hesitation in coming to you." Valentin shrugged. "If he took that to mean you should be in charge of running the estates, then surely that is a compliment?"

"You are his heir."

"And I have my own business to run." Val held his gaze, all traces of amiability gone from his face.

"So I should take on the job until you feel like dabbling in it yourself?"

"What the hell is that supposed to mean?"

"You know damn well what." Anthony glared at his brother. "As usual, you get to do whatever you please, and I have to sacrifice what I want to keep you and Father happy!"

Valentin raised one scathing eyebrow. "You don't know what you want. All you know is how to destroy yourself. I thought that if you knew Father and I believed you could run the estates, it might give you a purpose, a reason to succeed, a way out of this mess you have created."

Anthony planted his fists on Val's desk and leaned forward. "How dare you presume to know what I need or what I want? All you care about is yourself. That's all you've ever cared about."

"And you haven't?" Val suddenly stood up and faced Anthony. "You've spent the last few years trying to kill yourself. Does that show much care for your family or the people who love you?"

"That's a cheap shot, Val. And let's be clear on one thing: as far as our father is concerned, I don't exist. You are his heir; you even have a son to succeed you. I'm just supposed to lie back and do my duty to the family."

"Devil take it, Anthony, if I could give you the title and all the responsibility that goes with it, I would."

"Easy to say when it can't ever happen."

Val's eyes flashed. "Now who's being unfair? I didn't make up these ridiculous rules about who can inherit what. When I say I'd give it all up for you, I mean it."

Anthony raised his chin. "Don't patronize me. I know what you and Father think of me."

"And what is that?"

"That I'm useless, that I'm a child."

Val sighed and sat back down. "No, Anthony, that's what you think about yourself. Don't try to pretend any differently."

"I'm twenty-five, Val, I know what I am!"

"Do you really? And what is that?"

"The second son of the second wife of a marquis. A son who should stop complaining and do his duty."

There was a long silence while Valentin stared at him. "You really have to stop feeling sorry for yourself, Anthony."

"I do not feel sorry for myself."

Val shrugged. "Then I suggest you make the best of the situation. Prove to me and our father that you are capable of running the estate. In fact, let me make the decision easier for you. I don't want to see you back here for a month. That should give you enough time to investigate the Stratham estate books and come to a decision."

Anthony struggled to contain his temper. "If our positions were reversed, is that what you would do, Val?"

"Of course not, but then I am a fool. I live to antagonize my father. You are not like me." He held Anthony's gaze. "I've watched too many people I care about try to ruin themselves. I'd rather not have to go through it again."

"Father thinks I'm jealous of you."

"Are you?"

"I . . . don't know." Anthony let out his breath. "How could I be when you have suffered so badly, and I . . ."

Val leaned back in his chair. "You're not jealous, but I suspect you are angry with me."

"Surely they are the same thing?"

"Not at all. You're angry because I involved you with Aliabad."

Anthony took a step back. "I'm not going to discuss him with you."

"Why not?"

"Because it happened in the past, and it has no bearing on our present disagreement."

Val got up slowly, his eyes full of concern, yet Anthony still flinched away from him. "That is the most ridiculous thing you have said so far. What happened with Aliabad changed you."

"I *said* I did not want to talk about it."

"But you should." Val slammed his hand down onto the desk. "Dammit, Anthony, I know how it feels to be forced . . . to be raped . . ."

Anthony turned toward the door as nausea overwhelmed him. "I refuse to discuss this." He struggled to open the door and felt it shoved shut as Valentin reached him.

"Listen to me," Val said urgently. "It was not your fault. What happened to you was my responsibility, and you have a perfect right to be angry with me because of it."

Anthony closed his eyes, leaning his forehead into the harsh wood of the door. "Let me out, Val."

His brother didn't move so Anthony did. He managed to push past Val, open the door and escape into the morning.

An hour later, he found himself staring up at the facades of Angelo's fencing academy and Jackson's boxing salon, which were conveniently situated next door to each other on Bond Street. He flexed his fingers inside his gloves. Perhaps this was what he needed, the opportunity to pick a fight, to let the rage churning in his gut find a sanctioned "gentlemanly" outlet.

He relinquished the notion of boxing, having seen enough blood for one day, and entered Angelo's. A portrait of the great Chevalier de Saint-George hung on the opposite wall and seemed to gaze down with a critical eye on the proceedings in the almost empty room below. Anthony nodded at a couple of acquaintances and caught the fencing master's eye.

"Have you time to take me on this morning?"

"Always, sir." Henry Angelo bowed with a flourish. "If you would only practice, you could become a master."

Anthony barely raised a smile at that piece of outright flummery. He headed past the displays of foils and fencing shoes into the back of the house, where he deposited his coat, waistcoat and boots. It was early enough that the vast majority of his peers were still sleeping off the excesses of the night before. After an hour or two of mindless physical activity, he'd feel in a far better position to think about his next move. He walked back into the main salon and headed to the center of the room.

Angelo bowed low as Anthony stepped forward and the master presented Anthony with his favorite foil.

"*En garde. Pret. Allez.*"

Without thinking, Anthony settled into his fighting stance and crossed blades with the master. Luckily, fencing required his entire concentration, both in body and mind, in a lethal dance of attrition. It also sharpened his senses, made him calculate the risks, the parries, the potential blows.

After a long while, when his arm began to ache and his errors became more frequent, Angelo spoke again.

"*Halte.*"

Anthony disengaged his blade and bowed again, became aware of the spectators who had gathered around them. Angelo wiped his brow.

"That was excellent, my lord. If you practiced every day, you would be a worthy opponent."

Anthony nodded. "Thank you." He turned around and met the familiar derisive gaze of Lord Minshom.

"You are definitely improving, Sokorvsky."

Anthony started to walk and kept moving, his eyes fixed at some point beyond Minshom. He made it to the deserted changing room, heard the door click shut behind him and spun around. Minshom leaned against the door, his foil dangling in his hand, his expression far too amiable.

"Angelo is right. You could be good at this if you tried. But then you never try, do you?"

Anthony ignored him and looked around for a cloth to wipe his face. He flinched as Minshom's foil whipped past him, hooked into the white towel and whisked it away.

"I'm leaving, Minshom. Don't you have anything better to do than annoy me?"

"Not really." Minshom smiled, expertly flicked his wrist

and drew his blade across Anthony's cheek and the corner of his mouth. Stinging heat flowered over Anthony's skin, and he tasted the warm coppery taint of his own blood.

"What the hell was that for?"

"To teach you to pay attention."

Anthony set his jaw. "And what if I no longer want to pay attention to you? What if I have moved on?"

He winced as Minshom's blade darted out again and sliced through his shirt, leaving a stark line of red on his chest.

"You haven't moved on. I haven't given you permission to."

Anthony's hand clenched on the handle of his blade. "Minshom, I'm not in a good mood this morning. I'm also quite sure that I don't require your permission for anything."

Minshom's foil came up, but this time Anthony was ready. Metal rang together and their blades clashed. Too enraged to bother with the niceties of etiquette, Anthony shoved Minshom back against the wall and held him there with the weight of his body.

"I'm going to get changed, go home and have a bath. Now let me get on with it."

Minshom met his gaze, leaned forward and licked at the blood on Anthony's chin, then followed a slow salacious path along Anthony's bloodied lower lip.

"Are you sure about that?"

Anthony dropped his foil and jerked his head away from Minshom. He froze as the other man ran his fingers down the wound in his chest. His blood was on Minshom's fingers, in his mouth, on his tongue. He groaned as Minshom twisted his nipple and then sucked it into his mouth.

God, this was so wrong, yet so right. Bloodlust roared through him, and he struggled to avoid the trap of the familiar, the desiring, the wanting . . . the pain.

"No." Anthony pulled back, yelping as Minshom's teeth scraped over his nipple. "I don't want this."

Minshom raised his head. "Why not? I want it. You should stop saying words that mean nothing and use your mouth for a better purpose. I want your bloodied lips around my cock, sucking me dry."

"No." God, he could see it, him on his knees, Minshom over him, goading him on, laughing.

"You're hard, you want it."

Anthony stepped back, shaking his head, words beyond him. Minshom remained against the wall, stroked himself through his breeches.

"You want it, Sokorvsky. Kneel down and give it to me. Or is it true that you only fuck women these days?"

Anthony stilled. Did everyone think they had a right to rule him? Was he ever going to be allowed to be his own master? Cold fury filled him, replacing his anxiety and enhancing his arousal to the point of pain. He stared down at his fisted hands and then at Minshom.

With a curse, he grabbed Minshom by the throat, spun him around and shoved him over the nearest table. "You want it, Minshom? Then take it."

He reached around, grabbed for Minshom's cock and started to rub it hard through his breeches. Minshom groaned and tried to throw Anthony off. Furious now, Anthony ground his cock against Minshom's arse, felt his swollen flesh expand and burn against the buckskin of his tight breeches.

Even through his clothing, Minshom's big cock felt good in his hand—hot, wet with pre-cum and ready to explode. Anthony leaned harder on the man; bit his neck to hold him still like a stallion mounting a mare.

"You're good at giving it out, Minshom, so how about taking it? How about my cock slamming into your arse for a change?"

Minshom bucked hard and writhed underneath him, caught Anthony off balance and the two of them rolled to the floor.

Anthony kept his hand wrapped around the other man's cock and gasped as Minshom grabbed for his, squeezing it painfully, making him want to come.

Side by side, they wrestled for dominance. Anthony managed to get his hand inside Minshom's breeches and felt the metal piercing on the crown of the other man's cock graze his palm. He closed his fist around Minshom's shaft and pumped hard.

"Christ . . ." Minshom groaned as he shoved his tongue deep inside Anthony's mouth, working him to the rhythm of their combined fingers, the rhythm of rough hard sex.

Minshom climaxed, his hot cum pouring out over Anthony's still-working fingers, his shaft twitching and pulsing with every thick spurt. Anthony pulled his hand free and rolled away, got hold of Minshom's wrist and ripped it away from his cock. He refused to let that man make him come ever again.

He stumbled to his feet, grabbed his clothes and stuffed his feet into his boots. Minshom lay on his back, looking up at him, his dark hair disordered, his pale blue eyes glinting. Anthony's blood covered his face and chest, his own pre-cum darkened the buff color of his breeches around his groin.

"We're not finished, Sokorvsky."

Anthony buttoned his waistcoat, his fingers shaking and throbbing in time to his engorged cock.

"How many times do I have to say this? What will make you listen to me and leave me alone?"

Minshom laughed. "The fact that one day you won't get hard the moment you see me? The announcement of your wedding, perhaps?"

"Damn you to the devil, Minshom." Anthony shrugged into his coat and smoothed down his hair. The cut on his face had stopped bleeding, yet it still stung, much like Lord Minshom's remarks. "Next time I won't just bring you off—I'll fuck you until you're the one begging for mercy."

"And you think I would mind?" Minshom licked his lips and shivered extravagantly.

"Yes, because you consider me beneath you, much like everyone else in this damned world."

Minshom sat up and Anthony tensed. "But surely the balance of our relationship has just changed. Aren't you proud of yourself?"

"Proud of myself for hurting you, for proving that I can behave like an animal?" Anthony shook his head. "It makes me want to puke. The last person I want to be like in this world is you."

"What a pity. And I was hoping for so much more."

Anthony put on his hat and bowed. "Good morning, Lord Minshom, and go to the devil."

He walked out, ignoring the startled comments from Angelo about his face, and headed for the park. He couldn't go home—his father might be waiting for him—and he couldn't go to work because it seemed he was no longer employed. He sat down on a bench and stared at the hopeful sparrows gathering around his boots. He had nothing to give them, nothing to give Marguerite either, even though that was what he yearned for.

A sudden flurry of rain helped make his decision. Madame's was also out of the question because he wanted sex too much. He set off back through the park gates. Perhaps David would be home and at least willing to let him in.

13

"How nice to see you, *Maman*."

Marguerite smiled brightly at her mother, who was seated on the couch in her drawing room. Helene wore a dashing high-poke feathered bonnet and a blue pelisse that made her look as young as Marguerite. It was so unlike Helene to leave the pleasure house during the week that Marguerite was already wary.

"It is nice to see you too, my dear. I came to see how your love affair is progressing." Helene smiled. "Although I hardly need to ask. You are glowing."

Marguerite touched her cheek. So much for her mother keeping out of her love life. Whatever had happened to make Helene change her mind? Marguerite thought she looked pale, but perhaps her mother saw things differently. She was, after all, an expert in all things sexual and was never afraid to express an opinion.

"Everything is fine, *Maman*, thank you."

Helene cocked her head to one side, her blue eyes considering. "But you do not intend to share the intimate details with me, do you?"

"Not really."

Her mother's smile faltered. "And so it should be. As Philip keeps reminding me, you are a grown woman. I just wanted to make sure that everything was all right. I always felt that I let you down over Justin."

Marguerite tensed. "In what way?"

"In many ways. I wasn't there to advise you. I wasn't able to prepare you for your wedding night."

"Justin prepared me quite well enough for that, *Maman*. I don't think you should worry."

Her mother sat forward, hands tightly clasped together. "When I met with you in Dover after the wedding, I was worried you had been forced to wed."

"I knew that. I hope I convinced you it wasn't the case." She'd tried so hard to pretend to her mother that all was well, to make her leave so that she could get back to Justin and Harry.

"Indeed you did, but I was still unsure whether to tell you what I'd found out about Justin. With what happened with Sir Harry afterward, perhaps I should've been more direct."

"What about him?"

Helene shrugged. "It is not important now, is it? Justin is dead, and I would hate to sully his memory."

Marguerite gripped her hands together. "*Maman*, you came all this way to see me, you might as well tell me what you want to say. As we've already discussed, I am a grown woman."

"All right." Helene still hesitated. "You knew Justin came to the pleasure house as a guest of Sir Harry Jones?"

"Justin told me that."

Helene nodded. "Did he ever share with you what he did there?"

Oh God, her mother knew, had known all along . . . Marguerite swallowed hard. "You forget, Sir Harry came with us on our honeymoon. It became obvious to me that his relationship with Justin was more complicated than perhaps it should've been."

"That is what I thought too, although I never actually saw them doing anything indiscreet. From what I remember, they always slept with women." Helene paused. "It seemed to me that Sir Harry was in love with Justin. Was that how it felt for you?"

Her mother's voice was so soft, so understanding. Marguerite wrapped her arms around her waist. Could she share the truth with her mother or was it better to simply agree? Wouldn't it be better to lay the blame on Justin, who was dead, rather than on Sir Harry, who was still alive and yet unable to defend himself?

"I wasn't completely surprised when I heard that Sir Harry had challenged Justin to a duel," Helene continued. "He was probably incredibly jealous of you."

Marguerite closed her eyes. In truth, Harry had been the perfect gentleman. It was Justin who had proved to be the problem.

"Marguerite?"

She stood up and walked across to the window, presenting her mother with her back. "*Maman*, what exactly does all this reminiscing have to do with me embarking on a new affair?"

Helene sighed. "I just wanted to make sure you weren't still blaming yourself over what happened. Justin couldn't stop Sir Harry loving him and neither could you. Sometimes guilt and grief can affect how you choose a new partner."

Marguerite turned around. "Is this visit because you've found out whom I'm seeing?"

"Unfortunately, yes."

"And you think I've made a bad choice—again?"

"Anthony Sokorvsky is hardly an uncomplicated man."

"I know that he sleeps with men. He told me."

"He did?" Helene still didn't smile. "Well I suppose that is a start. Perhaps he'll tell you the rest of it before he breaks your heart."

"I'm not planning on letting him do that. We've barely become intimate as it is." Marguerite glared at her mother. "He has been nothing but kind and honest with me, and I resent you implying otherwise."

"Really." Helene got up and pulled on her gloves. "Then please feel free to ignore everything I've said to you."

"He is a good man, *Maman*." Marguerite pressed her hand to her heart. "I know it, here."

"I've known Anthony Sokorvsky for years, and I'm sure you're right." Helene's tight smile faltered. "I've always wished him well. I just didn't expect him to take up with one of my children. Promise me that you'll take care of yourself, Marguerite."

"What do you think he'll do to me?" Marguerite tried to laugh. "Beat me?"

"I . . ." Helene shook her head. "I'll pray for you, my darling."

"Surely that's a little melodramatic? I didn't think you believed in God anyway."

Helene gave her a quick hug and patted her cheek. "Since Philip reappeared in my life, I've realized there has to be a God somewhere. Now, please take care."

Marguerite sat back down as her mother left and stared at the unused tea cups. So her mother knew something about the intense nature of Justin and Harry's relationship. Did that mean others did too? And why was Helene so worried about her relationship with Anthony? He'd told her about his sexual peccadilloes, surely that was enough? Her mother seemed to be implying that his needs were far more complex and that Marguerite wasn't the woman to deal with them.

Goodness, why was her love life always so complicated? Was her mother right that her guilt over Justin made her incapable of choosing a proper mate? Marguerite scowled at her indistinct reflection in the silver tray. She liked Anthony; she trusted him. How much worse could his sexual tastes be?

And now she was at odds with her mother as well. She sighed. Why did it have to come to this? Why couldn't she find a man who was straightforward and easy to please? It was as if she couldn't make up her mind about what she wanted; her desire to be conventional was at war with her own sexuality.

A knock on the door made her compose her features into what she hoped was a welcoming smile. Had her mother come back or had Mrs. Jones finally remembered she was supposed to be a chaperone and gotten out of bed?

"My lady, are you receiving visitors?"

Marguerite smiled at her butler. "Who is inquiring?"

"A Lord Minshom, ma'am."

Now what was she supposed to do? Minshom must have seen her mother leave, so he'd know she was at home. And if he had seen Helene, had he recognized her? She could only pray he hadn't. After her scandalous conduct with Anthony that morning, could she risk offending an old family friend of the Lockwoods?

"Please tell him to come up, and bring some fresh coffee. And I wish to go out in about quarter of an hour, so have my carriage ready."

She waited while the butler left with the tea tray and then returned with a smiling Lord Minshom. He looked as if he'd engaged in some sort of physical activity, his pale blue eyes were animated, his cheeks flushed. He swept her an elegant bow.

"Good morning, Lady Justin. Thank you for seeing me."

"Good morning, Lord Minshom." She gestured to a seat on the couch opposite her. "Did you ride here? You look quite invigorated."

"Indeed I did, my lady. And before that, I spent an hour at Angelo's fencing establishment honing my technique."

"You enjoy fencing, sir?"

He shrugged. "It depends on my opponent. This morning's session was exhilarating, although I would probably call the outcome a draw."

"And I would imagine you prefer to win, sir."

He met her gaze. "I always do in the end."

The butler appeared with a tray of drinks, and Lord Minshom accepted a brandy while Marguerite poured herself some coffee.

"Was there something in particular you wished to see me about, Lord Minshom?"

He sat back, one long leg crossed over the other, his arm along the edge of the couch. "You doubt any man would seek you out purely for the sake of your company?"

Marguerite bit her lip. Did he intend to answer every other question with a barbed one of his own? She sipped at her coffee, refusing to gratify his ego with a response.

"Actually, there was something I wished to share with you." Lord Minshom put down his brandy glass. "It concerns Sir Harry Jones."

Marguerite stared at him and prayed the tension didn't show on her face. "What about him?"

"I've heard he is back in Town."

"That seems hard to believe."

Lord Minshom shrugged, the gesture elegant. "Why? It's not as if the Lockwood family is going to pursue him. Dueling is illegal. If they implicate Jones, they will also cast suspicion upon their son—and we all know whom they'd prefer to blame for the tragedy, don't we?"

Marguerite ignored his provocative remark and held his gaze. "But surely the authorities . . ."

"What authorities? From all accounts, the duel was carried out in a perfectly respectable manner. Even if Jones's peers don't like what happened, they can hardly condemn him. Of course, the coroner wasn't told about the duel, but he chose not to argue when Lord Lockwood informed him that there had been an unfortunate accident with a loaded gun."

Lord Minshom half-smiled. "Trust me; the Lockwoods are powerful enough to stop any further inquiry into Justin's death. And we both know that there are good reasons for that decision. What they choose to do to Sir Harry in private is another matter. I've already offered to 'speak' to Jones on their behalf myself."

"You haven't actually seen him then?"

"Not yet, but we were once quite . . . close. I suspect he might come to me for help."

Marguerite contemplated pouring herself more coffee but decided against it in case her hand shook too much and betrayed her agitation. Lord Minshom might appear relaxed, but he watched her with all the attention of a cat about to spring on a fat little mouse.

"If he does turn up, will you keep me informed?"

Minshom stood up and bowed. "Of course, my dear. I would hate for you to worry." He flicked her a knowing glance. "Although why you might think he would come after you is anyone's guess. He was the one who killed his best friend, wasn't he? Not you."

"And yet society is more likely to accept him back than they are to accept me or a man who fails to honor his gambling debts." Marguerite stood too and managed a curtsey. "Thank you for coming, my lord. I appreciate it."

"I always enjoy coming . . . to visit a beautiful woman. Do you have time for a ride in the park this afternoon? I'd be delighted to escort you."

"Unfortunately no, sir. I have a commission to finish for my mother."

Lord Minshom paused by the door. "Another of your miniature paintings or something more mundane?"

"Actually, it is a portrait of my mother's husband."

He nodded and she prayed his sudden interest in her mother would disappear in his curiosity about her artistic skills.

"I would like you to paint a portrait for me one day."

"Of your family, your children?"

His mouth twisted. "I have no children, none that I acknowledge anyway. I was thinking of a portrait of myself. It would save me having to seek out my reflection at every turn."

"I'm afraid I don't accept outside commissions, sir. I only paint for pleasure."

"And it wouldn't please you to paint me?"

She considered the interesting angles of his face, his high cheekbones, slightly slanted pale blue eyes, sensual mouth . . . Her fingers twitched as she imagined capturing the essence of his complex personality on less than two inches of porcelain.

"As I said, my lord, I paint only occasionally these days. I fear I'm not disciplined enough to take on real clients."

He inclined his head. "If you change your mind, I would be more than happy to sit for you."

She curtsied and moved past him to open the door. "I'll walk you down to the hall. I'm actually on my way out."

Minshom looked interested. "To visit the Lockwoods?"

"No, to pick up a new bonnet from my milliner."

"That sounds like much more fun."

She risked a smile at him. "I hope so."

He followed her down the stairs and retrieved his hat and gloves then waited with her until the butler announced her carriage was ready. Marguerite held out her gloved hand and Lord Minshom took it.

"Thank you for coming to see me."

He kissed her fingers and then straightened; cast a rueful look at the darkening sky.

"I wonder if I might ask a favor of you, Lady Justin? It looks like rain and I have no desire to get wet. Could you send my horse home with your groom and take me up in your carriage instead?"

Marguerite looked up, felt the first spots of rain on her face and inwardly groaned.

"Of course, Lord Minshom. Where would you like to be dropped off?"

"At my house? It is hardly out of your way."

He followed her into the carriage, took the seat opposite her and smiled. "Do I make you nervous, Lady Justin?"

Marguerite forced herself to look him in the eye. "Not at all, my lord."

"I think I do. I think you find me attractive and are trying to think of a way to flirt with me."

"I beg your pardon, sir?"

He sat forward. "You don't need to lie to me. A young woman in your position, widowed, alone, missing the delights of the marriage bed. It's hardly surprising that you start to cast your lures elsewhere."

"Believe me, I am not casting anything at you at all, my lord!"

"Are you sure, my dear?" He gave her a lazy smile. "Perhaps you have someone else in mind. On the day of the birthday party, I noticed you carried all the scandalous items necessary for an illicit affair in your reticule. I admire such organization in a woman, and I would be more than happy to sexually serve you."

Marguerite simply stared at him, feeling her cheeks redden as he continued to smile.

"There is no need to color up. I would be more than willing to fulfill any needs you have at your convenience." He slid his hand up from his knee to his thigh, and feathered his fingers lightly over his groin. "*More* than happy to oblige you. And I could promise you absolute discretion. The Lockwoods would never hear of your sexual dalliances from me."

She found herself staring at his fingers, realized he was half-erect, wondered how he would compare with Anthony, with Justin . . .

"I'm flattered by your gracious offer, my lord, but I have no need of your services."

"Because you are wedded to Justin's memory or because you have already found someone else?"

"That is none of your business, sir."

He laughed and gently squeezed his shaft. "Indeed it isn't, but as a past friend and a concerned relative of your husband, perhaps you might understand my interest."

"Are you suggesting that if I don't sleep with you, you might choose to reveal my actions to the Lockwoods?"

"As a member of the family, I believe I have a duty to protect the females of my line."

Marguerite managed a laugh. "Do you really think they would care?"

"It depends on who you are fucking, doesn't it?"

Marguerite blinked hard. How had their conversation degenerated to such an intimate level that he felt comfortable touching himself and using foul language in front of her?

"I think you should get out of my carriage."

Lord Minshom sat back, his hand still cupping his groin. "You wouldn't be disappointed. I'm an excellent lover, you know. Ask anyone."

Marguerite glanced out of the small window and saw they were approaching Lord Minshom's residence. The carriage slowed and then came to a halt.

"Good-bye, Lord Minshom."

He touched his hat, smiled and opened the carriage door, pausing to look at her. "In fact, ask Sokorvsky. I'm sure he'll give me a glowing recommendation."

The slam of the door made Marguerite flinch. What on earth had Lord Minshom meant? Was he implying that he'd been intimate with Anthony, or was he just trying to shock her? She stifled a sound halfway between a laugh and a sob.

Either Lord Minshom was prepared to do anything to get her into his bed, or he was letting her know that he knew about Anthony and was staking a prior claim on her new lover.

Marguerite covered her face with her hands. God forbid she found herself in the same nightmarish situation again, caught between two jealous men, unable to stop them from coming to blows, from trying to kill each other . . .

She needed to talk to Anthony, to find out where he stood in regard to Minshom, and without revealing exactly why she found the idea of being trapped between them too horrific to contemplate.

14

"Marguerite, what is the matter?"

Anthony stopped walking and stared down at his companion. They were supposed to be enjoying a companionable stroll through the park. He'd already made remarks about the mildness of the weather, the scenery, the ducks on the pond, and received hardly a word in reply.

"Will you at least look at me?"

She turned her face up toward his, and he registered the worry in her blue eyes, the dark shadows beneath.

"Are you still unwell?"

"No." She sighed. "I'm just trying to think what to say."

"To me?"

"Yes." Her quick smile was strained. "Four days ago my mother came to see me."

"And?"

"She knows about us."

Anthony grimaced. "I told the twins it would be impossible to keep that news a secret." He took her hand, placed it firmly

on his sleeve and resumed walking. The park was still bare of
foliage, no sign yet of the spring bulbs or the blossom. "And
what did your mother have to say for herself?"

"That you were not a good choice for a lover."

He stopped again as an all-too familiar sense of inadequacy
laced with frustration rolled through him. "Does anyone in this
damned world think I'm capable of anything?"

Marguerite tugged at his arm. "There's no need to shout;
everyone is looking at us."

"Let them look, or do you want me to leave? I'd hate to
spoil your afternoon with my loathsome presence."

"Now you are overreacting."

Was he? Briefly he closed his eyes and then fixed them on
the elaborate park gates. He hadn't been home or gone to the
shipping office for three days. David had given him a key to his
lodgings and left Anthony there to wallow in his own misery
while his friend was away on naval business.

He grabbed Marguerite's hand. "Come on."

"Where are we going?"

"Somewhere we can be private, or don't you trust me enough
to be alone with you?"

"Oh, for goodness' sake." Marguerite picked up her skirts in
her free hand and hurried along by his side. They reached David's
building, which faced onto the park, and Anthony pulled out
his key. She said nothing until he closed the door behind them.

"Where exactly are we?"

"Does it matter? It belongs to a friend of mine. We are safe
here."

She slowly took off her gloves and considered him. He tried
not to shift around as her sharp gaze took in his disordered linen
and badly shaved chin. He realized he wasn't prepared to be examined, dissected, found wanting—not by Marguerite, not by a
woman he desired. He scowled down at her.

"So what exactly did your mother say to make you so worried about being my lover?"

Her eyebrows rose. "There's no need to be so defensive. I didn't say I was worried."

"You didn't have to. It's obvious from the way you are behaving."

"You are impossible." Marguerite yanked at the cream ribbons of her bonnet until they loosened and threw the contraption on a chair. She stormed across to him and poked him in the chest. "Why did I bother to defend you to my mother when you have obviously given up on yourself?"

He caught her wrist, retaining his grip even when she tried to pull away. "What the hell does that mean?"

"My mother tried to tell me that your sexual needs were too extreme for me to imagine, let alone satisfy."

Abruptly his antagonism disappeared beneath his apprehension. "What exactly did she say?"

She looked up at him. "That you like men."

"You already knew that."

"I know, but she insisted you needed to tell me the rest."

Anthony found it much easier to watch her luscious mouth rather than react to her cutting words. He bent his head, captured her lips and kissed her as hard as he could. She made an exasperated sound and kissed him back, her teeth nipping at his already bruised lower lip, which made him instantly hard. He wrenched his mouth away, hissing as her teeth gouged his lip.

"Can we talk about this afterward?" Anthony said.

"After what?"

"After I've had you."

"Why would you think I'd agree to that?"

"Because you want me, and I'm offering you the perfect opportunity to use my body to release all your tension and anger."

He shoved his hand under her skirts, cupped her sex, and felt her moist core settle over the palm of his hand. "You want me."

He backed her toward the wall, kissed her mouth with a savagery he hadn't known was in him. She slid her hand into his hair, held him close, her fingers between them wrenching at the buttons of his breeches. He groaned and thrust his cock into her hand.

"Please . . ."

She guided him downward, and the dripping crown of his shaft bumped against the softness of her stomach, the hair beneath it, her clit and finally the welcoming opening below. He grasped her around the waist and lifted her onto him. He gasped at the tightness and fierceness of her grip on his shaft. Hard and fast this time, to slake the need and to forget himself in the welcome of her body.

Even as he pumped into her, he remembered to thumb her clit, to bring her with him to a crashing conclusion. He even remembered to pull out, to let his seed release on her belly rather than where he really wanted it, deep inside her.

"Hold on to me," he murmured, as he carried her into David's bedroom, her legs wrapped around him, their bodies still close and connected. He placed her carefully on the bed. She immediately rolled away from him.

"That wasn't fair."

"You didn't enjoy it?"

"Of course I enjoyed it, but sex is not a substitute for a serious conversation."

He came up on one elbow over her, smiled at her indignant expression. "Are you sure about that?"

With one deft motion, he threw her skirts over her head, exposing her sex, and licked his way through the wetness he'd helped create. She bucked against him, grabbed hold of his hair and pulled hard. He winced at the pain but didn't stop, driving his tongue deep, sucking her clit into his mouth until she whimpered and shuddered with release.

He moved off her and allowed her to sit up, trying not to smile as she fought her petticoats and patterned muslin skirts to reveal her flushed face. "Anthony Sokorvsky!"

He deliberately licked his lips, watched her eyes widen in response.

"Anthony . . ."

"What?" He sighed and flung himself down on his back, savored her taste in his mouth even as he braced himself for her next remark.

"My mother wouldn't say what else you liked in bed. Will you tell me?"

He'd known the question would come, but he still balked at answering it. How honest could he be, especially when he wasn't sure what he really did like? He stared up at the cracked ceiling.

"The thing is . . . I've changed."

Marguerite sighed. "You don't have to say that."

He rolled over to look at her. "But I have, you have no idea how much . . ." Dammit, the fact that he was lying there next to her having the conversation was astounding by itself, but he could hardly tell her that.

"Then tell me. You promised to be honest."

He stared at her. What *did* he like? He'd never been given the opportunity to form his own tastes, only accepted those that were forced on him. He looked over her shoulder at David's oriental cabinet. "Sometimes, I . . . like to be tied up."

She nodded, her expression as serious as he suspected his own was. "And what else?"

Oh God. "I also liked it when you pulled my hair hard, when you dug your nails in my back, made me hurt."

He held his breath, would that be enough? The rest of it he

was too confused to even consider. She looked away from him, down at her hands, and he swallowed hard.

"Why?"

"I beg your pardon?"

"Why do you like these things?"

Now he was the one to look away. There was no chance of him sharing that part of his life with her. "I don't know, and as I said, I'm trying to change." He hated the uncertainty in his voice. He sounded so pathetic, so needy and so defensive about the indefensible.

"And do you only like it when a man does these things to you?"

"I've never tried them with a woman." He forced a laugh. "Not that any woman would want to do such things."

"My mother obviously thinks I wouldn't."

He glanced up at her sharp tone, recognized the anger in her face. It seemed he wasn't the only one frustrated by his parents.

"She has no idea what I am really like. Why should she decide such matters for me?"

"Well, she does have a lot of experience."

She glared at him, hands on her hips. "So you agree with her? You think I'm too weak to deal with your needs?"

He sat up against the headboard, held up his hands. "I didn't say that."

She turned her back on him, and he flinched.

"Help me take this damned dress off."

"Marguerite?"

She glared over her shoulder at him. "Help me!"

He complied, undoing the ties and loosening her corset. He resumed his position cross-legged at the top of the bed as she struggled out of her clothes down to her shift. When the outline of her body was revealed in all its lush, flushed glory, his cock thickened and pressed against his untucked shirt. She gave him an impatient glance.

"Take off your clothes too. Do I have to do everything?"

He stripped, his excitement rising as she glared at him, his heart thudding in time to the pulse in his cock. He hadn't realized she had such a temper and was surprised at his eagerness to see where her anger took them.

"Now what are you going to do?"

Marguerite scanned the small bedroom, returning her gaze to Anthony. "This friend of yours, does he like to be tied up too?"

"Yes, he does, but . . ."

She jumped off the bed, "Then he must have something here to secure you with, yes?"

"You're going to tie me up?"

"Yes, why shouldn't I? I'm fed up with being treated like a porcelain figurine, protected and alone inside the china cabinet." She glared at him, dared him to challenge her, to tell her not to be silly, to *laugh*. He did none of those things and the understanding in his gaze almost made her forget her anger.

He shrugged. "I'm tired of people underestimating me too. I'm not going to stop you."

She headed for the chest of drawers and hesitated at the thought of invading another person's privacy.

"May I help you, ma'am?"

Marguerite gasped and spun around to stare at the man who leaned against the bedroom door. He was dressed in naval uniform, his hat in his hand, his long blond hair disheveled from the wind. He was also distinctly familiar.

"Captain David Gray, at your service, ma'am. We met at Madame Helene's." He nodded at Anthony. "I can only apologize for the interruption. I'll get what I need and I'll be off."

Anthony looked appalled as he scrambled to the side of the bed. "God, David, I'm so sorry. We'll leave immediately."

Marguerite's fingers curled into her palm until they bit into her flesh. He was probably mortified at being caught naked in his lover's bed with a woman.

But Captain Gray didn't look angry. If she remembered correctly, he was a friend of her mother's and Lisette's and therefore unlikely to betray them. She curtsied, difficult to do well when wearing only one's shift.

"Perhaps *I* should go and leave Captain Gray to satisfy your needs."

"Marguerite . . ."

Captain Gray smiled. "Please, both of you, stay here. I am the one who is de trop."

"And what if I asked you to stay?" Marguerite couldn't quite believe the bold words emerging from her own mouth.

Captain Gray hesitated. "Ma'am?"

"I want to tie Anthony up. Can you show me how to do it?"

The captain exchanged another longer glance at Anthony. "Sokorvsky?"

"I'm quite happy to be tied up, David. If Marguerite wants your help, I'm not going to stop her."

"Then I'd be delighted."

David put down his tricorn hat, took off his gloves and shut the bedroom door firmly behind him. Marguerite tried to breathe normally. He seemed to accept her seminakedness as nothing out of the ordinary and showed no tendency to salivate over her. And it wasn't as if she hadn't been naked in front of two men before.

"You need something strong but supple enough to tie well, if that makes sense." He stepped past her and opened the second drawer of the red lacquered tallboy. "I find long silk scarves work very well. Which color would you like?"

Marguerite peered into the drawer and saw a rainbow of colors. "Black, I think, do you have that?"

"Indeed I do." He extracted four scarves and handed them to her. "I suggest you tie a scarf around each wrist and ankle first and then attach him to the bed."

Marguerite almost wanted to laugh at his quiet, businesslike tone, but she didn't want to lose the anger inside her either. She turned toward Anthony on the bed, noted his barely concealed excitement, the heaviness of his straining cock quivering against his belly.

David bowed to Anthony, "I do apologize for coming back. I assumed my work would keep me out until the end of the week, but the ship I expected didn't arrive."

Anthony sighed. "I'm the one who should be apologizing. This is your home." He glanced at Marguerite. "This wasn't planned."

"These things rarely are." David's smile seemed genuine, his interest in the situation obvious even to Marguerite. "Shall we proceed?"

Marguerite climbed onto the bed and awaited further instructions.

"Loop the scarf around his wrist, tie a loose knot and then tie both ends to the bed frame."

"How tight should it be?"

David came up behind her and tugged at the scarf. "It depends on how much you want to mark him."

Anthony cleared his throat. "Tie it as tight as you want, Marguerite; I'll probably enjoy it."

She stared hard at the black silk scarf. Could she do this? Did she really want to? Perhaps her mother was right and she *was* too afraid. She tied the knot, heard Anthony's stifled gasp as she tightened it. Despite the fact that she was anxious, she was the one with the power this time, not a naïve young wife who didn't understand what was expected of her.

"Would you like me to help you?"

She blinked up at David who had come around to inspect her work, his expression carefully blank.

"No, I'd prefer to do it myself."

He nodded as if he perfectly understood. "Do you wish me to leave then?"

She studied him for a long moment, recognized the rising arousal in his sea blue eyes, the quickness of his breathing, the already prominent bulge in his breeches.

"I'd like you to stay. Perhaps you can check my work when I've finished."

"I'd be delighted; as Anthony already knows, I like to watch."

She continued tying Anthony up, avoided touching his erect cock as she moved around the bed. Soon he lay spread eagled on the covers, each limb attached to a bed post by a scarf. Marguerite knelt between his muscled thighs and simply looked at him, noting the slight red marks on his wrists and ankles, the tautness of the black silk, the play of his muscles under his skin.

"Do you like me like this, Marguerite?"

She looked up at Anthony's quiet question.

"Yes."

She felt a slight movement behind her and turned her head to stare at David. She'd almost forgotten he was there. His gaze was fixed on Anthony too, but she saw no sign of passion, just the experienced eye of a detached observer.

"Captain Gray?"

"Yes, my lady?"

"If you were alone with Anthony, what would you do next?"

He shrugged. "It's up to him. I don't believe in forcing a man to accept whatever I feel like giving him, although there are some men who do."

"And some men who like being forced, no doubt," Anthony murmured. "What would *you* like to do to me, Marguerite, now that you have me at your mercy?"

She shivered. This was bizarre; this whole situation was unusual. "Not hurt you, not force you."

"You could oil his skin, he'd probably like that."

Marguerite eyed Anthony's long powerful body, now displayed for her enjoyment, constrained by her hands. How would his skin feel straining and slick as she massaged oil into his quivering flesh?

"Do you oil him, Captain Gray?"

"Yes, I do, and please call me David. I also use oil for other reasons."

"When you fuck him, you mean?"

Surprise flickered in David's eyes followed by wry amusement and respect. "Yes, my lady, for when I fuck him."

Anthony groaned. "Marguerite, for a well-brought-up young lady, your language is appalling."

"I told you, I'm tired of being treated like an innocent. I'm a widow, not a shy debutante."

David handed her a vial of oil, and she turned back to Anthony. He flinched as she coated her fingers with oil and started to massage it into his chest.

"Dammit, you could've warmed it first."

She flicked his nipple. "I thought you liked it to hurt?"

His skin felt burning hot beneath her hands. She shaped his ribcage, the hollows of his stomach and the slight flare of his hips. He started to move under her, the slight undulation pulling on his bonds, making him strain toward her touch. His cock brushed against her arms as she worked, leaving streaks of pre-cum on her skin, on the fine lawn of her shift. She could smell his desire all around her.

"What about my cock?" he demanded hoarsely as she started to rub oil into his thigh.

"What about it?"

"Aren't you going to massage me there?"

"Not yet."

David's chuckle reminded Marguerite of his presence. He sat in a chair, one leg crossed over the other as he watched the action on the bed. He raised his eyebrows at her. "Do you still want me here?"

She smiled at him. "Do you always put your cock in him or do you sometimes use something else?"

"Marguerite!"

She ignored Anthony's strangled exclamation and kept her gaze on David.

"We could gag him, you know. That would keep him quiet." David smiled. "To answer your question, sometimes I use a carved phallus or short jade plug instead. Why do you ask?"

She shrugged. "I just wondered."

David stood up. "If such things interest you, take a look in the third drawer down in the tallboy. I'm something of a collector of the unusual and erotic." He bowed. "Now I really must leave you—I have arranged a luncheon engagement with your sister Lisette, and she doesn't like to be kept waiting."

"You won't mention me, will you?"

"Of course not. I'll be the soul of discretion." He winked at her, stroked a lingering path up Anthony's leg to his hip and then left, shutting the door behind him.

Marguerite returned her attention to Anthony, who was gazing helplessly at the door. She stripped off her shift. Anthony's eyes widened and he licked his lips.

"Come here and let me kiss you."

"*Non*, I haven't finished with you yet." She knelt between his legs and took the heavy crown of his shaft into her mouth and sucked hard, used her teeth to draw him deep down her throat.

"Oh God," he moaned and thrashed under her, his hips trying to lift, his heartbeat pounding loud enough to hear. "Yes, just like that, make me come, make me come hard for you."

She cupped a hand under his balls and squeezed, brought them tight against the root of his shaft until he started to groan with every pull of her mouth. He climaxed, his cock so far down her throat that she barely had to swallow to take all his cum.

While he recovered, she set about untying him, rubbed at the red spots on his wrists and kissing the soreness away.

"Did you enjoy yourself?"

She dropped the last of the scarves onto the bed. "Yes."

His smile was slow and lascivious. "So did I." He continued to watch her as she vainly tried to smooth out the wrinkles in the silk. "I certainly don't see you as a shy retiring debutante anymore."

She sniffed. "I'm glad to hear it."

"Perhaps your mother can be wrong. And if she can be wrong about her own daughter, perhaps she can be wrong about our relationship as well."

She met his gaze. Why had he mentioned her mother? Suddenly she didn't feel brave and daring anymore. Had she truly wanted to give Anthony what he craved or was she simply trying to prove a point to Helene?

"I never said I was prepared to give you up."

"But you thought about it, didn't you?"

"Of course I did. She is my mother; we normally agree on most things."

He sighed, shoving a hand through his already disordered hair. "I don't want to come between you and your mother, but . . ."

She moved closer to him, kissed his stubbled cheek and then his lips with a confidence she was far from feeling. "You won't."

He cupped her chin and waited until her eyes met his. "I haven't shocked you then?"

"Not yet."

"You have certainly shocked me. I didn't realize you had such a temper, but I'm not complaining."

Conscious now of the coldness of the room and her naked state, Marguerite slipped off the bed and picked up her corset and petticoats. Despite what he said, she knew she'd behaved appallingly, had lost her temper, allowed two men to see her naked and—even worse—enjoyed every moment of it.

"Let me help you."

She stood still as Anthony patiently laced her corset and tied the strings at her waist. He dropped her dress over her head, settled it around her and did up the fastenings.

"There, you look beautiful again."

"Scarcely that."

He chuckled. "God forbid I offend you. I meant you look presentable." He dropped a kiss on the top of her head. "What are you going to do about your hair? It looks like a bird's nest."

In answer she hunted up some hair pins from the floor and the bed, gave the ends of her hair a quick practiced twist and pinned the mass on the top of her head. She quickly added her bonnet and tied the cream ribbons, then curtsied to Anthony as he stared at her.

"Well, will I do?"

His smile was warm and full of admiration. "Perfectly." He hesitated, rubbing a hand over his naked chest. "Give me a moment to dress and I'll escort you home."

"I think I'd like to go by myself." She tried to hold his gaze and failed. "Do you mind?"

He stepped back, the laughter dying from his eyes. "Of course not. Perhaps I'll see you tomorrow?"

Marguerite picked up her gloves and reticule. "That would be lovely." Why had this suddenly become so difficult? She nodded awkwardly. "Good-bye then."

He didn't reply, and she almost tripped in her haste to get to the door and leave. Unexpected sunlight on her face made her pause at the main door. She'd forgotten it was still afternoon. How long had she allowed herself to be with Anthony and forget the outside world? She needed to get home, take a deep breath and think.

15

What the hell had he done now? Anthony shoved a hand through his hair and stared at the door through which Marguerite had departed. She'd seemed to like tying him up, exulted in it even, so why had she looked so forlorn and uncertain at the end? He sighed and bent to pick up his clothes.

Perhaps she'd gone along with what he suggested simply to appease him and hadn't enjoyed herself at all. Dammit, why should she want to watch a man beg? Women wanted strength in a male, the kind of man who'd give them children and protect them from the realities of life.

Anthony paused as he pulled his shirt over his head. But she'd let David stay. In truth, she'd asked for his advice, and she hadn't needed to do that. He wondered again exactly what had gone on during Marguerite's short marriage, what had been her relationship with Harry Jones and her husband. Perhaps her frustration at being seen as naïve came from what she had experienced. Had she suspected Justin and Harry were lovers? She'd seemed almost comfortable being with two men.

"Anthony, you are a fool."

He said it aloud, could almost hear Marguerite's distinctive voice echoing the sentiment. He frowned as he tucked his crumpled shirt into his breeches. He stunk more than a fishmonger's whore. It was definitely time to go home, replace his clothing and decide what to do next.

His father's mansion was almost as forbidding from the rear as it was from the front. Anthony slipped through the mews and into the kitchen, winked at the cook and started up the back stairs. He paused on the first level to hold the door open for a flustered-looking footman with a laden drinks tray.

He frowned as the sound of raised voices reached him. What in God's name were his father and Valentin shouting about now? He distinctly heard his name. With a sigh, he stepped into the vast empty hall and walked across to the library. The door was ajar enough for him to see his father confronting Valentin in front of the imposing marble fireplace.

He walked into the room and waited to be noticed, waited in vain as his father started speaking again.

"This is probably your fault, Valentin."

"I think not. You asked me to speak to him. You were the one who wanted him out of my business and into yours."

"Only because *you* refuse to face up to your responsibilities."

Val sighed. "This is not about me. Perhaps if we focused on Anthony, we might find some answers."

Anthony cleared his throat, and they both swung around to stare at him. His father spoke first. "Where the hell have you been?"

"Staying with a friend."

"And you didn't think to let us know?"

"Father, I'm almost twenty-six, not six. Why on earth would you want to know where I am?"

"Because . . ." The marquis glared at Valentin, his face still flushed with anger.

"Because you think Valentin has been leading me astray again?" Anthony stared at his brother. "He has been far too busy telling me to insinuate myself into the family business to bother about that."

"Perhaps Valentin has shown some sense for the first time in his life."

Val laughed. "Hardly. Can't you see that because of my interference, Anthony is as angry with you as he is with me?"

"Anthony isn't angry. He's always been an excellent son."

"Unlike me, of course."

Anthony knocked hard on the desk. "Perhaps you could both shut up and pay some attention to me for a change. I'm sick to death of being either ignored or talked about as if I'm not here."

The marquis frowned. "I hardly think that's an appropriate way to speak to your father and older brother. We were worried about you."

"Really? It's hard to tell." Anthony realized he was shaking as waves of heat rolled through him. He took a step forward until he was in between the two men. "You both treat me like a child."

"Don't be ridiculous."

Anthony forced a smile. "You see, sir? You can't even allow me to have an opinion, can you? Valentin is the only one in this family allowed to do that, isn't he?"

Val frowned. "He does have a point, Father."

Anthony snorted. "Don't try to placate me, Val. I know what you both think."

"And what is that?"

Anthony swallowed hard and forced himself to look his brother in the eye. "That I'm too soft, too vulnerable, too damned young to make my own decisions."

"We've already had this conversation, Anthony." Val pulled on his gloves. "I told you what I thought, and you refused to discuss it further. Maybe when you show the maturity to have that discussion, then I, at least, will begin to take you seriously. I cannot of course speak for our father."

Briefly Anthony closed his eyes, tried to gather his beleaguered resources. "Just because I was raped when I was nineteen does not make me less of a man." He took the time to glare at them both. "That's what you believe, isn't it? That somehow I need to be protected from myself."

Horror crossed the marquis's face followed quickly by pity. Anthony hated both emotions, needed nothing more to confirm what he'd long suspected. He'd never be worthy in his father's eyes, even less so now that his father knew the truth.

"I knew there was more to that kidnapping. Why didn't you tell me?" The marquis avoided Anthony's gaze and rounded on Val, his voice rising in accusation.

"Oh for God's sake, Father! This isn't about Val. It's about me."

"Anthony . . ." In an unseen display of unity, Val crossed the rug to stand by the marquis's side. The formidable likeness between them shocked Anthony to the core. "That really wasn't helpful."

Anthony's hands tightened into fists. How dare Val try to make him feel guilty for speaking the truth. "Did it ever occur to either of you that I like what I do in bed?"

"But you don't."

"How the hell do you know?" Anthony realized he was shouting and that he didn't care who heard him.

"Because I've been in every possible sexual situation imaginable, and *I know.*"

"Just because you didn't enjoy something means I can't? We are only half brothers. Perhaps my tastes are different from yours."

"How would you know what your tastes are when you've allowed them to be dictated by rape?"

The marquis suddenly moved as if to shield Anthony from his brother. "That's enough, Valentin."

"But, sir . . ."

"I *said* that's enough."

Anthony bowed to his father. "Am I supposed to thank you for saving me from the lash of Val's tongue? As I've been trying to tell you for the last few minutes, I do not need your protection."

"There is no need to speak to Father like that, Anthony."

Anthony laughed. "Well, there's something. I've managed to get you defending each other. But then why should I be surprised? It's always been about you two, hasn't it? I'm just a side show. My mother and my sisters are all secondary to your precious relationship."

The marquis's expression tightened. "You will go and change, present yourself to your mother, who is worried sick about you, and come back to my study."

Anthony picked up his hat. "I'll certainly go and see my mother, but I'm not coming back here to be shown the error of my ways or have you feel sorry for me."

"Then where will you go? This is your home."

"Actually, this is *your* home, Father, and one day, when he stops being so pigheaded and realizes he wants it, it will be Valentin's. It's probably time I found somewhere else to live anyway."

The marquis lifted his chin, his gray eyes cold. "And how will you afford that when I cut off your allowance?"

"I'll survive. In truth, thanks to Val, I'm more employable than most other noblemen. Perhaps this is the only way I can prove to you both that I'm not what you think, that I can succeed by myself without being cosseted."

Valentin smiled. "Good luck." He shot an irritated glance at the marquis. "And before you start, I promised Anthony I'd not tell you what happened with Aliabad. I honored that request. It was the least I could do."

"Valentin," Anthony said. "I don't need your pity or guilt either."

Val turned back, his expression chilly. "My feelings are my own. If I'm not allowed to speculate about yours, don't you dare do it to me."

"Agreed." Anthony nodded at his brother and then at his father. "I'm going to see my mother. I'll be in touch about the rest of it."

The marquis swallowed hard and put his hand on the desk as if to steady himself. "I would appreciate that."

Anthony fought an unheard of desire to kneel at his father's feet and bawl like a babe. He had to see this through. He had to prove that he was more than capable of running his own life.

"Good morning, sir."

He turned his back on his brother and his father and hurried up the stairs to his room.

"What do you mean I have visitors? I'm in the bath! Tell them to go away!"

Marguerite glared at Mary, her maid who stood by the door to her bedroom, hands clutched around a drying cloth.

"Not that kind of visitor, my lady, just your family."

"Tell them I'll be down in a minute."

"Yes, my lady. Mrs. Jones is entertaining them quite nicely, but they were asking for you."

"Help me dress, then."

Marguerite sighed and stood up, allowing the steaming fragranced water to stream down her body. After her unexpectedly erotic afternoon, she'd hoped to bathe, have her dinner in bed, and go to sleep. Her skin still felt hot, as if all her senses were on fire. She wished she'd overcome her fear and stayed to make love with Anthony again. Perhaps he could've tied her up that time . . .

She blinked away that salacious thought and thrust her arms into the sleeves of the green flowered muslin gown her maid held out to her. Facing her family with thoughts of Anthony in her mind would not be a good idea.

At least she hadn't started to wash her hair. While her maid brushed it out and repinned it, Marguerite checked her reflection in the mirror. Her cheeks were flushed and her lips a little swollen, but that might be explained away by her bath.

"There, my lady. You look lovely."

"Thank you."

With a grateful nod, Marguerite picked up her skirts and descended the stairs to the drawing room. Mrs. Jones waved at her from her seat behind the tea tray. Even from a distance, the smell of brandy on her breath was all too evident.

"Oh, there you are, my dear; I was just telling your father how famously we've been getting along."

Marguerite glanced at Lord Philip Knowles, who winked at her. He was her mother's husband but not her father. It wasn't worth correcting Mrs. Jones. In the few years she'd known him, Philip had certainly done everything in his power to treat her like one of his own children. He sat between the twins on the couch, his relaxed manner a quiet testament to his wealth, intelligence and good taste.

Marguerite liked him immensely. He was the only man who had ever been able to deal with her mother as an equal without resenting or trying to possess her. Philip stood up and bowed, then stared at Christian until he followed suit.

"I apologize for visiting you so late, but I was at my bankers', and your mother asked me to pop in and see how you did."

"Why didn't she come herself? Is she unwell?"

Philip's eyebrows rose. "Not at all. She is simply too busy, and she was concerned about you."

Marguerite immediately felt guilty. She already sounded defensive and she hadn't even sat down. Exactly how much had her mother told Philip, and why hadn't she come herself? It was most unlike her. A cold sensation settled low in Marguerite's stomach. Perhaps Helene really had washed her hands of her eldest daughter and her inconvenient choices. But wasn't that what Marguerite had wanted? Now she wasn't so sure.

"We didn't go into the bank." Lisette smiled at Marguerite. "Apparently, I'm a distraction and Father fears Christian will start asking for more money."

"Hardly that." Philip chuckled and sat back down, his amused gaze on Christian's stony face. Sitting as he was, between the twins, Marguerite could trace their likeness to each other, their shared heritage and their deep connection. The twins were as dear to her as she hoped her own children would be, but she'd never known a father's love.

"Oh, dear."

Marguerite jumped as Mrs. Jones dropped a tea cup and bent to pick it up, almost dislodging the entire drinks tray.

"It's all right, ma'am, I've got it." Christian located the cup, which had rolled under his chair, and replaced it on the tray.

Mrs. Jones hoisted herself out of her chair and stared distractedly at the door. "I'll go and get another cup. I'll be back in a moment."

Marguerite waited until her chaperone left the room and the gentleman resumed their seats before defiantly pouring herself a large shot of brandy. The taste reminded her of Anthony, and she licked her lips, wondering what he was doing now, whether he slept or whether he lay awake thinking about her, touched himself as he did.

"Marguerite, are you listening to me?"

With a guilty start Marguerite looked up and into Lisette's laughing eyes. "I'm sorry, Lisette, what were you saying?"

Lisette smiled at her. "I was just remarking that before the cup fell, your chaperone was rummaging in her reticule as if her life depended on it."

"She was probably looking for her gin bottle." Marguerite shrugged. "That's why she excused herself, to get a new one."

"She hardly seems like an adequate chaperone, my dear," Philip said, his keen gaze on Marguerite. "Are you sure you want her?"

"I don't want her; I need her. She allows me to live alone. If I complain about her to the Lockwoods, they might make me move in with them, and that I couldn't stand." Marguerite glared at her brother and Philip. "It is so unfair that ladies are so constricted."

"I agree." Christian nodded. "But as a widow, you have more freedom than most."

"I know that." Marguerite turned back to Philip before her brother could elaborate. "Was there anything in particular my mother wished to say to me, sir?"

"Not that I recall. She was simply concerned that you hadn't made any, um, rash decisions as to your future."

Marguerite put down her glass. "Oh, is that all? Nothing much then, only that she doesn't trust me to make any decisions at all."

"That's not what Philip said, Marguerite," Christian interrupted her. "And to hell with being tactful, we're all concerned about you."

"Why?"

"Because of Anthony Sokorvsky."

Marguerite fixed him with her best glare. "*You* were one of the people responsible for my meeting him!"

Christian shrugged. "I didn't expect you to go this far."

"Have you all been discussing me, then?"

Lisette nodded. "Of course we have. We're your family."

"No, you're not." Marguerite stood up and gripped the back of the chair. "Not if you think it gives you the right to tell me whom I can bed. I'm the widow of a peer, not an innocent un-married girl."

Philip laid a hand on Christian's arm, the quiet gesture enough to stem the anger brewing on her brother's face and his impul-sive step toward her. "I think what the twins are trying to say is that they are worried about you."

"As is my mother, apparently."

"Yes."

Marguerite inclined her head a glacial inch. "Thank you all for your concern, but I am quite capable of dealing with An-thony Sokorvsky. If I need any help, I will ask for it."

"Sokorvsky isn't doing this because he's enamored of you," Christian said. "He's doing it to avoid a scandal."

Marguerite met his glare head on. "I know. He told me."

"He *told* you?"

"Yes, imagine that, two adults having an honest conversa-tion about their relationship. Isn't it refreshing?"

"And you're not disturbed by what he said?"

"I'm a grown woman; I've been married before. I under-stand that not all men have the same sexual inclinations."

"But *Maman* didn't think you knew about Justin and Sir Harry," Christian said. "*Mon Dieu*, she wasn't even sure herself . . ."

"Christian."

Christian closed his mouth and nodded at his father. "I apol-ogize, sir, that is none of my business."

"How about apologizing to me?" Marguerite countered as anger finally forced its way through her tiredness. "I'm the one you're insulting. Why is it all right for you and Lisette to enjoy yourselves at the pleasure house when I should not? Does hav-ing a titled father make you somehow more immune to scandal than a Bastille-born bastard like me?"

Lisette stepped in front of Christian, her chin raised, hazel eyes fired up for battle. "That's not fair, Marguerite. Christian was only trying to help."

Marguerite was the first to look away. She knew they meant well, but at this moment she hated their solidarity and their legendary closeness, hated *them*. "Perhaps you should go."

Philip came around the twins and took her hand, enclosing it between both of his. "I'm sorry, Marguerite, I didn't bring them here to start an argument."

She struggled to smile. "I know. I just wish everyone would stop trying to protect me from my own choices."

He squeezed her hand and brought it to his lips. "That is the nature of loving someone though, isn't it? I love your mother, but I've had to learn to allow her the freedom to make her own decisions and, God forbid, her own mistakes."

He looked over his shoulder at the twins, who were whispering to each other, their heads close together. "I've also learned that being a father to adult children isn't easy."

"Have you met Anthony Sokorvsky?"

"Yes." His expression became more guarded. "Why do you ask?"

"Because I value your opinion?"

He winced. "And despite that flattery, I'm not going to tell you what I think of him. Didn't you just say that you were entitled to make up your own mind? If you have accepted him, faults and all, what else is there to say?"

She stared into his eyes and slowly nodded. "I won't let him hurt me."

Philip bowed. "I'm not sure anyone can guarantee that in a relationship, but you are an intelligent woman, and I'm sure you'll make the right decisions."

"Thank you for your support."

His smile was wry. "I'm not sure I support your particular 'choice,' but I'm certainly not going to interfere unless you ask me to." He turned to the twins. "Say good-bye to your sister, and let's be off."

Marguerite walked slowly toward the twins, but neither of them moved. To Marguerite, their expressions were identical, unreadable and infuriatingly familiar. She let her tentative smile die and simply nodded.

"Good-bye then, give my best to *Maman*."

Lisette glanced at her silent brother before she answered. "We will."

As she watched them leave, Marguerite was aware of an unpleasant tightening sensation in her chest. For years, it had been her and the twins against the world. They'd grown up together in the nunnery orphanage and hardly seen their mother, who was trapped in England during the war. Marguerite had loved them, mothered them and cried with them. Now it seemed she was outside that charmed circle. Had Philip stolen her place or had she pushed her own way out?

Mrs. Jones came back into the room and looked around. "Did they leave?"

"Yes."

"Oh, how disappointing! I was looking forward to talking to Lord Philip."

"So was I." Marguerite sat down with a thump and finished off her neglected brandy in one long swallow. "I think I'll go to bed."

Mrs. Jones waved a note in front of her face. "I almost forgot. Lady Lockwood's footman dropped this off for you."

"Thank you."

Marguerite took the note with her as she made her way up to bed. Was it yet another invitation insisting she masquerade as a valued member of the Lockwood family? When would that charade end? Would she ever feel completely wanted and welcomed simply for herself? Her mother had Philip, the twins had each other, and who did she have?

She thought she'd had Justin, had been prepared to do any-thing to keep him, and even then, she'd failed. Her eyes filled with tears, and she hurried to rip open the covering sheet. In-side, there were two folded notes addressed in unfamiliar hand-writing. The first was from Charles's wife, Amelia, and was an invitation to a party that weekend at their country house in Essex.

The singularity of such an invitation stopped her tears. Amelia had never liked Marguerite, so why on earth was she being in-vited to such an intimate gathering? She opened the second sheet, read the short sentences and all became clear. Lord Min-shom informed her that he'd arranged for her to meet clandes-tinely with Sir Harry Jones at the house party, and that it would be her last chance to see the man before he left England again.

Marguerite laid the notes on the top of her vanity and smoothed out the sheets. A weekend in the countryside would get her away from her family and perhaps help her understand the reasons for her husband's untimely death.

The thought of having to deal with Lord Minshom gave her pause. There was something about him that both repelled and fascinated her. How could she ensure her safety and yet still see Harry? She forced her tired mind to concentrate. What would Amelia do if Marguerite asked to bring Anthony with her?

Amelia would be delighted. She'd see it as a way to destroy Charles's affection for Marguerite and perhaps even repeat the scandal to Lady Lockwood. And maybe that wouldn't be a bad thing after all . . . She would write to Amelia, ask if she might bring Anthony and pray that she could deal with the specter of Sir Harry Jones once and for all.

16

Marguerite breathed in the icy autumn air as Anthony's curricle swept up the long driveway to Locking Hall. She'd defied convention, left Mrs. Jones happily ensconced at home, and driven down to Charles and Amelia's little place in the country in an open carriage alone *with a man*. As declarations of intent went, it was quite a statement.

She grabbed a loose blue ribbon as it threatened to rip free of her bonnet, laughing as she retied the bow under her right ear.

"You seem very cheerful today."

She glanced across at Anthony. He looked handsome in his dark blue driving coat, black boots and buckskin breeches. His booted feet were planted firmly on the floor of the curricle, his hands relaxed on the reins. As they'd navigated their way out of London, he'd proved to be an excellent whipster.

"I am. I'm escaping my family for the weekend."

He grimaced. "I'm escaping mine too. I've decided to find my own set of rooms."

His tone didn't encourage questions, but she didn't care about that. After all, he'd promised her honesty.

"I have my own house and they still come after me."

His expression tightened. "They do?" He clicked to his horses, and they started to slow. "Mayhap I'll start looking for a castle with a drawbridge. My father probably owns one somewhere. If I'm dragooned into becoming his estate manager, I'll probably find out for myself."

"He wants you to run the estates?"

"Unfortunately, he does, and for once Valentin supports him."

"Isn't that a good thing?" Marguerite asked tentatively. "Doesn't it show that he trusts you?"

Anthony flicked a glance at her. "Strange, I don't see it like that. It's just another way for my father and Val to keep an eye on me, to control me, to keep me from disgracing the family."

The hurt in his voice resonated within Marguerite and made her want to reach out and touch him. "I understand. You fear you'll never be free of your father's interference."

He laughed, the sound carried off by the wind. "And I can't really leave. My mother is married to him, remember? And she would be devastated if I walked away. God, what an unholy tangle . . ."

Marguerite stared hard at the beech trees edging the drive. "How nice to have someone who wants you to stay. Neither of the families I'm supposed to belong to seem to need or want me anymore."

She refused to look at him, set her teeth on her lower lip to stop it from shaking. He guided the horses to the edge of the driveway and stopped the curricle. She gasped as he drew her into his arms and held her close, then she allowed herself to subside like a foolish girl against his broad chest.

"Marguerite . . ." She made the mistake of looking up, saw her tiny reflection mirrored in his dark blue eyes. "If you don't think you're wanted, why did you accept this invitation?"

She lowered her gaze to stare at the embossed silver buttons of his coat. Trust Anthony to reach into the very heart of the matter. How much of her true undertaking did she want to reveal? She had hoped for more time to ascertain that Harry was actually there before she revealed anything to Anthony. The whole weekend might just be part of some cruel joke on Lord Minshom's part.

She sighed, her breath condensing in the cooling air, and put her hand on Anthony's shoulder.

"I can't tell you exactly why yet. But this visit could help me understand Justin's death."

"Ah." Anthony brushed her mouth with his gloved fingertip. "Then I can scarcely complain, although if that is the case, I'm still not sure why you asked me to come with you."

"Because I might need your help. Is that reason enough?"

His expression gentled, and he angled his head lower, licking a line with his tongue along her closed lips. "Yes." He straightened and retrieved the reins. "Shall we proceed?"

Marguerite took a deep steadying breath. "I'm glad you are with me, Anthony. I don't think there is anyone I would rather have by my side."

He went still and looked back at her. "Thank you."

She tilted her head up to look at him. "Is that all you have to say?"

"It's all I'm able to get out at the moment." He sighed. "Your faith in me is a new experience. No one else thinks I'm capable of doing anything except ruining my life."

"My family says the same about me."

He smiled and she smiled back, aware of the growing connection between them, the sense that she had truly found a man who understood her. He bent to kiss her cold cheek.

"Then perhaps we should prove them wrong together?"

"Perhaps we should." Marguerite nodded decisively.

His laughter warmed her. With a light flick of his whip, he set the horses in motion and they headed to the front of the house.

A footman ran down the shallow worn steps to greet them

and to assist Marguerite out of the curricle. While she waited for Anthony to confer with the stable hand, she looked up at the mellow red front of the house. Ivy grew around the diamond paned windows, and rose stems climbed around the door. If Justin had lived, this would've been his country estate until his father died.

Marguerite felt no sense of ownership. Her marriage had been so brief that she'd never even visited the house. She had no sad memories to spoil its obvious charm and beauty. Smoke rose from the ornate chimney pots and curled around the roof line before drifting lazily toward the almost barren trees.

Anthony touched her arm. "Are you ready to go in?"

She placed her fingertips on his sleeve, picked up her skirts and walked into the house. Whatever happened during her stay, she was determined to face it with as much grace and courage as she could muster. Another footman led them into a sunny drawing room where Amelia sat by the fire, her embroidery hoop in her hand, a bored expression on her round face.

Marguerite fixed on a smile. "Good afternoon, Amelia. I hope you are well?" She glanced up at Anthony. "May I introduce you to Lord Anthony Sokorvsky?"

Amelia dropped her embroidery on the floor, her mouth a perfect O. She craned her neck to look behind Marguerite. "Where is Mrs. Jones?"

"She decided not to accompany me. Lord Anthony very kindly brought me down in his curricle."

"You were alone?"

Marguerite pretended to frown. "Well hardly that, Amelia. We were together."

Anthony nudged Marguerite and swept Amelia a perfect bow. "Good afternoon, my lady, and thank you for inviting me into your home."

Amelia smiled distractedly at Anthony and continued to stare at Marguerite as if she'd never seen her before. Marguerite hoped she looked calm and confident. It was harder to pretend she hadn't behaved shockingly than she had imagined. She had no idea how Lisette carried it off so convincingly, but perhaps it was time she learned. Amelia got to her feet and held out her hand to Anthony.

"It's a pleasure to meet you, my lord." She cast Marguerite a sly glance. "I'm even more intrigued about how you came to meet my dear sister-in-law."

"Oh, through mutual friends. Isn't that always the case?"

"I suppose it is." Amelia beckoned to a footman. "Please show my guests to their rooms." She nodded at Marguerite. "And we'll see you down here for dinner in an hour or so?"

"That would be lovely, Amelia," Marguerite said. "Is Charles here?"

"No, I believe he's out shooting at some kind of bird. He should be back soon. I'm sure he'll be delighted to see you both." Amelia studied Anthony. "Especially you, my lord."

"I'm looking forward to meeting him as well. I know Marguerite holds him in high regard."

With a last cordial nod in Amelia's direction, Anthony escorted Marguerite back into the hall and up the carved oak staircase. To her surprise, the footman led them to adjoining rooms. She remembered to thank him as he closed the door behind him. Her luggage sat in a pile on the blue rug in front of a welcoming fire.

With a sigh, she took off her bonnet, set it on the dressing table and studied her face. Despite the openness of the carriage she looked remarkably well, her cheeks flushed from the cold and wind, her eyes bright.

A knock on the door made her straighten and turn away from the mirror. A young woman entered the room and bobbed a curtsey.

"Good afternoon, my lady. I'm Rachel. I'm here to unpack your luggage and help you change."

"That would be lovely." Marguerite smiled and resigned herself to not getting a moment to see if Anthony was all right. He'd seemed more than capable of dealing with Amelia. His manners were always exquisite, his countenance serene. In truth, she suspected he was as good at hiding his inner turmoil as she was.

As she helped the maid unpack, Marguerite pondered his revelations about his family. Did they disapprove of his sexual tastes? Was that why he was being forced to move out? Despite being at odds with her own family, she still believed that when they realized she was happy, they'd come around to her involvement with Anthony.

She stared down at the petticoat she was attempting to fold. Would Anthony ever receive that acceptance? And if not, how would he deal with it? She would hate to lose him.

By the time Marguerite emerged from her room, darkness had fallen and the candle sconces in the hallways had been lit. Anthony leaned against the wall beside his door, immaculately turned out in shades of brown and black, his dark hair glinting in the soft light. He bowed and offered her his arm. "You look very nice. Blue suits you."

"Thank you. Were you waiting for me?"

"Of course I was. Do you think I want to brave your relatives alone?"

"They aren't that bad. I'm quite fond of Charles. He's always been very kind to me."

"I'm sure he has."

His dry tone made her look up at him. "Do you mean because he got to inherit everything instead of Justin?"

"Good God, no! After seeing how his wife reacts to you, I *meant* that he's probably infatuated with you."

"It's true that Amelia doesn't like me. I've never bothered to ask why. I always try to be nice to her."

"And that probably makes her dislike you even more." Anthony continued down the stairs until they reached the bottom and then stopped. He cupped Marguerite's chin in his hand so she had to look at him.

"Why don't you believe you have a right to be part of the Lockwood family?"

"Because they didn't want me. After Justin's death, they tried to annul the marriage, tried to pretend it had never happened."

"But you know it did. Why don't you act as if you believe it?"

"That is hardly fair. I've done my best to fit in."

"Have you?"

She swallowed hard. "Yes, I have, and it's no use. How would your father feel if you brought home a girl whose mother was a notorious brothel owner and your father . . . your father wasn't even named, because . . ."

Anthony's fingers covered her mouth. "Don't."

She shoved his fingers and his sympathy away. ". . . not even your mother knew who he was, because she was forced to bed so many men in the Bastille." She choked a laugh. "I could have royal blood or the blood of murderers in my veins. What a perfect addition to an aristocratic family."

She wiped hastily at her eyes and glared at Anthony. "Don't you dare feel sorry for me."

"I won't." He brushed her cheek once, twice, taking the tears and some of the hurt away. "You are an amazing woman, Marguerite. Any man should be honored to have you in his family." He held her gaze, kissed her fingers and placed her hand back on his sleeve. "Now, let's go and make ourselves pleasant to our hosts, and perhaps you'll finally tell me what on earth we are doing here."

Marguerite was right; the Lockwoods didn't like her. So why had she braved their chilly disapproval? Anthony observed the various members of the intimate gathering as they sat around the dining room table. Eleven chairs were full. The twelfth guest apparently delayed in London. Four of the couples, including their hosts, were members of the Lockwood clan, and none of them, except Charles, bothered to address a word to Marguerite unless forced to out of politeness.

Marguerite seemed as serene as ever, her smile charming, her interest in the conversation around her genuine. Was he the only one who knew how hard this was for her? How much effort it took to pretend that everything was fine? He knew. He'd played the same game his whole life. He tried to make up to his father for Valentin's loss by being the perfect son, tried to fade into the background and pretend that nothing had changed when Val returned . . .

At least on the top floor of Madame's pleasure house he'd been allowed to attend to his own feelings, his own needs. To be recognized for what he was, rather than ignored or found wanting. He picked up his glass of red wine and drained it. Marguerite's courage humbled him, made him realize how far he still had to go to find himself.

"Sokorvsky, are you enjoying the wine?"

He turned to look at his host, his empty glass still in his hand. Charles Lockwood clicked his fingers and a footman instantly refilled it.

"The wine. Is it to your liking?"

"It's excellent." Anthony put down his glass and gave his full attention to Charles, who didn't look particularly friendly. "Thank you for inviting me for the weekend."

"I didn't invite you. Marguerite asked if you could come."

"But you could've said no."

"I was going to, but my wife had already sent you an invitation."

Ah, so Charles believed in getting to the point. Anthony smiled. "Well, however it happened. I'm still grateful."

"Why?"

"Because I always enjoy Marguerite's company."

"She permits you to address her by her first name?"

Anthony met Charles's furious gaze. "She does."

Charles busied himself lighting a cigarillo and didn't offer one to Anthony. "I still consider Lady Justin part of this family."

"Really?"

"Of course I do. And as such, she is still under my protection."

"Do you think I mean to harm her?"

Charles scowled. "I've heard about your ramshackle ways, Sokorvsky."

"I'm surprised you have time to listen to gossip, Lockwood. I never do." Anthony sipped at his wine, wondered if the rest of the diners were straining to hear the muted conversation at the head of the table. "I have a great deal of respect for Marguerite."

"I'm glad to hear it. She's not been widowed for long."

"More than two years, I believe."

"Is it that long?" Surprise mixed with sadness filled Charles's eyes. "It feels like only days since my brother died."

Anthony let out his breath. "I knew your brother. He was a true gentleman."

"Yet you are spending time with his wife."

"His *widow*. You knew Justin better than anyone. Do you think he would want Marguerite to mourn him for the rest of her life? Wouldn't he want her to be happy?"

"In principle, I agree with you." Charles sighed. "In my heart, I find it difficult to let her go."

"I can understand that. She is a wonderful woman."

They both looked down the table toward Marguerite, who looked back, a puzzled expression on her face. Anthony winked, and she relaxed and turned back to her neighbor.

"She likes you, doesn't she?"

"I hope so. She can certainly trust me."

"Then I suppose I shouldn't interfere." Charles leaned close. "To be frank, I was surprised when Amelia suggested Marguerite attend this house party. They have never been close. Perhaps Amelia did it to show me that Marguerite doesn't need me anymore."

"I'm sure that was part of it. But, please, Marguerite is very fond of you. I'm sure she'll want to remain friends."

"Don't worry about that. I'll always look out for her, whether she likes it or not."

Anthony raised his glass to Charles. "I'll consider myself warned."

Anthony's gaze was drawn back to Marguerite, who was smiling at something the man sitting next to her had just said. Damnation, he wanted her. He wanted to take her upstairs, strip away her finery and make love to her until she cried out his name and begged him never to leave her.

Could he tell her everything? Could he share the excruciating details of his sex life and hope she would still want him? He glanced around the table. God knows, he wanted someone to know who he really was, someone who cared.

The door to the dining room opened, and a cold draft ruffled the tablecloth and the soft dresses of the ladies. Anthony looked up and the welcoming smile on his lips froze. Lord Minshom's languid gaze swept everyone at the table, paused at Anthony and moved on to Charles. He inclined his head.

"I do apologize for my late arrival. I hope you've left me something to eat."

17

While Lord Minshom made himself comfortable at the dining table, Marguerite's attention was drawn back to Anthony. His gaze was fixed upon Minshom's face, but his expression was unreadable. Foolishly, she hadn't thought that her nemesis would actually be a fellow guest. She'd assumed Minshom would stay with Sir Harry, wherever he was hiding. Had she done the right thing bringing Anthony or had she inadvertently made things worse?

"Lady Justin, how lovely to see you again. I trust you are well?" Lord Minshom's voice carried clearly across the table to her. There was no chance of pretending she hadn't heard him. She met his stare with one of her own and watched his eyebrow rise.

"I'm quite well, thank you."

"Excellent."

Minshom's cool gaze moved to Anthony, and Marguerite found herself tensing.

"And Sokorvsky. What brings you here?"

Anthony just looked at him, his hand fisted on the table-cloth. Amelia giggled.

"You'll never guess. Lord Anthony came with Lady Justin."

Charles cleared his throat. "Actually, darling, Lord Anthony was invited by us, as were all our guests, and we're delighted to see him."

Minshom smiled. "As am I. We've spent some interesting evenings together, haven't we, Sokorvsky?"

Anthony kept his gaze on his hand wrapped around his wine glass. "In the past, perhaps."

"Oh come, come, surely not that long ago?"

Marguerite tried to catch Amelia's eye. Surely it was time for the ladies to leave the men to their port? She didn't relish the spectacle of Lord Minshom toying with Anthony. The tension between the two men was almost palpable.

"In fact, I seem to remember encountering you at the theater the other week." Minshom nodded at Marguerite. "You were escorting Lady Justin."

Marguerite frowned. Minshom's tone implied that she was somehow irrelevant, that something far more important had occurred between Anthony and him at the theater than she knew about. She fixed on a polite smile.

"I don't remember seeing you there, Lord Minshom. Did you enjoy the play?"

"I scarcely remember the play. I'm always more interested in the people."

Amelia picked up her fan and smiled at the ladies. "Shall we leave the gentlemen to their port?"

Marguerite was the first to rise. She guessed the conversation had become too staid for Amelia's liking. Before she left the room, she tried to catch Anthony's eye, but he refused to look at her, his attention fixed on his wineglass. Part of her wanted to stay and protect him, from what she wasn't quite sure. But hadn't he complained that everyone tried to mollycoddle him? Perhaps he needed to face Lord Minshom by himself.

Anthony watched the ladies depart, all too aware that Marguerite had tried to get his attention but completely unwilling to give it to her. She hadn't been surprised by Minshom's arrival. Had she known he was coming? And if so, why had she brought Anthony face-to-face with a man he despised? Did she somehow know of the connection between them—that Minshom had sworn to do anything to get him back under his thumb?

He glanced over at Minshom, who sat opposite him, and saw him smile at one of Charles's remarks. Perhaps he had it the wrong way round. Minshom knew of his connection with Marguerite. Had he told her to bring Anthony as a guest? He sighed. Unless there was a connection between Marguerite and Minshom, that idea was equally ridiculous. And Marguerite had sounded sincere when she'd told him she needed him. At this particular moment, he needed to believe that more than he needed to breathe.

"Cat got your tongue this evening, Sokorvsky?"

Anthony finally looked up at Minshom. Despite having no facts to go on, he knew in his gut that Minshom represented some kind of danger to Marguerite. The odds of them meeting in the same house on the same weekend were far too great. He had to find a way to honor his promise to Marguerite but not let Minshom rile him.

"Good evening, Lord Minshom."

"Are you surprised to see me here?"

Anthony shrugged. "I'm always surprised to see you."

Minshom leaned across the table as Charles headed toward the decanters on the sideboard. "I'm connected on my mother's side to the Lockwood family. They consider me a cousin."

"That explains it, then."

"You're not concerned about sharing a house with me?"

"Why should I be?"

"Because sometimes it is hard to resist temptation."

"Perhaps it will be good for you."

Minshom's smile flashed out. "My, the little boy is finally showing his mettle. I was talking about you being unable to resist me, not the other way around."

"I know what you meant. It doesn't mean I have to agree with you. I'm not the one doing the chasing this time."

Minshom's light eyes narrowed. "You think I came here for you?" He laughed. "Your conceit is almost amusing. I came here for a completely different reason. You are not the only person I have an interest in." Minshom got up and bowed. "Now, please excuse me. I have to go and change and then come down and charm the ladies. Lady Justin is very beautiful, isn't she?"

Anthony barely managed to stay in his chair as Minshom headed for the door. With provocation like that, how the devil was he expected to deal with Minshom over the next two days? He poured himself a glass of port when it circled the table again and drained it in one swallow. When would Charles end his excruciatingly boring conversation about hunting and reunite with the ladies?

Half an hour later, Marguerite sat next to Anthony in the drawing room, a cup of tea balanced on her knee and one wary eye on Lord Minshom, who was talking to Amelia. The room was decorated in overly fussy pink stripes and clashing florals that made Marguerite feel quite dizzy. She risked a glance at Anthony and a smile, but he didn't respond. She hadn't been able to conceal her reaction to Minshom's appearance, and she thought Anthony had noticed. She braced herself for the questions she knew would follow.

If only she'd realized exactly how strained the relationship between Minshom and Anthony was. In Minshom's presence,

Anthony's easy charm had deserted him, leaving him grim and unsmiling, and his suspicions on obvious display.

"Did you know Lord Minshom would be here, Marguerite?"

"Why are you asking me?"

"Because I don't like the man, and he seems to be taking quite an interest in you."

"Perhaps he admires me."

"He told me you were beautiful."

She winced. "He would."

"So you admit to having an acquaintance with him?"

She turned to look up at him, kept her gaze steady. "I've met him at the Lockwoods', and he escorted me home once. I'm not sure if that constitutes an acquaintance."

"Do you like him?"

"*Non.*"

"Good. I suggest you keep away from him."

She raised her eyebrows. "You say 'suggest,' yet it sounds more like a royal command. Perhaps we should discuss *your* acquaintance with Lord Minshom rather than mine."

Anthony frowned. "Any association I had with him is in the past. I loathe the man."

"Such strong sentiments for such an apparently minor relationship."

"I didn't say it was minor. I . . ."

"Goodness me, are the love birds quarrelling?"

Marguerite looked up to find Lord Minshom in front of them and tensed when he drew up a chair and sat down. He'd changed into a dark blue coat, silver waistcoat and tight black pantaloons which clung to his long legs.

"Surely that is none of your business?" Anthony asked.

Minshom looked pained. "You used to have such excellent manners, Sokorvsky. Whatever happened to them?"

"Perhaps I reserve them for those who deserve my respect."

"And if I don't want your respect?"

Anthony smiled. "Then surely we are even." He took Marguerite's hand. "Do you wish to see the gardens?"

She refused to meet his intent gaze or react to the pressure of his grip on her wrist. If Lord Minshom wanted her to meet with him, she needed to endure his conversation for a little while longer. In truth, it would almost be better if Anthony stormed off in a rage and left her alone with Minshom, although she didn't relish that either. She opened her mouth to reply to Anthony, but Minshom got in first.

"It is a little too late to be wandering outside, don't you think?"

"I wasn't asking you, Minshom."

"I was answering for the lady. I would hate to see such a delicate flower catch a cold."

Marguerite placed her hand over Anthony's and gently squeezed, drawing his attention back to her face. "I fear Lord Minshom is right. It does look rather chilly out there. Perhaps we should wait until the morning."

"Well, then would you like to take a stroll around the room and stretch your legs?"

Minshom chuckled. "I believe Sokorvsky is trying to get rid of me, Lady Justin. Perhaps he's afraid I'll steal you from under his nose."

She raised her chin. "That is most unlikely, seeing as I enjoy his company immensely."

"More than you enjoy mine?"

"I didn't say that, my lord."

Minshom raised his eyebrows. "Is that what brought you two together? Your dislike of me? How amusing. I've never seen myself in the role of cupid before."

Anthony looked down at Marguerite. "To be perfectly frank, when I'm with Lady Justin, I can't say I think of you at all."

Lord Minshom placed a hand over his heart. "I believe my feelings are hurt." He got up and gave them an elaborate bow, reached for Marguerite's hand and brought it to his lips. "Perhaps I'll see you in the morning?"

Marguerite folded her fingers around the scrap of paper Lord Minshom pressed into her palm and tried to look unconcerned. Anthony didn't bother to reply as Minshom retreated, pausing to talk to Charles before leaving the room.

"Thank God he's gone."

"You were rather rude to him, Anthony."

"Rude? The man deserves to be hung, drawn and quartered, and you think I'm rude?"

"It's not like you."

He sighed, "I know, but Minshom makes my skin crawl."

"Why?"

"Because . . ." He studied her, his usually calm expression absent. "I can't tell you here. Perhaps later."

"Tomorrow?"

He hesitated. "Later tonight when I creep into your bed?"

"I don't remember agreeing to that." *How on earth was she going to meet with Lord Minshom if Anthony was by her side all night?*

He stared at her, his smile dying. "You don't want me?"

"Of course I do. It's just . . ." She looked desperately across at Charles. "I'm in Justin's old house."

"Ah, I see. You're afraid of offending someone who is already dead."

"That is scarcely fair, Anthony."

"I don't understand why you arranged for me to accompany you here if you didn't want me."

"I told you why I wanted you here."

His shrug was dismissive. "To support you, to be your friend."

"Is that not enough for you?"

"I suppose it will have to be."

"Now you sound like a petulant child."

He held her gaze. "A child wouldn't want you the way I do."

She briefly closed her eyes. "Anthony, why are you making this so difficult?"

"I don't know." He studied her intently. "Perhaps because you still haven't told me exactly what is going on?"

Frustration rose inside her and battled with her conscience. "Do you think I came here to sneak off and indulge in a night of passion with Charles or Lord Minshom?"

"Well, that would certainly make sense of it all."

Heat rose on Marguerite's cheeks. "There's no need to be sarcastic. I do not want to bed another man!"

"Then why are you behaving so oddly?"

"If by 'oddly' you mean that I took exception to you assuming you were welcome in my bed, then yes."

"I did not 'assume'; I thought we were going to be honest with each other."

She stood up, snapped open her fan and plied it vigorously. "As honest as you are about your relationship with Lord Minshom?"

"Hold on a moment, you can't just change the subject like that and expect me to respond."

"I'm not changing the subject. You questioned my honesty; I'm simply repaying the favor."

Anthony rose too, making Marguerite aware that their argument had gotten out of hand and was attracting a fair amount of interest.

"I will tell you anything you want to know about that man in private."

She sighed. "And look, our argument has come full circle. We're back to Lord Minshom again."

"So we are, and that's exactly what he probably intended, isn't it?"

They stared at each other for a long moment and then Marguerite headed for the door. In the deserted hallway, Anthony caught up with her and grabbed her hand. "Please don't let him come between us."

Marguerite eased her hand out of his grasp and placed it flat on his chest. She had to stop Anthony from following her. She had to make it impossible for him to come to her room that night.

"He can only do that if we give him the power to hurt us. Rather than worrying about me, perhaps you should be concerned about yourself."

"In what way?"

"You told me you hated everyone protecting you, but as soon as Lord Minshom confronted you, you tried to get away from him."

"I was trying to protect you! Isn't that what you asked me to do?"

"So you say, but I'm not the one who is afraid of him, am I?"

Anthony stepped back, the harsh angles of his face stark against the blazing blue of his eyes. "You think I'm a coward, don't you? The kind of man who hides behind a woman's skirts."

Marguerite held her ground, aware that she was hurting him. But she had no choice. Hopefully Anthony would still be prepared to listen to her when she was able to tell him the truth. And what she was saying was true; she really didn't understand his relationship with Minshom.

"I think you fear him, though I'm not sure why."

"But you're not interested in allowing me access to your room tonight to explain myself. You're more worried about what Charles will think of you taking a lover than in sorting things out with me."

Marguerite simply stared at him as panic gripped her and paralyzed her thoughts. What could she say?

Anthony bowed. With all the good humor stripped from his face, he resembled his older half brother.

"I'll bid you good night. But perhaps I'm not the only one being contrary. If you're too afraid to offend the Lockwood family, why on earth did you decide to bring me down here with you? What happened? Did you lose your nerve or am I suddenly not good enough anymore?"

He turned on his heel and headed back down the hall toward Charles's oak-paneled library, where the roar of male conversation already resonated. Marguerite stared after him. The urge to follow and slap his face for his outrageous suggestions was so strong she had to clench her hands into fists. She was trying to protect him from Minshom, didn't he see that? Didn't he understand that the last thing she wanted to do was drag him into a situation that might not even happen?

She ran up the stairs and all the way to her bedroom, her heart thumping in her chest. Perhaps she wouldn't bother to hear him out about Lord Minshom after all. Perhaps she'd ignore him for the rest of the visit and flirt with Charles to annoy Amelia instead.

She slowly opened her fingers to reveal the folded paper Minshom had pressed into her palm, took off her gloves and opened the note. It told her to meet him at the south gatehouse at midnight. Marguerite glanced at the clock on her mantelpiece. It was already past eleven and, if she remembered correctly, the gatehouse was at least a ten minute walk from the house.

She'd have to change, put on more serviceable boots and something warmer than the thin silk of her blue evening dress. She glanced uncertainly at the servant's bell. Would she be able to get out of her dress without assistance? She didn't want to waste time explaining her sudden need to change her dress to a maid or, even worse, have Anthony hearing her next door and coming in to help her undress.

Luckily, the small puffed sleeves slid easily off her shoulders and allowed her to wiggle around and gain access to the buttons at the back of the bodice. After a few contortions, she managed to get the dress off and find something plainer and warmer in her closet.

After another quick glance at the clock, she pushed her feet into stout walking boots and grabbed her hooded cloak. Hardly daring to breathe, she checked the connecting door between her suite and Anthony's was locked and headed for the door.

Laughter and music rose from the rooms below, and cigar smoke mingled with brandy and perfume permeated the stuffy hallway. Marguerite drew her hood over her hair and went down the servants' stairs, pausing at each landing to get her bearings before finding herself in a cold stone passageway beside the kitchen.

She took a deep breath and then tiptoed past the half-opened kitchen door and out into the gardens. It took her a few moments to adjust her vision to the dimness of the light, and then she set off, following the brick-edged path around the house and to the southern end of the park, where the smaller of the two lodges lay.

The beginnings of a frost glimmered on the pathway and the well-cut lawns and gilded the bare trees with silver. Marguerite shivered as she passed into a copse of trees hugging the edge of the ornamental lake and was swallowed into the shadows. Her hand closed around the small pocketknife her mother had given her for her eighteenth birthday. Not that she'd ever had to use it on anyone, but she'd been taught how to defend herself, something her mother considered every woman should know.

The lodge came into sight, its red brick solid and reassuring, as was the light in the window. Marguerite paused to gather her thoughts and calm her breathing. Minshom was far too astute to appear before without a plan or a show of confidence, even if it was put on. She continued up the brick path. Noting the side door was slightly ajar, she put her hand on it. She had to go through with this. She had to confront Sir Harry and lay her past to rest.

* * *

Anthony attempted another smile at one of Charles's terrible jokes and took refuge in his glass of brandy. It was past midnight. Could he make his excuses and go to bed? Surely no one would miss him now, or, after seeing him argue with Marguerite, assume he was up to no good. He set his glass back carefully on the table, his fingers shaking. How much had he drunk? Would he even be able to make it up the stairs without assistance? He cleared his throat.

"Good night, all."

Charles slapped him on the back, his drunken amiability in sharp contrast to his wariness at dinner.

"Good night, Sokorvsky. See you in the morning."

Anthony took the candle from the footman stationed in the hall and walked slowly up the stairs. He paused at Marguerite's door but saw no light under it. Had she gone to bed in a rage? He leaned in closer to the panels, tried to calm his breathing to listen for some sense of her, but he felt nothing.

He continued on to his room and pushed open the door. Unfortunately, Marguerite hadn't chosen to jump into his bed either. With a sigh, he set the candle down and walked across to the roaring fire. He felt off-kilter, his past and his secretly longed-for future weighed in the balance, forced together into the unlikely scenario of a weekend in the country. Minshom could destroy him with one word, and yet Anthony couldn't hate him as much as he wanted to. The man still had the power to excite him, to lead him on, to make him dread disclosure, yet desire it at the same time.

"Damn him."

Anthony hunkered down on his haunches and stared into the flames. Did he really want Minshom to tell Marguerite his secrets? Would that somehow make it easier, to be forced to confess, to blurt out his worst desires under threat of pain and punishment? God, he despised himself sometimes. Marguerite was right to doubt him and his courage.

There was a knock at his door, and he got to his feet. A young maidservant bobbed him a curtsey, her smile nervous.

"Good evening, sir."

"Good evening, may I help you?"

The maid juggled the pile of folded clothes she carried and hitched it higher on her hip. "I'm supposed to be looking after the lady in the next room. It's the first time Cook has let me out of the scullery to see if I'd be any good at it, you see."

Anthony tried not to look puzzled as he waited for her to continue.

"The thing is that I don't know if the lady is still downstairs or if she's gone to bed or . . . what." The maid looked hopefully up at him.

"And what do you want me to do about it?"

She frowned. "Well, I don't know if I should go in there or not. What if she's asleep?"

"Have you asked Cook what to do?"

"I can't. She'll say I should know and that I'm just not ready to be an upstairs maid, but I am ready, I really am."

Anthony patted the girl's shoulder. "I'm sure you are, but I still don't understand the problem. Why don't you just pop your head quickly around the door and check if the lady is in bed, and then close the door again?"

The maid's lower lip trembled. "Because the door is locked, and I can't find the spare key."

"Ah." Anthony glanced at the door that connected his suite to Marguerite's. How kind of the fates to smile on him in this particularly appropriate fashion. "Do you want to use the door in here?"

"If that's all right with you, sir, and you won't tell Cook that I interrupted you and lost the key and everything, sir."

"Of course I won't tell her. Now come along, we'll try the door together."

Anthony followed the maid over to the door and waited as she tried to turn the handle.

"It's locked, sir."

"So it is. Well, I suppose that means the lady doesn't want any visitors tonight."

The maid rummaged in the pocket of her apron. "But I have the key for this door, sir."

"Of course you do."

Anthony thought about sending the maid away, but realized he was far more interested in seeing if Marguerite was in bed than the maid was. And for God's sake, he wasn't going to do anything, just check that she was indeed where she said she would be and leave.

"Try it then."

The door opened with a soft click, and Anthony and the maid peered into the gloom. Marguerite's familiar flowery scent invaded Anthony's nostrils, and he breathed in deep.

"I can't see her, sir."

"Neither can I."

Anthony's throat tightened as he realized the elusive perfume was the only evidence of Marguerite in the room. Heat coiled in his body, leaving him shaking and almost light-headed. He looked down at the maid.

"I'm sure she'll do without your services tonight. Leave the clothes by the bed, and tell Cook your lady was asleep and didn't need your help at all."

"But isn't that a lie, sir?"

He forced a smile. "Not really, she's probably fallen asleep in one of her friend's rooms, so I doubt she'll be back until the morning. I know she wouldn't want you to get into any trouble on her account."

Anthony fished in his pocket and found half a crown, held it out to her, keeping his tone light and unconcerned. "Take this for your trouble and get yourself to bed. You probably have to be up early in the morning."

The maid studied the coin and then Anthony. "That's very kind of you, sir, but my mother said never take money from a gentleman, because before you know it, he'll be taking liberties with you."

Anthony managed a laugh and walked back to the door leading into the main hallway. "Not this gentleman." He opened it with a flourish and tossed her the coin. "Your mother is a wise woman. Good night my dear."

She walked past him with exaggerated care. He wasn't sure if she feared he'd ravish her or take the money back. Either way, he wanted to reassure her that nothing would happen.

"Good night, sir, and thank you."

His smile vanished as he closed the door behind her. Where the hell was Marguerite, and what the devil was he supposed to do now?

18

"Ah, there you are, Lady Justin. Or may I call you Marguerite? We are practically related."

Marguerite halted at the entrance to the snug kitchen. Lord Minshom sat by the open fireplace, an earthenware mug cradled in his hands, one booted foot propped up on the scrubbed pine table. There was no sign of the real occupants of the lodge, although a fire burned in the hearth and a kettle steamed on the stove as if waiting for their return.

"Where is Sir Harry?"

"Oh, he's not here yet. He's supposed to arrive tomorrow evening on his way back to the coast."

"Then why did you ask me to meet you here?"

Lord Minshom leaned back in his chair and stared up at her. The smile in his eyes died. "To see if you were capable of obeying orders. Many women promise much and fail to deliver."

Marguerite fingered the knife in her pocket, trying to remember all the places she might wound an unsuspecting man and render him helpless.

"Well, I've proved I'm punctual, so I'll bid you good night."

Minshom slowly shook his head as if admonishing a child. "There's no need to be so abrupt. Don't you want to share some of this excellent coffee with me? I'm sure you're chilled from your walk."

"Not really."

"You don't like me, do you?"

"I don't trust you, sir."

"Fair enough."

Marguerite tensed as Lord Minshom got to his feet. Even though he wasn't a particularly big man, the small kitchen seemed to shrink around her.

"Isn't there anything you'd like to ask me about, say Anthony Sokorvsky, for example?"

"Any explanations I need can come from him."

"So he hadn't told you much about our relationship then?"

"He's told me everything I need to know. That it is in the past."

"And you believe him?"

"Yes."

He chuckled. "And if I tell you that as far as I am concerned, I still own him, will that change your opinion?"

"You cannot 'own' another person, sir."

"Really? Not even if they offer themselves to you, body and soul?"

Marguerite took a step back and came up against the door frame. "No, sir."

"We'll have to see about that, won't we?" Lord Minshom observed her through narrowed eyes, and she tensed for flight. "Perhaps you and I can sit down and work out a more civilized arrangement. It's not as though Sokorvsky would mind being shared, is it?"

"Good night, Lord Minshom."

He blew her a kiss. "Good night, Marguerite. I'll expect you tomorrow at the same time."

"And will Sir Harry be here?"

Minshom shrugged. "You'll just have to wait and see, won't you?"

Marguerite turned on her heel and left with as much dignity and speed as she could muster. Fear trickled an icy path down her spine as if she feared a knife or a shot in the back. Minshom was indeed a devil. She hardly knew him, and yet she was slightly afraid of him. If Anthony had really been in his clutches, how had he survived?

She slowed to a walk as the sturdy walls of the main house came into view. She needed Anthony to help her deal with Lord Minshom, but after her earlier panicked dismissal, did she still have the right to ask for his aid? If she went to him now, explained herself and told him the truth, would he turn from her in disgust?

She twisted her hands together. Why was it so hard to make up her mind? She really needed to stop vacillating. It wasn't surprising that no one took her seriously.

Marguerite took a deep breath and stared up at the outline of her bedroom window. For the first time in her life, she didn't want to wait to confront Anthony; she was tired of waiting for people to acknowledge her. She opened the back door into the house and headed straight up the servants' stairs. Despite the relatively short time since her departure, the house was quieter and more settled.

A faint light flickered under Anthony's door. Marguerite whispered a prayer of thanks. She'd go into her own room, change into her night things and risk Anthony's wrath by invading his room through the connecting door between them. At least she wouldn't have to stand out in the hallway knocking and quietly begging to be let in.

She undressed quickly, warmth stealing over her as her body adjusted to the temperature of the room and shook off the coldness of the night. Should she take her hair down? She glanced at her pale reflection. Of course she should. If she was pretending she'd woken up and come to Anthony's room in a sudden fit of remorse, she'd better look as if she had been sleeping.

Her fingers closed around the handle of the door that separated their suites. To her surprise, the latch clicked open before she could even insert the key. Had she forgotten to lock it after all, or had someone been into her room? She pushed the door until she could see into Anthony's room, relieved that it didn't creak.

Only one candle illuminated the space. Anthony sat by the fire, his face in profile. His white cravat and coat hung over the back of the chair and his boots had been kicked off. Gathering all her courage, Marguerite stepped into the room, the wooden floor cold on her bare feet until she reached the comfort of the fireside rug.

"Anthony?"

He didn't look up, just continued to stare into the fire, one hand moving rhythmically in the shadows of his groin. Marguerite moved closer until she faced him and could see exactly what he was doing. His fingers were wrapped around his erect cock, which was itself wrapped tightly in leather straps.

"What are you doing?"

"You informed me that you were unavailable so I decided to pleasure myself."

Marguerite bit her lip at his flat tone. "You do not seem to be enjoying it."

His smile wasn't reassuring. "Trust me, I am."

She gestured at the tight binding around his cock. "It looks painful."

"It is."

"Is this for my benefit? Who exactly are you punishing? Am I supposed to feel guilty because I wouldn't let you into my bed?"

He shrugged. "If you like. It's as good a reason as any to excuse my perversions."

"I wanted to talk to you, but perhaps I should wait until the morning."

"Perhaps you should."

The anger and frustration she hadn't dared to show Minshom coalesced like a fist in her chest. There was obviously no other way to get his attention than to finish this. She stepped between his open thighs and grabbed his wrist, stilling his movements.

"Unless you'd rather I helped you 'enjoy' yourself?"

He raised his head and looked at her for the first time. Lust and anger swirled in his blue gaze, held her prisoner and made her swallow hard. "Why would you want to do that?"

"Because I'm sorry for walking away from you this evening? Because I want to see how you taste?"

He shuddered so violently she felt it through her fingers on his wrist.

"Do what you want."

Marguerite sank to her knees and stared at his straining leather-clad shaft and balls. Pre-cum seeped through the strips, darkening the leather, especially at the crown. She touched the strap that curved under his balls.

"Where did you find the leather?"

"In my luggage."

"You brought the straps with you for this purpose?"

"No. It's simply a spare strap used to secure luggage in the curricle. It just happened to suit my needs."

"Ah." Marguerite leaned closer, inhaling Anthony's scent and the muskier tones of the leather. His politeness ignited something fierce inside her. She was tired of being ignored, of being overlooked. Whatever was going on, she *was* determined to get his full attention.

With deliberate slowness, she licked a path from his balls up his shaft and circled his crown. His breath hissed out as she nibbled on the leather. She took her time then, investigated every gap in the leather with the tip of her tongue, sucked on the ties at the base of his cock, tugged at them until his hips lifted off the chair toward her mouth. His hand fisted in her hair.

"God, Marguerite."

"Don't touch me."

She waited until he subsided back into the chair, until his hands returned to grip the arm rests. She had his attention now in every quivering inch of his cock. And, *mon Dieu*, she liked it, she liked ordering him around. Could she make him beg?

Anthony gripped the arms of the chair until his fingers hurt. Marguerite's tongue flicked out again, and he tensed and then groaned as she licked a lascivious trail around his balls. She inserted a finger behind the constraining leather strap, tightening it further, adding more strain to his desperately aroused cock.

It wasn't supposed to have happened this way. He'd fully intended to wait until morning and confront her when he was calmer, when his completely foreign wave of anger and possessiveness had died down. But she'd come to him, caught him at his most vulnerable and totally surprised him.

She tightened her fingers on the leather around his balls, bringing his shaft away from his belly, causing his blood to pump so hard he felt it in every tortured breath. Not that he should be surprised. She'd constantly proved that there was far more to her than superficial beauty. Wasn't that exactly why he liked her so much? Would she like it if he begged? He swallowed a moan. He was about to find out.

"Please, Marguerite."

She didn't stop the torment, took the first inch of his tortured cock inside her mouth and sucked. He couldn't help the surge of his hips, the instinctive urge to thrust deeper, for her to take all of him.

"Please . . ."

She folded her fingers around the base of his shaft and swallowed the rest of him. Heat seared through his cock, his groaning echoed every pull of her mouth as she forced his cum up his shaft to explode into her mouth.

"God . . ."

He shuddered and writhed as his pumping cock fought the conflicts of the binding to completion, to satisfaction, to utter bliss. He collapsed back into his chair, his breathing ragged, his heart thumping so hard it threatened to burst from his chest.

Marguerite sat back and wiped her hand over her mouth. He didn't dare look at her, concentrated on untying the leather strap and using his handkerchief to clean himself off.

"Should I go back to bed now?"

He stopped. He knew he had to look at her and confront her with his painfully acquired knowledge. "*Back* to bed?"

Her eyes widened. "*You* unlocked the door, didn't you? Were you spying on me?"

"Actually I was trying to help your maid. You locked her out. She had a key to the internal door, which I allowed her to use."

He was proud of the calmness of his voice after such erotic intimacy, after she'd lied to him.

"So which one was it? Charles or Minshom?"

Marguerite got to her feet and retreated behind the chair opposite his, one hand clenched on the top of the delicately carved frame.

"Minshom."

Fury shot through him. "Really? Did he teach you how to do that?"

"Suck a man's cock?" Marguerite raised her chin. "I already knew how to do that, and you know it."

Anthony managed a dismissive smile. "Was he any good?"

"At what?"

"Fucking."

She glared at him for so long he thought he'd go blind. "Do you really think I'd sleep with him?"

"Why not? You sleep with me." God, had he really said that? Was he comparing himself to Minshom, competing with him?

Marguerite briefly closed her eyes as if she couldn't bear to look at him. But he wasn't ready to apologize to her yet. She was the one who'd lied to him, had consorted with his worst enemy.

"I didn't touch him. I'm afraid of him."

Anthony went still. "What the hell does that mean?"

"I'm afraid of him. I was hoping you'd be able to help me."

"That's why you asked me to accompany you down here, to help you with Minshom?" He laughed. "Then why lie to me and go off and meet him by yourself?"

She met his dismissive gaze, her eyes desperate. "Because I didn't realize he would actually be a guest at this house and that he would try to create discord between us. I thought to meet him privately. And I hoped I wouldn't have to ask for your help."

While he thought about her words, Anthony took a moment to tuck his cock away and button his breeches. "Is he your lover?"

"Of course not! Didn't you hear what I said?"

"I'm afraid of him, and he's fucked me." She didn't look surprised by that revelation. God knows what else Minshom had said about him. But she was here, wasn't she? She'd come to him despite everything.

"Is Minshom blackmailing you?"

"Not really."

He gestured at the chair opposite him. She sighed and came around to sit in it, drew her knees up and encircled them with her arms.

"Then why did you meet with him?"

"He knew Justin."

"So?"

"He also knew Sir Harry Jones. Apparently, Harry is back in the country."

"And Minshom claims to know where he is."

She half-smiled. "Exactly, and he said he would arrange for me to speak to Harry."

"Ah . . ." Anthony stared down at his clasped hands and addressed them rather than Marguerite. "And why is it so important for you to speak to Sir Harry?"

"Because he was there when Justin died."

"Do you think he has the answers you seek?"

"I don't know, but I have to talk to him, have to try . . ."

He looked up again, heard the strain in her voice, the misery that the years had failed to extinguish. Despite all his reservations about her consorting with Minshom, he could understand that need. God knows he'd lived every agonizing empty minute of it with his father after Valentin's kidnap and his eventual return.

"Do you trust Minshom?"

"*Non.* That's why I asked you to come with me."

"But as I'm sure Minshom has already pointed out to you, I am not exactly a hero."

"Do you think I would believe anything Minshom said to me?"

He smiled at her indignant expression and reached across to take her hand. "I'll help you."

"Thank you. I know after the way I treated you at dinner I don't deserve it."

"I'm beginning to understand that having me in your bed when you were attempting to meet Minshom might have been a little inconvenient."

Her answering laughter was almost a sob. "Oh God, Anthony, I was so frightened . . ."

He stood up and pulled her into his arms, bringing her back to sit on his lap. "I assume, since you are still asking for my help, that he didn't produce Sir Harry?"

She leaned into him, resting her head on his shoulder. "He didn't. I wasn't even surprised. I'm not sure if he intends me to meet with Harry at all." She shivered. "It's as if he likes to play with people, to watch them suffer like a cat with a mouse."

Anthony stroked her hair and drew her even closer. "I'll be with you next time, I promise, whether Sir Harry turns up or not."

She sighed and cuddled close. "Thank you."

He kissed the top of her head. He should be thanking her. She'd given him an opportunity not only to help her come to terms with her past, but to finally show Minshom he was a lot stronger than he looked.

"Will you come to bed with me now, Marguerite?"

She touched his cheek. "I'd like that."

He smiled into the darkness as warmth coalesced around his heart. "I'd like that too." He slid a hand around her neck and tilted her face up to meet his. When he kissed her, he caught a hint of leather and his own cum on her lips and was instantly hard.

Marguerite sighed and kissed him back, her tongue tangling with his, her fingers settling into his hair. He picked her up, walked across to the big four-poster bed and placed her gently in the center. She watched him pull off his shirt and step out of his breeches. After the strain of the leather binding, his cock was overly sensitive, but he didn't care. This was about Marguerite's pleasure, not his own. This was about learning what pleased her.

"I want you, Marguerite."

He knelt on the bed and simply stared down at her. Her long hair was spread out around her, and her dark eyelashes were lowered to conceal her expression. Anthony brushed his fingertip over the curve of her cheek and traced the edge of her mouth. Went lower to her throat and then circled her nipple through the thin muslin of her nightgown.

She sighed as he increased the pressure of his fingertips, drew the small nub tight before sucking it into his mouth. She liked that, her body arching into him. In truth, so did he. Not all men were so responsive. His fingers found her other nipple, worked that to a hard pulsing tip too, before he used his mouth to make it even harder.

He raised his head, saw that she was watching him and returned to kiss her mouth. Her tight nipples grazed the hair on his chest as she moved in rhythm with him. He pushed his knee between her thighs, pressed it to the intimate flesh he intended to arouse to the point of ecstasy. Soon her sex softened and creamed for him, the damp fabric of her nightdress riding up on his knee.

"Can I take this off you?"

In answer she sat forward, allowed him to pull the voluminous garment over her head and toss it to the floor. Even in the dim candlelight, her body looked magnificent, her breasts high, her waist small enough to encompass with his hands, her sex . . . His throat dried as he contemplated that neat triangle of hair. Such delights she concealed, such softness and strength, such feminine weapons to make a man scream and beg for release.

He kissed her flat stomach, nuzzled her belly button and

moved lower, using the tip of his tongue to lick at her already exposed clit. She didn't stop him when he crawled between her legs and spread them wide enough to accommodate his shoulders. He kissed her sex again, his lips meeting hers, his tongue spreading them to sample the delights of her wet and welcoming channel.

He drew back to look at her, saw her fierce concentration on what he was doing, the way her hands clutched at the bedclothes, the shallowness of her breathing. Perhaps it was time to push her a little, to discover the extent of her sexual curiosity, to allow her the freedom to express what she needed from him—things he suddenly realized he'd never been allowed to do, his sexual tastes dictated and forced by the demands of others.

"You enjoyed sucking my cock, didn't you?"

"Of course." Her voice was so soft, her smile so intimate, that his cock jerked and filled out even more.

"You enjoyed seeing me bound as well, didn't you?"

"Yes." She licked her lips as his fingers traced a lazy path around her clit, stroking and petting it, making it swell even more.

"It's a shame you don't have a cock. I think I'd enjoy tying it up." He slid one finger inside her and withdrew it, repeated the slow penetration as he talked. "Watching you come against your bindings, watching you beg me to give you release."

She shuddered as his thumb covered her clit, joined the slow rhythm of his lone finger.

"I've seen something you might enjoy though." He flicked her swollen clit, pinching it between his finger and thumb until she moaned. "Perhaps you've already tried it at the pleasure house."

"Tried what?" She gasped as he added another finger, her body stretching to accommodate him, to draw him deeper.

"A clamp here." He touched her pussy lips. "Or here." He

circled the fingers already working her clit. "I understand that it has a similar effect to the leather straps. It keeps you stimulated and aroused. Perhaps we should try that when we next visit the pleasure house. I like the thought of you decorated like that."

She came hard against his two embedded fingers, grabbed at his arm, dug her nails deep as she cried out. He didn't stop working her, added a third finger and lengthened the stroke of his movements until the palm of his hand met her pussy with every stroke.

"I'd like to see you come for me like that. Even better, I'd like you to wear the clamps for me all evening so that I could touch them whenever I wanted and drive you wild. I'd make you wait until I had my mouth and fingers on you, make you beg before I'd take them off and fuck you."

He glanced up at her, saw her eyes were closed, her mouth a tight line as a second climax approached. He drew his fingers out until they were barely inside her, bent his head to suck her clit into his mouth and heard her scream as she came again, her thighs clamping around his head while she bucked against him.

He struggled free and stroked his cock, brought it close to her wet sex and rubbed the crown against her clit.

"Do you want me?"

"Yes." Her terse response aroused him almost as much as the cream pouring from her sex. He placed his aching cock at the entrance to her channel, pushed in a half inch and held still. "Are you sure?"

"Yes!"

He smiled down at her. "Touch your breasts for me, make your nipples hard." Her hands cupped her breasts, her thumbs settling over her rosy nipples. She sighed as she touched herself, making Anthony's cock twitch and jerk, to demand completion inside her. He wanted to flood her sex with his seed, make her his, show her that no other man would love her the way he did.

Despite his possessive thoughts, or perhaps because of them, a drop of common sense forced its way to the surface of his fevered mind.

"Do I need to pull out?"

"*Non.*" She opened her eyes to stare at him, her hands stilling on her breasts. "Are you making love to me or not?"

Some perverse demon made him continue. "You came prepared to seduce me, then." He held still, his cock barely inside her. "Did you think it was the only way to persuade me to help you?"

He flinched as she shoved at his chest and rolled away from him in a flurry of bedclothes.

"Yes, of course, that's exactly what I did. How could you doubt it?" She grabbed the sheet, clutched it to her breasts. "Do you really think that's all I came for? Do you *really believe* that's all you are to me?" She swung her legs over the side of the bed, tugged at the sheet until it followed her and wrapped it around her body.

Anthony sighed and stood up too, spreading his hands wide. "Marguerite, don't do this, don't . . ."

"Don't what? Leave?" She looked magnificent in her rage, hair tumbling down her back, blue eyes flashing, cheeks flushed with arousal. "As I'm only interested in fucking you to get what I want, and I've done that, why shouldn't I leave?"

His temper stirred and rose to meet hers. He blocked her exit, put his hands on her shoulders and made her face him. She made him angrier than any woman he'd ever met, but she wasn't afraid of him. What the hell could he say to stop her walking out? He took a deep shuddering breath.

"I'm not used to trusting anyone."

"So?"

"I'm used to being fucked and forgotten."

Marguerite continued to stare at Anthony, one hand wedged between them, gripping the sheet, her knuckles jammed against his chest. He took another breath, lowered his head until his forehead rested on the top of her head.

"I'm not used to someone . . . to anyone, wanting to be with me without expecting something in return."

Now she felt guilty, because in a way, he was right. She'd come into his room quite prepared to do anything to make him help her again, not thinking that he might view her panicked response in a more cynical, yet so vulnerable, light.

"You're right. I did want something from you." He stiffened and made as if to step back. She brought her hand around the back of his neck to keep him close. "But it wasn't just about the sex. I simply wanted to be with you."

He sighed. "God, I'm sorry. I'm woefully inadequate at this. I'm used to dealing with men who simply want to fuck me and walk away."

Marguerite closed her eyes at the bleakness of his tone. How horrible to see making love in terms of being forced, not considered or cared about. It sounded as if he was talking about little more than prostitution.

She pushed at his chest until his head came up, and then stood on tiptoe to kiss him. "I don't really want to leave. Perhaps you can persuade me to stay?"

His arms locked around her, and he deepened the kiss, picked her up until her sex was crushed against the hardness of his shaft and held her there. She squirmed against him, her recently doused passion quickly reignited as his kisses became rougher, his thick cock slippery and wet with pre-cum.

She wrenched her mouth away from his. "Please, don't fuck me; make love to me."

In answer, he backed her up against the wall and slid his cock inside her, began moving hard and fast. She grabbed onto his shoulders, anchored her feet on his hips and held on, allowing him to dictate the pace, the urgency, the frantic drive for completion.

As she climaxed, she hoped he knew that this was nothing to do with commerce and everything to do with emotion. She hoped he knew that she wanted him too so badly . . .

19

For Marguerite, the next morning passed in a daze of polite conversation punctuated by intervals when she forced herself to eat whatever was put in front of her and pretended to listen to the whispered gossip swirling around her. The afternoon progressed so slowly she wanted to scream, and as the conversation centered on Amelia's pregnancy, Marguerite had nothing to say, nothing to add that might not be misinterpreted as jealousy, sarcasm or both.

To her secret relief, the men had gone out shooting, or some such manly sport. So she didn't have to contend with Anthony's concern or the barbed comments of Lord Minshom. She could only hope Anthony had the sense to keep out of Minshom's way.

"Marguerite?"

She smiled vaguely into Amelia's irritated face. "I'm sorry, Amelia, did you say something?"

One of the other women sitting in the circle of chairs around the cozy fire in the cluttered drawing room tittered. Marguerite recognized her old tormentor, Amelia's cousin Drusilla, who was still unmarried and had somehow convinced herself that Marguerite had stolen Justin from under her nose. She was famous for her cutting set-downs and complete lack of humor.

"Mayhap Lady Justin is wondering how to placate Lord Anthony Sokorvsky when he gets back from his shooting expedition." Drusilla looked down her long nose at Marguerite. "In my experience, gentlemen do not like it *at all* when a lady shows them up in company."

Marguerite put down her tea cup and faced Drusilla. "You're quite right, Drusilla. Men don't like to be questioned do they?" She glanced around the avid circle of listeners. "But surely it is our feminine duty to ruffle their self-importance occasionally?"

Two of the married women chuckled. Drusilla's cheeks reddened, and she glared at Marguerite. "Perhaps *some of us* prefer to behave in a more ladylike fashion, particularly *those of us* who should know better."

"You are too hard on yourself, Drusilla." Marguerite smiled sweetly. "Just because you pride yourself on your honesty doesn't make you a pariah to all men."

"Indeed! Perhaps I was talking about you, Lady Justin. A woman whose husband is scarcely cold in his grave racketing around with another man."

Marguerite refused to allow Drusilla's aggressive tone to intimidate her. Perhaps it was time to bring her simmering dislike out into the open, to dispel a few rumors once and for all.

"My husband died two years ago. I'm sure he'd want me to be happy again, and I'm hardly 'racketing around.' I'm visiting my brother-in-law and his wife for a restful weekend in the countryside."

"In the company of another man."

"Who is another invited guest in this house."

"Not that I wanted either of you here," Amelia muttered.

"Then why invite us?" Marguerite looked inquiringly at

Amelia. Would Amelia admit she'd asked Marguerite both on Lord Minshom's behalf and to expose her affair with Anthony in an unfavorable light to Charles? Marguerite didn't think Amelia would do either. She hated not to be liked and approved of.

"Amelia invited you because her husband gave her no choice," Drusilla said. "Although, perhaps having seen the way you treat Lord Anthony, Cousin Charles will speedily revise his good opinion of you."

"Perhaps he will. But I suspect his good sense will prevail, and he will simply be happy for me."

Drusilla laughed. "You're expecting Lord Anthony to propose to you?"

Marguerite raised her eyebrows. "Why not?"

It was strange: she'd never thought of marrying Anthony, never wanted to be married to anyone ever again. The idea seemed ludicrous. Anthony deserved someone young and innocent and . . .

Marguerite realized Drusilla was speaking again.

"*Why not?* Because, if you'll excuse my bluntness, Lady Justin, a man doesn't need to buy the cow when he has already tasted the cream."

A collective gasp rippled through the other women. Marguerite realized she wanted to laugh. Was Drusilla really so naïve about what men wanted? Perhaps she was. Perhaps Marguerite was the one who was out of step with society. But what was new about that? Her mother had hardly brought her up in a conventional manner.

"What an incredibly coarse comparison. I confess I'm quite shocked." Marguerite got up and curtsied to the assembled women. "I think I'll go and lie down and try to pretend you didn't embarrass yourself by saying that out loud, Drusilla."

Drusilla opened her mouth, but Marguerite was already moving toward the door, head held high. Her mother had taught her never to be ashamed of herself or to explain or defend her actions.

She reached her bedroom and lay back on the cream satin counterpane, stared up at the elaborately decorated ceiling. Peace surrounded her for the first time that day.

Could she really imagine Anthony married to one of the fresh-faced innocents who made their debut every Season? His sexual tastes were far too complex to be satisfied by a young virgin. Restlessly she kicked her slippers off. But was that quite true? She'd been an innocent when she married Justin, and yet she'd quickly acquiesced to his unusual sexual requests.

But she suspected Anthony's needs were more complicated than she, or perhaps even he, knew. That didn't scare her though— it just made her more determined to find them out. Marguerite's slight smile died. Anthony had never suggested marriage to her. He was obviously content with their original bargain to support each other through the Season and to be friends.

She rolled over on her stomach and buried her face in the pillows. And that was enough for her, wasn't it? Having Anthony for a friend had proved to be a blessing in many ways. She hadn't expected a marriage proposal, had she?

The dainty clock on the mantelpiece struck six times, and Marguerite groaned. Six hours until she was due to meet Lord Minshom again, and hopefully, Sir Harry. How on earth was she going to get through them? Instinct told her to make her excuses and stay in her room for the rest of the evening, but she couldn't do that. Drusilla would take it as an admission of guilt, and Anthony needed her help to fend off Lord Minshom.

And she was done with hiding, with trying to please everyone and not pleasing herself at all. It was ironic that her liaison with Anthony had put her at odds with the Lockwoods *and* her own family. If that taught her anything, it was that she could never win and might as well be herself.

With a sigh, she got off the bed and rang the bell. If she was going to face the assembled company for dinner, she was determined to look her best.

Anthony knocked twice on the inner door between his suite and Marguerite's and waited for a response. Just as he raised his hand to knock again, the door opened and the maid he'd met the previous night emerged. She curtsied to him and smiled.

"Good evening, sir." Her voice descended to a shrill whisper. "And thanks for your help last night!"

"You're welcome." Anthony nodded at the grinning maid. "Is her ladyship ready to go down to dinner yet?"

"I am." Marguerite answered for herself. "Come in, Anthony, and close the door, you're creating a draught."

With a wink at the maid, Anthony stepped past her into the room and found Marguerite sitting at her dressing table powdering her face. He strolled over to drop a kiss on the top of her head and was greeted with an expanse of lush bosom that made him instantly hard.

"Good evening, my lady. You'll be pleased to hear that I kept out of Minshom's way today, or perhaps he kept out of mine. He didn't stay all day, said he had errands to run. Let's hope they involved Sir Harry Jones."

Marguerite sighed and met his gaze in the mirror. "I'm still not convinced Sir Harry will turn up, are you?"

"It depends what Minshom is really after, doesn't it? If he truly wishes to help you, I'm sure Sir Harry will be produced. If he's just trying to get revenge on me for leaving him, the outcome is less certain."

"Of course, you were lovers."

Anthony froze. He'd forgotten how little Marguerite knew about him and Minshom. She met his horrified gaze in the mirror, her expression tranquil and reached up to pat his hand that rested on her shoulder.

"It's all right. Lord Minshom told me he wanted you back, or that he was quite happy to share."

Anthony shuddered. "We weren't exactly 'lovers.' I don't want to go back to him. I'd rather die."

He hoped she heard the determination in his voice and knew that he spoke the truth. He tensed, wondering what else Minshom had told her about their unequal relationship.

"I can understand that. He seems a most unpleasant man."

"Trust me, he is." Anthony moved closer and squeezed Marguerite's shoulder, desperate to touch her fine skin and forget Minshom.

"You look particularly lovely tonight, my lady."

"Thank you." Her smile was wry. "I feel as if I'm readying myself to go into battle."

"You anticipate a struggle?"

She glanced up at him and the diamond and sapphire necklace around her throat glittered in the candlelight, making him blink.

"Don't you?"

He held out his hand and she got up, shaking out the skirts of her pale blue, high-waisted, silk gown. Diamonds encircled both her wrists and swung from her ears. Although she was smaller than him, he sensed her strength of purpose, her courage, her resolve. Suddenly he wished he had something to give her, something of value to show the world how much he admired her.

"I'd like to buy you jewels."

Marguerite's eyebrows rose and she shrugged. "There's no need. I feel conspicuous enough already." She touched his arm. "And you've already given me much more than mere jewels."

He stared down into her eyes and, finding a sense of acceptance he'd never had before, swallowed hard. "Did you manage to amuse yourself without me today?"

"I managed to antagonize one of Amelia's old cronies by refusing to be ashamed of my liaison with you." She smoothed a hand over the silk of her dress. "That's one of the reasons I decided to dress up tonight. I want her to see how happy I am with my choice." She reached up and straightened Anthony's cravat. "You must promise to look equally delighted by my company."

"That won't be difficult. You are a delight." For an instant she looked away from him, and he caught her chin. "Why do you find it so hard to accept a compliment?"

"Probably because I'm used to being overlooked for my mother and the twins."

"They neglected you?"

"*Non*, they are just . . ." She shrugged. "So much more interesting than I'll ever be."

He kissed her nose. "I know how that feels. My father and brother are the same." She looked at him, her expression serious until he cleared his throat. "But I see you, Marguerite. I see the strength and the honesty in you, and I'll always appreciate that."

Her eyes filled with tears, and she hastily dabbed at the corners of her eyes. "Now you have made me cry. How do you expect me to make a grand triumphant entrance at your side if my nose and eyes are red from weeping?"

"You'll still outshine them all." He took his handkerchief from his pocket and gently patted the tears. "There, you look beautiful."

She grimaced at him but didn't speak, waiting until he put his handkerchief away to take his arm. He opened the door out into the hallway and looked down at her. "Is there anyone in particular you wish me to be obnoxious to, or shall I just practice a look of general slavish adoration?"

She laughed, the sound warming him as they approached the stairs. Even the sight of Minshom dressed in black and silver prowling the hallway below didn't destroy his sense of wonder, of delight in her company. When all this was over, when she'd met with Sir Harry and hopefully found the answers she wanted, he'd tell her everything, the whole sordid pitiful story.

"Anthony?"

He didn't realize he'd stopped moving until Marguerite spoke. Could he do that? Could he share not only the depths of his depravity but his utter humiliation? Share the needs he wasn't sure he could suppress even though he wanted her more than he'd wanted anything in his contemptible life?

He guided her back into the shadows at the top of the stairs. Perhaps Valentin was right, and it was time to stop running away from the things he couldn't change.

"Marguerite, when we get back to Town, may I come and call on you?"

"Of course you may. Why do you ask?"

"Because . . . because I want to be honest with you."

She bit her lip and held his gaze. "I would like that. Perhaps by then I will be able to be honest with you too."

Relief washed over him, and he brought her hand to his lips. "Thank you."

Marguerite allowed Anthony to lead her into the drawing room and fixed a dazzling smile on her lips. No one here would know her inner turmoil, the sense that Lord Minshom was poised to disrupt her peace forever. Had Anthony understood what she'd said to him, that she had more truths to reveal, more secrets than he might imagine?

She hoped so. Hiding the truths about her marriage from everyone, perhaps even from herself, was a burden she would be grateful to relinquish. And who better to understand her than Anthony? A man who had made his own difficult sexual choices in the past and lived to regret them.

And then there was the matter of Justin's death at the hand of his best friend. If she could find some peace from meeting Sir

Harry, all the torment would be worth it. She glanced up at Anthony's handsome face. He concealed his troubles almost as well as she did—the outsider in a family, much like her, the one always striving to fit in, to be acknowledged, to be loved.

She squeezed his arm, aware of the strength concealed by the fine broadcloth, the heat of him, the fire within. How strange that fate, in the shape of her brother and sister, had brought them together.

"Marguerite? Is something wrong?"

Anthony looked down at her, his expression concerned, and she smiled into his blue eyes.

"No, my lord. In truth, I'm glad you are with me tonight."

"So am I."

His answering smile was as warm and admiring as she could have wished. It didn't matter what humiliations Lord Minshom made her endure. She was no longer alone, and if she concentrated on the future, a future which might contain the complex man by her side, she was also certain of success—wasn't she?

20

Marguerite watched as Anthony carefully closed the door back into the main house. She drew her cloak around her and headed for the path between the kitchen garden and the wilderness beyond. With his longer stride, Anthony caught up with her within a few paces. Like her, he wore a black cloak and dark clothing, but his head was uncovered, his hair blowing in the bitterly cold wind.

The clock in the stable yard struck the quarter hour, and Marguerite paused in the shelter of one of the tangle of old holly trees and faced Anthony.

"Are you sure you want to do this?" She'd asked him the same question at least a hundred times. His answer was always the same, so she wasn't quite sure why she insisted on repeating it.

"I'm sure. I'll give you a quarter of an hour to complete your business with Sir Harry. If he doesn't appear or if anything changes, come to the door of the lodge and signal to me. I'll be with you in an instant."

Marguerite nodded and held out her hand, found herself

dragged into a fierce embrace, Anthony's mouth locked on hers for a deliciously deep and lingering kiss. When he drew back, he caressed her lower lip with his thumb.

"Don't do anything foolish, will you?"

"Like what? Brain Lord Minshom with a candlestick?"

"Exactly. I'd rather like to do that to him myself, so don't hesitate to call me."

"Such double standards, my lord."

He smiled and his teeth glinted in the moonlight. "Just be careful. Minshom is a wily opponent."

"I know that." She stood on tiptoe to kiss his cold cheek. "Let's just pray all goes well and that I don't need your help after all." She stepped away from him, achingly conscious of the sudden lack of warmth and the strength of his embrace.

As before, the door into the rear of the lodge stood slightly ajar. She entered the hallway and pushed open the kitchen door. Lord Minshom stood by the fireplace, hands clasped behind his back. His black coat lay over a chair by the table, and he looked remarkably at home. He glanced up, his expression cordial.

"Ah, good evening, Lady Justin. I'm so glad you decided to return."

Marguerite inclined her head a regal inch. "As I recall, you gave me very little choice in the matter. Is Sir Harry here?"

"Not yet. There are a few things I need to discuss with you before he arrives." He gestured at the table. "Won't you sit down?"

Even though her knees were shaking, Marguerite held her ground. "I don't believe there is anything we have to say to each other."

Minshom strolled across to the table and took a seat, crossed his booted feet and looked up at her. "Well, there you are wrong, my dear. In order for you to see Sir Harry, I have a few conditions of my own."

"Then perhaps I'll leave." Marguerite curtsied low. "I resent being played like a fool. I think I'd rather not know your little plans."

"Really? You'd rather my version of the events surrounding your marriage were made public than hearing the truth from Sir Harry? He certainly had some very interesting things to say about you."

Marguerite moved closer to the table and grabbed the back of a chair for support. "And you expect me to believe you've talked to him? I doubt that."

He reached inside his coat, drew out a folded parchment and laid it on the scrubbed table top. "Not only did I talk to him, but I got him to write down exactly what happened between him and Justin." He met her gaze, his pale blue eyes hard. "All of it, from the very beginning. The poor fool thought I meant to help plead his cause." His soft laughter chilled her. "As if I would."

"Then what do you want and why are you doing this?"

"Sit down."

Marguerite complied, her knees giving way gracefully as she sank onto the hard rush seat. Minshom toyed with the blue ribbon wrapped around the folded parchment.

"There are two reasons. The first is that I want justice for my cousin. Justin didn't deserve to die, and Sir Harry will pay for that. The second is more personal." He looked at Marguerite. "I want to deal with Sokorvsky once and for all. Luckily for me, you are rather intimately connected with both men."

"So I am actually irrelevant?"

"Well, hardly that. You are an interesting woman, Marguerite, as is your mother." He paused as if waiting for a reaction. "You always reminded me of someone and eventually I worked it out. You are Helene Delornay's daughter."

"That is scarcely a secret, sir. I'm very proud of my mother and have never tried to hide the relationship."

"But everyone else has, haven't they? Between the meddling

Duke of Diable Delamere and Viscount Harcourt DeVere, your origins have been kept quiet, haven't they?"

A cold ball of fear settled in her chest like a tight fist, but Marguerite didn't say anything. Lord Minshom smiled.

"In truth, I only realized who you were when I caught a glimpse of your mother visiting you at home. It was enough for me to make the connection and follow up with some more solid investigating of my own."

"So?"

"So, I wonder how the Lockwoods felt about their precious son and heir marrying the bastard daughter of a whore?"

"The Lockwoods knew everything they needed to know."

"I doubt that." He held her gaze. "And even if they did, I'm not sure they'd wish the rest of the *ton* to know the kind of woman their son chose to marry, do you?"

Marguerite gathered her courage, wondered how many minutes had passed since she'd walked into this emotional battlefield.

"If you spread this gossip, the only person you will hurt is Justin and the Lockwoods, not me. I'm already considered a pariah; this will certainly not alter their opinion of me."

Minshom raised his eyebrows. "I must commend you, Marguerite—your calmness is remarkable, especially for a woman."

"I suppose I should thank you for the compliment, but I'd rather finish this conversation as quickly as possible and leave." She half-rose from her seat. "Have you finished trying to blackmail me?"

"Not quite." His smile disappeared. "If we ignore the feelings of the surviving Lockwood family, there is also the little matter of your marriage and Justin's reputation to consider."

"What do you mean?"

"You cared for Justin, didn't you?"

"Of course I did. I loved him."

"And yet you slept with his best friend."

There it was, the accusation she'd been expecting. And as she had always feared, it was far more devastating to hear it spoken out loud rather than whispered behind her back.

"If you asked Sir Harry about his relationship with Justin then you know what I did, and why."

"I do know, but I'm quite willing to make you the scapegoat for Justin's death. A jealous husband tries to shoot the best friend who has cuckolded him with his own wife and ends up dead. Now that is something the scandal sheets would love to hear the details of. It's the story that everyone has been gossiping about for the last two years, why not bring it out in the open and make it the truth?"

"Because it isn't the truth."

"It's the truth I intend to tell if you don't agree to my conditions."

Marguerite stared at Lord Minshom and saw no hint of compassion on his hard face. "Why would you do that to me? As you said, I am nothing to you."

He shrugged. "And thus disposable. In one single blow I can ruin you, protect Justin, and destroy Sir Harry's chances of ever being accepted back into English society again."

Marguerite licked her lips. Her mind seemed to have frozen into ragged shards. There must be a way out of this trap, but she could no longer see it. She couldn't betray Justin, but the thought that all the blame for what had happened should rest on her was intolerable. She'd just started to find herself, to believe she was worthy of love, to breathe without fear . . .

"What do you want Lord Minshom?"

"In order for me to keep me quiet about Justin and to get your own chance to speak to Sir Harry?"

"Yes."

Minshom leaned forward. "I want you to call Sokorvsky. I

know he's out there. And when I've finished with him, I'll tell you where to find Sir Harry."

"And what guarantee do I have that you'll leave me and Justin alone afterward?"

He patted the pile of parchment. "I'll give you this to burn and leave Sir Harry to his own conscience, as long as he stays out of my way."

"Anthony is worth so much to you?"

"Anthony is . . ." He paused. "Anthony deserves to pay for daring to leave me, for thinking he could have you instead."

"Are you jealous, Lord Minshom?"

"Jealous of you?" He stood and loomed over her, forcing her to look up at him.

"Why would I be jealous of a woman? Sokorvsky needs a man to master him, and he knows it."

"And yet, he chose to be with me." She tensed as Minshom's expression went blank. He slowly produced a pistol from his coat pocket and pointed it at her.

"Go upstairs and into the first bedroom on the right. Take off your dress and sit in the chair facing the door."

"Are you going to shoot me if I don't do what you say?"

"Do you wish to take the risk?"

Marguerite shook her head. One thing had become clear to her: in order to safeguard both the past and her possible future, she was willing to endure his confrontation with Anthony. "Do you give me your word that Lord Anthony will survive your encounter?"

He pointed toward the door, taking her elbow to help her up the narrow stairs. "You care for him, then?"

"Yes."

"He'll survive. I've never killed one of my lovers yet, although I've come close." He laughed, the sound echoing up the stairs. "Sokorvsky would probably like being fucked to death."

Marguerite stumbled, and he shoved her up the final steps and into the bedroom. A fire had been lit and candlelight illuminated the small space. A four-poster bed draped in brown quilts dominated the room. A wooden chair sat opposite the bed facing the door.

"Take off your dress."

"Why? Are you intending to rape me too?"

"I try not to fuck women. In my experience, they cry and break far too easily." He turned her around, pulled off her cloak and tugged at the laces at the back of her bodice. He bit her throat, and she jerked her head away.

"I want Sokorvsky to think the worst when he bursts in here. I want him to imagine my hands on you, my tongue in your mouth, my fingers buried in your cunt."

Marguerite tried to wrench away from him, but his hands held the laces of her gown, and he yanked her back like a toddling child or a disobedient horse. She shuddered as he dragged down her bodice and then her petticoats, forced her to step out of them, leaving her in her corset, stockings and shift. His hands cupped her breasts, his thumbs over her nipples.

"You are beautiful, Marguerite. I'm almost tempted to find out what Sokorvsky sees in you, to explore all your delicious possibilities." He angled his hips against her buttocks until she could feel the hot press of his cock.

"You've even made me hard. It's a long time since I've allowed a woman to have that effect on me."

"Perhaps you're losing your touch?" Marguerite gasped as he suddenly pushed her toward the chair. His smile was not reassuring.

"Perhaps I am." He sat down in the more comfortable wing chair by the fire and crossed his legs. "Now we just have to wait for Sokorvsky."

* * *

Anthony checked his pocket watch for the hundredth time and then returned his gaze to the gatehouse. There was a light in the kitchen and one in the room directly above, but the rest of the house remained dark. There was no sign of any horses or indication that Sir Harry had arrived, but that didn't necessarily mean he wasn't already there.

Damnation, what on earth was going on in there? Anthony exhaled and watched his breath condense in the frigid air. In the distance, the clock in the stables chimed the half hour. He couldn't wait any longer; Marguerite might be in trouble. To his relief, his fears for her safety far outweighed his fear of Minshom. He set off down the brick path to the kitchen door, let himself in and studied the deserted kitchen.

Where were they? Had they left through the front door when he was hiding in the bushes? Surely he would've heard them. He inhaled the floral scent of Marguerite's perfume, and the more masculine smell of brandy and the particular brand of cigars Minshom favored. Retreating, he checked out the dark front parlor and an office, found the door to the cellar locked and chained.

There was still a faint light coming from one of the rooms upstairs, but why would Marguerite have agreed to go up there with Minshom? Anthony gripped the knife in his pocket and headed back to the foot of the stairs. With as much care as he could, he climbed the steep carpeted steps and paused on the small square landing. Light shone from under the door to his right. After a deep breath, Anthony turned the handle and stepped over the threshold.

The first thing he saw was Marguerite. He frowned as he realized she was half undressed, her gown pooled at her feet, her gaze distraught. He took half a step toward her and was brought up short by a familiar drawling voice.

"Good evening, Sokorvsky."

He turned toward the fire and the single candle and saw Minshom stretched out at his ease in one of the wing chairs.

"What the devil have you done to her?"

"Nothing yet, although she truly is a luscious piece, isn't she?"

Fury roared through him, followed by cold resolve as his mind tried to make sense of the scene. God dammit, if he'd laid one finger on Marguerite, Minshom was a dead man. He picked up her gown and threw it into her lap.

"Come on, Marguerite, I'll take you back to the house."

Minshom raised his arm, pointed a dueling pistol at Marguerite's head. "No, you won't. She stays here. I'll let her go when I've finished with you."

Ignoring Minshom, Anthony turned to Marguerite and held out his hand. "Don't listen to him; he's bluffing. He won't kill you; he's not that stupid."

Marguerite bit down on her lip. "I can't leave, Anthony."

"Why the hell not?"

"I agreed to stay because . . ."

Minshom interrupted Marguerite. "Because I promised to show her all the juicy details about our relationship. Isn't that right, my pet?"

Anthony stared at Minshom, his mind curiously calm. "You can't make me do anything I don't want to do."

Minshom's smile widened. "Oh, but I can. That was the part you always liked best, remember? I don't have to kill her, Sokorvsky. Even a slight wound can fester, become infected, and lead to a slow, lingering, painful death. I'll say the same to you as I said to your lover: Are you prepared to risk it?"

Anthony locked gazes with Marguerite. "If you want to leave, I'll make sure he doesn't shoot you."

"But I don't want him to shoot you either." Her quiet, reasonable reply almost made him want to smile. How like her to be so pragmatic.

"I'd much rather it was me, Marguerite, really."

Lord Minshom shifted in his seat. "This is all very edifying, but neither of you are leaving until I'm satisfied. Marguerite, tell him you want to stay and then be quiet."

"Why would she want to stay?" Anthony turned to Minshom. "What possible sick gratification can you get from making her witness you forcing me to have sex with you?"

"I don't need to force you. You've always been more than willing." Minshom nodded at Marguerite. "I knew he liked men before I even met him. He fagged for my cousin at Eton, enjoyed being fucked even then."

"Hardly. I had no choice. None of us did." Anthony grimaced at the memory. "Your cousin was twice my weight and three years my senior. He also embodied your family's renowned appetite for savagery and bullying, which made him impossible to fight off for long."

"Poor Sokorvsky, always the victim, always the one not to blame." Minshom steadied his elbow on the chair arm, keeping the pistol trained on Marguerite. "I suppose what happened when you were nineteen wasn't your fault either, was it?"

Shock flickered across Anthony's face and he notably paled. Minshom gestured at Marguerite, who remained in her chair, hands gripping the sides as she watched them both, hardly daring to breathe.

"Did he tell you about that, Marguerite? Or perhaps your mother did. After all, it happened at the pleasure house."

"She told me nothing." Marguerite hoped her calm response would help Anthony gather his wits, show him that she refused to be shocked by anything Lord Minshom intended to say to her.

"As I understand it, dear Anthony got mixed up in some nefarious sexual business with his half brother Valentin involving a Turkish gentleman named Aliabad."

"And what does that have to do with you, Lord Minshom?"

Minshom shrugged. "Nothing, I suppose, but for Sokorvsky, it helped cement his sexual tastes, made him crave pain and humiliation."

Briefly Anthony closed his eyes and then refocused on Marguerite as if she were the only person in the room and that he was speaking to only her. "After Aliabad raped me, I refused to have sex with anyone for years. That's what he made me crave—nothing."

"But you eventually came around, and that's when I met you on the top floor of the pleasure house, seeking . . . What exactly were you seeking, Sokorvsky?"

Marguerite tried to picture the top floor of the pleasure house. She'd only visited it a couple of times; the extreme sexual practices enjoyed there hadn't excited or intrigued her.

Anthony cleared his throat. "I'm not sure what I was seeking, but I found you, and you were quick to tell me what you wanted."

"So it's my fault you are as twisted and needy as you are? I made you want sex to be as painful and humiliating as I could make it?"

"I wanted sex, yes."

Marguerite bit her lip as Anthony simply stared at Minshom, his face heartbreakingly open, his expression unguarded. Yet she didn't see weakness or neediness, she saw a quiet strength that perhaps Anthony wasn't even aware of. Her hands fisted at her sides. She wanted to go to him, to enfold him in her arms and tell him it didn't matter, that she would make everything right for him.

"Stay there, Marguerite. We haven't finished yet."

She blinked at Minshom's harsh command, realizing she'd been poised to leave her seat. Anthony's clear blue gaze flicked over her and then returned to Minshom. "Don't tell her what to do."

"Why not? Is that your prerogative? Is that why you like her so much?"

Minshom stood up and came up behind Anthony, resting the small pistol on his shoulder, still pointing at Marguerite. He slid a hand into Anthony's pockets and removed the knife and the pistol Anthony had concealed there.

"I'll keep the knife. It's much easier to hold than a pistol." Minshom dealt with his gun and then the one he'd taken from Anthony and tossed them onto the seat of the wing chair. "Don't try to use them against me, Marguerite; neither of them are loaded now."

"But I could still hit you over the head with one, couldn't I?"

"You really are quite amusing, my dear, but you should know that I'm not afraid to defend myself, even from a woman."

Marguerite couldn't believe she'd actually said the words out loud. Lord Minshom had the nerve to smile as if she'd made a joke. Anthony said nothing, his attention on Minshom as he resumed his position behind him. He flinched as Minshom curved his arm around his waist and then dropped his hand to cover Anthony's groin.

"Does she do what you tell her to? Or is it the other way around? Is she happy to hurt you to give you sexual release?"

"I wouldn't ask it of her."

Anthony flinched as Minshom twisted the fabric of his breeches, dug his fingers into the curve of his balls and kneaded his cock. Minshom smiled at Marguerite. "But surely you know that she likes the unusual. Why else would she have married Justin Lockwood if she wasn't prepared to be . . . accommodating?"

"I don't know what you mean." Anthony's voice sounded strained as if he was fighting the pressure of Minshom's fingers, and the obvious and gradual swelling of his shaft.

Marguerite shivered; perhaps this wasn't about Minshom

showing her how perverted Anthony was after all. Perhaps it was far more personal.

"Marguerite, didn't you tell Anthony about the true nature of your liaison with Justin?" Minshom tutted. "And I thought you told me you believed in being honest."

"I do."

"Yet you omitted to mention that you shared a bed with your husband and his lover and fucked them both?"

Marguerite focused her gaze on Minshom's hand which was roughly fondling Anthony's cock through his breeches. She couldn't bear to look up, to see the shock she knew would be on Anthony's face.

"What Marguerite chose to do in her marriage is nothing to do with you." Anthony's quiet voice penetrated Marguerite's haze of guilt.

"Really?" Minshom asked. "Yet Justin was my cousin. I believe I have a right to ensure that his reputation, even in death, is spotless. If his wife cuckolded him, surely the world should know?"

"You forget, I knew Justin. He was scarcely an innocent."

Minshom laughed. "Are you suggesting my cousin encouraged his wife to indulge in an affair?"

Anthony looked straight at Marguerite. "I'm not sure. Perhaps Marguerite would like to tell me that part of it herself, in private."

He swallowed a gasp as Minshom's hand jerked hard on his cock.

"Oh, no, Sokorvsky. *Nothing* is private between us. Don't you remember how that felt? How you used to beg to be fucked, to be beaten, to be used as I saw fit?" Minshom chuckled. "How many men fucked you, came in your mouth or in your arse at my command?"

Anthony grimaced and closed his eyes as if he couldn't bear

to remember. Marguerite pictured it instead, Anthony being repeatedly taken, naked, alone, hurting . . .

"I don't care."

"I beg your pardon?" Minshom said.

"I don't care if he had fifty men a night." Marguerite forced back her tears. "He had no choice, you said so. You said you forced him."

"And you admire a man who allows himself to be used like that? A man so weak that he can't say no?"

She opened her eyes wide. "But he did say no, didn't he? That's why we are here now and why you are behaving like a pathetic, discarded lover."

Minshom's face stilled as did the hand that gripped Anthony's cock. "You would know all about that, wouldn't you, my dear?" he purred. "When you realized Justin had only married you to conceal his affair with Sir Harry, you must've been furious."

"That's not how it happened . . ."

"Didn't you know that? Justin told me he was looking for a suitably ignorant female to marry. The kind of woman who would be so grateful that she wouldn't care what he got up to in the bedroom. But it was even easier for him than that, wasn't it? Because you not only condoned his behavior but embraced it."

"Leave her alone."

Anthony stirred, tried to turn, but Minshom held him close, the knife edge biting into his throat. His cock throbbed along with the sting of the blade. Did Marguerite realize that in defending him, she had pushed Minshom too far, that now he would have no compunction in bringing her down?

"Shut up, Sokorvsky. Perhaps it's time you realized Marguerite isn't quite as pure and lovely as she appears. She married Justin, found out he was fucking Sir Harry, and deliberately tried to come between them." Minshom's laugh was deadly. "Perhaps even literally. She pretended to like Harry, all the while whispering lies and poison into his ear about how Justin no longer needed him or wanted him now that she was around."

Anthony glanced at Marguerite, who seemed to have shrunk back into her chair, her eyes wide and terrified.

"It's hardly surprising that Sir Harry picked a fight with his best friend, is it, when a woman like Marguerite starts to meddle?"

Anthony licked his lips. "It is hardly Marguerite's fault if her husband cannot manage his affairs. She was married to him; surely she had a right to be first in his affections?"

"And the way to do that was to fuck his best friend? To ignore her wedding vows and conveniently end up a widow?"

Marguerite shook her head as if words were beyond her. Anthony drew an unsteady breath. Had she instigated a ménage à trois within her own marriage, and was Minshom really implying that she had caused her own husband's death?

"I don't care." He echoed her earlier words, hoping she realized it. "I don't care if she fucked them both."

He almost groaned as Minshom gave his cock one last savage twist and then shoved him forward. He stumbled and fell to his knees, braced a hand on the floor to stop himself falling forward. He managed to look behind him and saw Minshom heading for the door.

"What are you doing?"

"I'm leaving. I've never heard such pathetic drivel in my entire life. I fear the pair of you are beyond my help."

"Your help? You call this *help*?"

Minshom's eyebrows rose. "You deserve each other. You are both weak and easily manipulated. There is no enjoyment left even in tormenting you."

Anthony got to his feet, conscious that Marguerite hadn't

moved or said anything since Minshom's last diatribe. He advanced slowly toward Minshom, who had opened the door.

"Then you are done with us?"

Minshom bowed. "I believe I am."

"Good."

Anthony raised his fist and plowed it right into Minshom's smiling face, did it again and watched Minshom's legs buckle and him fall backward down the stairs to land in an untidy heap at the bottom. Without another glance he slammed the door shut and locked it.

21

"Marguerite, are you all right?"

Anthony went down on his knees beside her chair, and grabbed hold of her hands.

"Why did you do that?" she whispered.

"What?"

"Knock Minshom out. Now he can't tell me where to find Sir Harry."

Anthony let go of her hands. She watched distantly as his expression darkened.

"After all that just happened, why the hell are you still worried about Sir Harry?"

Marguerite licked her lips. "I only agreed to stay with Minshom because he promised to tell me where Harry was."

"And I thought you'd stayed for me."

"You don't understand . . ."

Anthony got off the floor and walked away, coming to a stop in front of the fireplace, his back still facing her. "I think I do. I'd assumed you were grieving for a dead man, not pining for another. Minshom had it wrong, didn't he? You were in love with Sir Harry, not Justin."

Marguerite blinked as searing color flooded her cheeks, slowly shook her head, even though she knew he couldn't see her. "That's not true. Lord Minshom deliberately tried to mislead you; are you going to believe him over me?"

Anthony finally swung around, one hand still cupping his groin as if to ease the ache of Minshom's touch. He sighed and didn't really look at her. "It doesn't matter. We can't choose whom we love, can we?"

Marguerite rose to her feet, advanced toward him and slapped him as hard as she could on the cheek. He grabbed her wrist when she attempted to do it again.

"What the hell was that for?"

"For believing Minshom, for pretending you didn't care what I'd done and then throwing it in my face."

"I'm hardly doing that. On the contrary, I just told you I understand!"

She struggled to speak through the tears crowding her throat. "You understand nothing. Perhaps Minshom was right and you only understand pain." She pushed his hand away from his groin, replaced it with hers. "Perhaps this is all you need from me."

His expression darkened. "Don't do that. I'm far too close to coming."

"Because Minshom made you hard? Is that what you meant about not being able to control whom you love, because you still love Minshom?"

God, she hated what she was saying, hated herself, but the need to hurt, to take the pain howling inside her and hurl it outward consumed her. Anthony knew—he knew what she'd done, and sooner or later he'd realize how unfit she was to be associated with him. Better to end it now, better to send him away before it hurt too much and destroyed her.

"Christ, I *loathe* Minshom, I *never* loved him. Don't you know that? Don't you understand anything about me at all?" Anthony was yelling, his face flushed, his blue eyes narrowed with anger. "I'm sick of being told what to do and what to think."

"I'm not telling you what to do. I'm trying to make you listen to me."

"Then do it without touching me, without . . . Christ, what's the use? Minshom's already convinced you I'm a pathetic weakling."

"No he hasn't; I'm just trying to . . ."

Anthony held up his hand. "Marguerite, when you touch me, all I want to do is throw you on that bed and shove my cock inside you, use it as *I* wish, rather than how Minshom *thinks* I should. I'm sure you don't want that, so please, get dressed."

Marguerite retreated to the chair, picked up her dress and petticoats and tried to put them on. Her fingers trembled so badly she could barely get the fine satin over her head.

"Oh, for God's sake." Anthony muttered. He appeared at her side, his intent gaze fixed on the swell of her breasts, the tightness of her nipples. He placed his hands on her shoulders and the dress fell from her fingers.

"Marguerite . . ." His mouth descended over hers, the savagery of his kiss a challenge she couldn't resist. She wrapped her arms around him and kissed him back, nipping at his lower lip, his tongue. Exchanging anger for lust seemed almost too natural, the desire to mark him, make him groan and beg not for Minshom but for her.

He angled her back toward the bed, his body heavy and hard on top of hers, his knee parting her thighs. He didn't stop kissing her, their mouths fused together, heat binding and blinding them, the need insatiable. She gasped as he freed his cock from his breeches and his knuckles grazed her mound. And then he was inside her, his shaft pressing deep, her back arching to take him all in.

"Marguerite, yes . . ."

He pounded into her, his thrusts fast and hard, relentless. She didn't complain, her body far too busy keeping him close, wrapping her legs around his hips to hold him within the cradle of her thighs. His kiss mirrored his movements, possessing her mouth as he possessed her body, utterly dominant, utterly in control.

His fingers slid between them, found her clit and worked it until she was coming and screaming his name into his mouth. His kiss dissolved into a gasp for air, and he bucked against her as the heat of his cum spurted deep inside her. When he rolled off, he stayed on his stomach, his face buried in the pillows.

Marguerite moved slowly off the bed and bent to retrieve her clothes. Surely now they were done? She'd never imagined allowing a man to take her like that, so completely, so absolutely. Having heard about her marriage, did Anthony now consider her fair game? She stared at her petticoats, fumbling as she attempted to tie them around her waist.

"Let me." Anthony was beside her again, setting her to rights, tightening her laces, doing up buttons, straightening her bodice. Almost unnoticed, her tears trickled down onto the dark blue satin, staining it black. This was the end; this was the last time he would ever want to touch her. She swallowed hard.

"Are you done now?"

His fingers stilled. "What?"

"Are you done proving to yourself that you can fuck a woman?"

In the silence that followed, she could clearly hear the irregular thump of his heart and his shallow breathing. Anthony stepped away from her and did up his breeches, picked up his gun and stuffed it into his pocket. She raised her chin and tried to make him look at her, but he avoided her gaze.

"My lady, if you wish to leave, I need to check on Minshom."

He sounded formal, all the anger stripped from his voice. Unable to reply, Marguerite simply nodded and waited by the fire as he opened the door.

"He's gone." Anthony sounded as stunned as she felt. "Obviously I didn't hit the bastard hard enough. I'll make sure he isn't loitering in the kitchen, and then you may come down."

His voice faded as he clattered down the stairs. Marguerite blew out the candles and left the room bathed in the warm glow of the fire, wondered distantly who lived here, who had been forced out to accommodate the selfish desires of Lord Minshom.

"You can come down, my lady."

Marguerite picked up her skirts and headed down the stairs, found Anthony in the kitchen. He gestured at the table. "I think Minshom left you something."

She picked up the bundle of parchment tied with the blue ribbon. At least she had that, Sir Harry's account of the duel, even if she didn't have him in person. She clutched the papers to her chest as Anthony draped her cloak around her.

"Are you ready to leave?"

She nodded again, still unable to speak, and walked past him into the hallway and out into the cold bleakness of the night. The stable clock chimed once. Was it only an hour since she'd walked into Minshom's trap? Only an hour since he'd deliberately revealed his own version of her brief marriage to Anthony, the man she'd come to care for? She stopped walking, turned toward his dark shape.

"It wasn't like that."

"I beg your pardon?"

"My marriage. It wasn't like that at all."

"Marguerite, it really doesn't matter does it? It's in the past."

"Not if Lord Minshom decides to gossip about it."

There was a long silence as he considered her. "I won't let that happen. I promise you."

"Why?"

"Because as I told you, I don't care what happened between you, Justin and Harry."

"Why not?"

He shrugged. "Because you are my friend?"

Ah, she'd forgotten that. She'd forgotten that just because she'd come to want him as more than a friend didn't mean that he had. In truth, after what he'd just heard about her, his diplomatic retreat was all too understandable.

"I will take care of Lord Minshom myself."

He shifted in the darkness and laid his hand on her arm. "Marguerite, you don't have to do that. I'm quite capable of taking him on."

Tears crowded her eyes, falling down her cold cheeks in hot, angry waves. "What are you going to do? Challenge him to a duel?"

"If necessary."

"And you think I would want that? Another man dead on my account? More gossip?"

"Marguerite . . ."

She pushed past him, picked up her skirts and ran for the house, the tears now pouring down her face. Were all men fools? Was Anthony about to make the same mistake Sir Harry had made and risk everything to save her reputation? She would not let that happen again. She would not; she'd kill Lord Minshom herself before she allowed Anthony within a mile of him.

She realized she was standing in the center of her bedroom, her breathing so loud she couldn't even hear the clock. She hurried to lock the door between her and Anthony's suites and checked the main door. He wouldn't be able to get to her here, not that he would want to . . .

With a sob, she fell to her knees, pressed her hands to her face and let the tears fall. Anthony had protected her from Lord Minshom, offered himself in her stead, refused to allow Minshom to destroy either of them. He'd also shown great courage when his worst secrets were revealed, refusing to allow Minshom to dominate or shame him. She realized she was proud of him. He might have unconventional sexual tastes, but he was no longer enslaved by Minshom.

And even if he'd been shocked by Lord Minshom's revelations about her, he hadn't shown it, hadn't allowed his anger and doubts to surface until after he'd disposed of his nemesis. Marguerite raised her head to stare into the fire. She should be grateful to him for that, even though he seemed to believe she'd really been in love with Harry.

How had he come to that conclusion? It was no more accurate than Minshom's version of the truth. She glanced at the door to Anthony's suite. Was it worth trying to tell him how it had really been? She shook her head. No, because he'd probably say that it didn't matter, that she could've fucked a whole regiment of Sir Harry's and he would still pretend to be fine with it.

All she could do was to arrange to go back to London without having to see either Lord Minshom or Anthony again. Resume the quiet uneventful life she'd envisaged before Anthony had arrived to unsettle her. Despite his promise, once he'd thought about her past, she doubted he'd ever want to see her again.

She stifled a sob and continued to cry silently, a necessary skill learned in the loneliness of the nunnery school when any sound at night would result in a beating. She didn't want Anthony to hear her, didn't want anyone to know how bleak her future now looked.

Anthony let himself into his room and took off his clothes, left them lying on the floor in a pile. He walked across to the china wash jug and poured water into the matching cream basin. The coldness of the water suited his mood, shocking his senses much as the events of the evening had.

God, what had he done? Taking Marguerite like that, using her to prove something to himself. No wonder she was disgusted with him. He sighed and dropped down onto the side of the bed. What a mess. Minshom had told Marguerite the worst of his sexual secrets and then shocked him by revealing that Marguerite had secrets of her own.

And despite what he'd tried to say to Marguerite, he had been shocked. Worse still, Marguerite had seen through him and realized it as well. He shoved his wet hair back from his face, shivered as freezing water drops rained on his bare shoulders. What the hell had been going on in that marriage to make Marguerite cuckold her husband with his own lover?

He focused on the rug at his feet and made himself think logically. Much better to think than to dwell on the fact that Marguerite knew the worst about him . . . He forced his thoughts away from his humiliation.

None of the explanations he'd heard about Marguerite's marriage made sense, not if he factored in what he knew of her, or thought he knew. It was as if Marguerite had decided she was guilty and had deliberately set out to hurt him, to force him away from her. And she'd damned near succeeded. For a moment, he'd been so confused that he had to put some distance between them.

With a shudder, he got under the covers and lay down. Whatever happened, they weren't done. He would insist on seeing her in London whether she liked it or not. He smiled savagely at the ceiling. He'd finally beaten Minshom, and Marguerite had helped him do that. She might think she was unworthy of him, but he knew better, knew she'd helped him become the man he should've been all along.

She now knew the worst about him, but he still wasn't clear about her past, and he wanted to be. He needed to find out exactly what she had done. He closed his eyes. One thing was clear to him: there was no way in hell he was ever going to lose her again.

22

"I'm fine, Mrs. Jones, really I am." To Marguerite's dismay, Mrs. Jones continued to flap around her as she tried to climb the stairs. "I'm just fatigued by the journey."

She entered her bedroom and tried to shut the door behind herself, but she wasn't quick enough to evict her companion, who was still eying her with every appearance of concern. Marguerite took off her bonnet and rubbed her aching temples. Rather than drive back with Anthony, she'd begged a ride from one of the other couples. Unfortunately, the couple she'd chosen hadn't enjoyed their weekend together, and she'd been the unwilling witness to a fine display of marital disharmony for the entire three hours of the journey.

"I'll get them to send you up some tea, shall I?" Mrs. Jones asked.

"That would be nice, and perhaps a tisane for my headache." She managed to smile. "Thank you, Lily."

"It's nothing, my dear." Mrs. Jones sniffed. "Even though you've taken to jaunting off around the countryside without me, I am supposed to be your companion."

"Indeed you are." Marguerite closed her eyes as her maid pulled off her boots and unbuttoned her pelisse. "I think I'll drink my tea and go to bed for a while."

In truth, she couldn't wait to be alone in her own bed, to find shelter in the familiar. To try to pretend that she hadn't been engaged in a torrid affair with the son of a marquis but had simply dreamed it all.

It felt like she had barely closed her eyes before there was a commotion outside her door and a familiar voice demanding to see her. Even though she knew it was no use, she rolled into the far corner of the bed and put her pillow over her head.

"Marguerite, I know you're in there."

She opened one eye to glare at her sister Lisette. "I'm asleep. Didn't Mrs. Jones tell you?"

Lisette sat on the side of the bed, making the mattress dip and bounce Marguerite toward her.

"She did, but I want to know what happened this weekend."

Marguerite sat up and eyed her sister. "I thought you weren't talking to me. And how do you know what I did this weekend anyway?"

Lisette smiled. "I have my sources. In truth, the whole family knows you went to Charles Lockwood's country house with Anthony Sokorvsky." She leaned forward. "How was it?"

"None of your business."

"Marguerite! You have to tell me something." Lisette folded her arms. "I'm not leaving until you do."

Marguerite grabbed her cream silk dressing gown from where it lay at the foot of her bed and put it on. She caught a glimpse of her reflection in the mirror, knew she looked like a pale ghost next to Lisette's liveliness and golden beauty.

"I really don't have anything to tell you."

"But Mrs. Jones said you returned without Anthony. So something must have happened."

Marguerite closed her eyes. "Lisette, will you just go away?"

There was silence, and then she felt Lisette's hands close over hers. "What's wrong? You can tell me."

Her sister's suddenly gentle tone was enough to start Marguerite crying again. God, she was sick of crying over men and the ruin of her reputation.

"Marguerite . . ."

"I can't tell you." She managed to choke out the words. "It's too complicated."

"Did Anthony Sokorvsky hurt you?"

The steel in Lisette's voice almost amused Marguerite. Despite her sister's deliberately frivolous exterior, she was as sharp and protective as their mother.

"No, he was the perfect gentleman. He was . . ." She shook her head. "It wasn't him, it was me. I'm the one who ran away."

Lisette drew Marguerite closer, put one arm around her shaking shoulders and held her tight. She lapsed into the colloquial French they'd grown up using. "Ssh . . . you are perfect, you are my big sister, you deserve the best man in the world, and if Anthony Sokorvsky isn't good enough for you, then so be it."

"He is good enough," Marguerite said fiercely. "I'm not good enough for him."

"I doubt that." Lisette handed Marguerite her handkerchief. "Please don't cry. Come home and talk to *Maman,* and we'll sort everything out."

Marguerite took the handkerchief and wiped at her tears, looking her sister in the face for the first time. "*Non,* Lisette. I don't think even *Maman* can fix this."

After she finally got rid of Lisette, Marguerite's day dragged on interminably. She'd spoken to her housekeeper, dined with Mrs. Jones and retired to her sitting room to contemplate the fire and supposedly embroider a set of handkerchiefs for Philip's upcoming birthday. When she was sure she was alone, she took out the package Lord Minshom had left her and put it on her lap.

Her fingers shook when she attempted to untie the blue ribbon. Did she really believe this was Harry's account of the events surrounding the duel, or was the whole thing merely a fabrication, another twist in Minshom's plan to blacken her name? It was also possible that Minshom hadn't intended her to have the information at all and had left it at the cottage by mistake. She tugged uselessly at the knotted ribbon, and then used her embroidery scissors to saw through the silk.

She unfolded the pages; the top piece was written in a different handwriting than the rest—Minshom's hand. She whispered the words he'd written into the stillness.

"Sir Harry is staying at the Jugged Hare Inn by Saint Katherine's dock until Tuesday morning when he will take a ship back to France. I suggest you go and meet him. Yours, Minshom."

She glanced at the clock. It was already seven o'clock and dark outside. Could she persuade Christian to come to the inn with her? Sir Harry would be gone by the next morning, and she could hardly expect Anthony to oblige her. She placed her hand flat over the page, felt the rough edge of the ink from Minshom's flashy signature under her palm. Why would Minshom choose to help her now? Did the man have a conscience after all?

"Anthony?"

Anthony looked up to see Valentin standing in the shadows at the door to his office. He stacked the pages left on his desk into a neat pile and closed the last ledger.

"Good evening, Val."

Valentin strolled farther into the office, his keen violet gaze assessing both his brother and the contents of his desk.

"You're here very late. It's almost seven."

Anthony gave him a brief smile. "I know, and I also know I'm not supposed to be here at all."

"As to that," Valentin said, "perhaps I was a little hasty. I never meant to imply that your work here wasn't appreciated."

Anthony raised an eyebrow. "Are you sure you're feeling well, Val? I've never heard you sound so conciliatory."

His brother shrugged. "Maybe I've learned my lesson and decided not to meddle anymore."

Anthony sighed. "I'm glad that you did. I realized there was some truth in what you said. That I needed to assert myself, to decide what I wanted out of life, rather than forever seeing myself as a victim."

"Did I really say all that? I thought I just told you to find a new job." Val sat down in the chair in front of Anthony's desk and studied the toes of his well-polished black boots.

"You know it was much more than that." Anthony let out his breath. "And I've decided to do what you suggested. I'll talk to Father; see if I can lift some of the burden of the estate from his shoulders."

"You don't have to do that." Val frowned. "You were right: that was an incredibly selfish suggestion of mine." He winced. "Sara and Peter haven't let me forget it."

"Val, I am seriously worried about you. Since when have you ever cared what anyone else thought?"

Val got up and walked across to the grimy window, his expression obscured by the gathering shadows in the ill-lit room. "Since I realized that despite my doubts, my son might not thank me for repudiating his heritage, for denying him his rank and place in society."

Anthony could only stare at Valentin's rigid back and marvel at the change in his brother. If that was what loving someone did to a person, he was all for it. He cleared his throat.

"I'm quite happy to help deliver that inheritance to Alexis, even if you don't want it. After all, that's what family is for."

"Damnation, I should be doing it, but I'm not ready."

Anthony smiled at his brother's halting admission, knowing that he was being asked for help and that for once he was able to provide it.

"I'm delighted to oblige, and I promise not to skim off too much money from the estate in my role as dastardly poor relation."

Valentin swung around and stared at Anthony. "I know you won't."

Anthony found it hard to look away from his brother. For the first time, he felt they were equals, that by conquering his demons he was able to see his brother more clearly. Not as the man who'd returned to steal Anthony's place in his father's affections, but as a man who felt as uncertain of his place as Anthony did.

"I've finished with Minshom."

"I'm glad to hear it. Does he understand that too?"

Anthony glanced down at his bruised knuckles. "I believe he does."

"Good, and how goes your affair with the beautiful Lady Justin Lockwood?"

"What affair would that be?"

Valentin returned to his seat, his smile superior. "The one that everyone is talking about."

"Minshom told her that the only sex I enjoyed involved pain and humiliation."

"Ah, and how did she react to that?"

"She defended me, said she didn't care."

"A remarkable woman, then."

It was Anthony's turn to pace the room. "She is, but, the thing is, I do have peculiar sexual tastes. Sometimes I like to be tied up, to be dominated, to . . ."

"And you don't think she will be able to tolerate such behavior or provide you with those things?"

"I don't know."

"Have you asked her?"

Anthony ran his hand through his hair. "No, it's complicated. She has secrets of her own, and there are reasons why she doesn't want to see me again."

"And you're going to let her do that to you? Let her get away without being honest with her?"

Anthony stared long and hard at Valentin. "No. You're right. I'm not going to let her walk away from me with things so unsettled."

Val got to his feet. "Bravo, little brother." He paused. "Sara lets me be myself. She knows that I need a little variation in my sex life. She understands and even enjoys the occasions when Peter and sometimes Abigail join us. So there are women who can understand, if they love you. I'm proof of that."

He frowned as he reached the door. "And if you share that information with anyone, I'll not only deny it, but I'll take great pleasure in beating you to a pulp. Good night, Anthony. I'll make sure your wages are sent on to you. I know where you live."

"Good night, Val." Anthony picked up the papers from his desk and placed them on top of the heavy accounting book. "I've finished all my work and left instructions for Taggart to clear up anything else that comes up."

When he heard the outer door bang, he realized he'd been talking to himself. Clearly uncomfortable in his role of confidant and mentor, Valentin had already left. Anthony hefted the pile of papers into his arms and walked through into the main office. He carefully deposited the stack on Taggart's neat desk and took a last long look around the shipping office. He'd learned a lot, but it was definitely time to move on and create something for himself.

He took a deep breath, inhaled the familiar smell of ink and spices and slowly let it out again. Time to talk things through with his father and then see if Marguerite would ever listen to him again.

"You want me to take you where?"

Marguerite tried to conceal her irritation as Christian slowly put his spoon down and stared at her across the kitchen table. He was working his way through a large bowl of chicken soup; the fragrant smell made Marguerite feel sick.

"To the Jugged Hare Inn."

"Why would I want to do that? Don't you have a perfectly good house of your own to get drunk in?"

With a thump, Marguerite sat down in the seat opposite Christian and tried not to glare at him. He'd taken off his coat and sat at his ease in his silver waistcoat and shirtsleeves. She glanced at Madame Dubois, who was busy stirring something on the stove and lowered her voice.

"Christian, could you stop being sarcastic and simply help me?"

He regarded her for a long minute as he continued to chew his food. "Does this have something to do with Anthony Sokorvsky?"

"Why do you ask me that?"

"Because I've heard that the Jugged Hare is a haven for men who prefer the more extreme sexual practices or like to dress up as women."

"And you assume Anthony would want to meet me there."

Christian leaned forward, his expression darkening. "If you don't know about Sokorvsky's sexual tastes by now, you don't know him at all."

"I know what he's been forced to do. I know he wants to change." Marguerite met Christian's glare full on. "And this conversation isn't about him anyway."

"God, I wish I'd never introduced you to him."

"Then why did you? I've wondered that myself."

"Because I knew about Justin's particular tastes, and I reckoned after he died, that you were concealing what you knew about him as well."

"So you introduced me to another man who likes men?"

"I introduced you to a man struggling to overcome his demons, a man I hoped would help you discover what you really wanted in a mate as well." Christian put his elbows on the table and pushed his hands through his thick blond hair. "Look, both of you seemed unsure of what you needed. I hoped you might work it out together."

Marguerite studied her younger brother with close attention. In his ability to gauge the sexual tastes of the members of the pleasure house, he was even more like their mother than Lisette. Was he right? Had he seen something in her and Anthony that would bring them together? She couldn't think about that now; all her attention had to be on her meeting with Sir Harry.

"But truly, this isn't about Anthony. This is about the past, about Justin."

Christian sat up straight. "Why do you need to meddle with the past? What about your future with Sokorvsky?"

Marguerite looked down at her clenched hands. "There is no future with Anthony. He thinks he knows what happened with Justin and Harry and . . . me."

"What did you tell him?"

"I told him nothing. Lord Minshom took care of that."

"*Merde.*" Christian rose to his feet, determination etched on his handsome features. "Of course I'll take you. I'll just get my cloak."

23

His father and mother hadn't been home and neither, apparently, was Marguerite. Anthony tried not to grind his teeth as all his plans to miraculously sort out his future in one evening evaporated. He'd left the Stratham mansion and now stood staring at Marguerite's butler—again.

"If her ladyship is out, may I speak to Mrs. Jones?"

"I'll see, sir."

Anthony was left fuming on the step, the door firmly closed in his face. Servants always had a way of knowing what was going on upstairs, and Anthony reckoned they already knew he was no longer in favor with their mistress.

"Lord Anthony?"

He nodded at Mrs. Jones, received a warm smile and a burst of gin-laden breath in return.

"Good evening, Mrs. Jones. I was wondering if you could tell me where Lady Justin has gone. I was supposed to meet her here."

Mrs. Jones frowned. "She seemed settled for the night and then she suddenly came running into the kitchen where I was having a comfortable chat with the cook, demanding an escort to her mother's place of business. Of course, I don't go there with her, so she took one of the footmen."

"And how long ago was that?"

"Not so long ago, my lord, probably less than half an hour."

He tipped his hat to her. "Thank you, Mrs. Jones, you have been most helpful. I'll make sure she gets home safely."

Before she had even shut the door, he was racing down the slippery steps and toward the main thoroughfare, where he hoped to pick up a hackney cab. Rain skittered sideways across the filthy cobbled street, obscuring his vision. Whatever Marguerite was going to do, his instincts told him it wasn't good. He flagged down a cab, hopped in and gave the driver Madame Helene's direction.

Marguerite hadn't contacted him or asked for his help; she'd chosen to go to her mother instead. But he didn't care. She might try to back away from him, to push him out of her life, but he wasn't going to allow it. They'd both broken through their pasts to find themselves, and if he had to drag her into that new future kicking and fighting him, he'd do it, not just for himself but for her.

His knowledge of the layout of the pleasure house exceeded most members', so after greeting the footman stationed in the hall, he headed straight down the back stairs to the kitchen. He halted at the door, wiping rain drops from his face in a vain attempt to improve his vision.

"Good evening, Anthony."

"Good evening, Madame."

Even as he continued to search the busy kitchen for Marguerite, he managed to bow to Helene. She walked toward him, her pale yellow skirts rustling, and effectively blocked his path.

"Are you looking for anyone is particular?"

He met her gaze. "Your daughter. Is she here?"

"Marguerite?" Helene raised her eyebrows. "Now why would you want to see her? I thought she had given you your marching orders."

"She tried to."

"And?"

"I refuse to accept them."

Helene continued to study him, all traces of her usual relaxed smile absent. "I'm not sure whether that is a good thing for either you or Marguerite. Perhaps you can help me decide."

"She knows the worst of me, and yet she refuses to denounce me. How can I offer her anything less than the same?"

"She told you about her marriage?"

"Some of it, but not, I fear, the whole. I think she believes herself unforgivable."

"As you do."

"As I did. Marguerite has helped me realize that there is always hope as long as people who love you believe in you."

"Marguerite was always a clever woman."

Anthony leaned his shoulder into the doorframe, needing the support of something solid. "Then help me find her, help me show her that whatever happened in the past, she is still loved."

He heard his own words, realized he meant them far more personally and profoundly than he had ever meant anything in his life before. Madame Helene stood on tiptoe and kissed his cold wet cheek.

"She has gone out with her brother. I believe they are going to the Jugged Hare Inn at Saint Katherine's dock."

"Why in God's name are they going there? Did Minshom set it up?"

Helene shrugged. "I do not know, but they are to meet someone important there."

"Sir Harry Jones, I'll wager."

"I won't bet against you this time, my lord." Helene lightly slapped the side of his face, her expression hard. "But if you make my daughter unhappy, I will make you wish you had never been born, title or no title, influential family or not."

"I understand, and I will try to avoid such a fate." He grabbed her hand and kissed it. "Thank you. I'll go after them."

"Tell the footman stationed at the back of the house to give you a horse. There is always one saddled and ready to ride."

"You think of everything, Madame."

Helene curtsied. "I try to. Good luck, my friend."

Anthony crammed his hat back on, brought the horse's head around and set off again, this time in the direction of the Thames. He'd heard rumors that the Jugged Hare was a Molly house, although he'd never been there himself. Was Sir Harry hiding there? It would be just Minshom's idea of a joke to host his former acquaintance in a house of such peculiar ill-repute.

Whatever Madame Helene thought, Anthony was sure Minshom was involved somehow. The timing and choice of venue bore his hallmark. It was highly possible that Minshom had sent Marguerite a note sharing Sir Harry's supposed whereabouts, thus setting her up for a second emotionally disastrous encounter.

He tightened his grip on the reins, urged the horse forward through the deserted streets. He wasn't going to allow Minshom to dictate what happened this time. With Christian's help, he would make sure that Marguerite was shielded from the worst Minshom could throw at her.

"How on earth are we supposed to find Sir Harry among this crowd?" Marguerite asked as Christian used his shoulder to create a path through the throng of merrymakers in the public bar of the inn. The air was thick with an acrid mixture of wood smoke, cheap gin and strong perfume.

"We're not."

"Then how are we going to find him?"

"We'll ask the landlord."

Marguerite sighed; such a prosaic answer and so unexpected from Christian. The scene at the inn was enough to keep her mind occupied. Amongst the loud, colorful throng, it was almost impossible to tell which were real women and which men. From past conversations with her mother, Marguerite knew that apart from the obvious, the size of a person's feet and hands often gave away their sex. As soon as she dropped her gaze to the floor, she began to make sense of the nature of the relationships around her.

She watched Christian talk to the landlord and wondered if he realized how many of the other customers were staring at his tall elegant form. She had no idea what her brother thought of the lascivious winks and shouted comments. His sexuality remained a mystery to her. According to Lisette, he was willing to sample everything on offer at the pleasure house but seemed to view it all quite dispassionately.

Christian beckoned to her, and she obediently made her way to his side, the hood of her cloak still obscuring her face from the cheerful masses. He bent toward her to be heard above the rising torrent of banter and catcalls.

"He says they have a Jonas Harry staying here in room five but not a Harry Jones."

Marguerite winced. "Really. Shall we go and check if there is any likelihood of them being the same man?"

"I think we should."

Christian's breathtaking smile flashed out. One of the Mollys pretended to swoon, and screeching, fell back into his lover's arms in a swirl of dirty petticoats. Christian took Marguerite's hand and stepped around the couple with a deferential bow, which simply provoked more playacting and whooping.

The upstairs landing was narrow and stank of spilled beer and urine, but at least they were alone. Marguerite touched Christian's arm.

"You don't have to come in with me."

He kept walking and knocked loudly on the scarred oak face of the fifth door. "Are you insane? Of course I'm coming with you."

Marguerite sighed. Her brother's instinct to protect her had been well-developed in their lonely childhood. She could hardly expect him to abandon her now. Tears pricked at her eyes, and she grabbed at his hand.

"You must promise me not to be shocked by anything you hear, by anything that Sir Harry says . . ."

Christian stared down at her. "Marguerite, you are my sister; nothing you do will change that. I'll love you regardless; we all will."

She'd thought she'd lost her family, but she was wrong. They were all around her, supporting her, not judging her, ready to help her if she'd let them. Christian knocked again and this time got a response as the door was unlocked from the inside.

Marguerite held her breath as it opened a scant inch to reveal the haggard face of Sir Harry Jones. Christian smartly stepped to one side so that Harry could see her. The door swung open, and after one last reassuring nod from Christian, Marguerite stepped into the room.

It stank of brandy and cigar smoke and the greasy remains of the badly cooked food piled in half-finished platefuls on the small desk. Clothes hung at random over the backs of the two rickety chairs, along with stockings, waistcoats and under things.

"Sorry about the mess. I wasn't really expecting visitors." Sir Harry cleared his throat and started gathering up his belongings and throwing them into an open trunk so that Marguerite could sit down.

"Didn't Lord Minshom tell you I wanted to speak to you?"

Despite her fears, her voice sounded reassuringly normal. Sir Harry stared at her, one hand smoothing over his unshaven chin. He seemed to have aged ten years since she'd last seen him, all the joy in his face exterminated, all the hope gone.

"I told Minshom I would be quite happy to see you, but I haven't heard from him in days."

Marguerite tried not to show her concern. What had happened to Minshom after Anthony had hit him? Had he crawled away somewhere to die? A tap on the door made her jump. Christian produced a pistol from his pocket and motioned for both her and Harry to stay still.

The knock came again and then the door handle slowly turned. Marguerite's gaze fixed on Harry's horrified face. Was it Minshom come to complete his revenge, or had the authorities finally caught up with her dead husband's lover?

"I apologize for turning up late, but Marguerite didn't tell me the correct time for our appointment."

Christian sighed and put his pistol away. "Sokorvsky."

"What are you doing here?" Marguerite stared at Anthony, her heart hammering so loudly she imagined they could all hear it. Despite her fear, she drank in the sight of his disheveled black hair and determined expression.

"Because I deserve to know the truth."

"You don't 'deserve' anything." God, she was frightened, so frightened by the intensity of his blue gaze, of the knowledge and supreme confidence burning there, as if he knew her through and through.

He shrugged. "You're right, I deserve your contempt for what I am, but you don't hate me do you? So why should I hate you?"

Sir Harry cleared his throat. "Excuse me, Marguerite, but who is this man? And what does he have to do with my relationship with you and Justin?"

Anthony bowed. "I'm Anthony Sokorvsky, a friend of Marguerite and her brother."

Sir Harry eyed the door, his throat working convulsively. "Delighted, I'm sure, but I'm still none the wiser as to what you are doing here."

Anthony sat down on the side of the unmade bed, his expression gentle, his gaze fixed on the other man. "I'm trying to understand what makes a man kill his best friend, and what makes a woman lie to protect the men she knew."

Sir Harry exhaled and sat down suddenly in the other chair facing Marguerite. Christian resumed his position against the door, his gun in one hand.

"I told Minshom everything. I even wrote it down for him." Harry looked up at Marguerite. "Didn't he even give you that?"

Marguerite drew out the sheets of closely written parchments and put them on the table. "I haven't read them yet. I wasn't sure Minshom could be trusted to tell me the truth."

Harry laughed, the sound bitter. "Minshom is a complete bastard."

"That we can all agree on." She leaned forward, trying to catch Harry's eye. "Will you tell me the truth?"

He glanced around at Christian and Anthony. "In front of them?"

She nodded. There was nothing left to lose. If Anthony wanted to hear the awful facts of her marriage, she no longer had the energy to prevent him. What happened after that, she would leave in God's hands.

Harry started to speak, his voice low, his expression uncertain. "I wasn't surprised when Justin wrote and told me he was getting married." He sighed. "He'd already told me that he would have to do it for his family's sake. He was the oldest. I understood that. But I didn't expect him to marry someone like you."

He lifted his gaze to Marguerite. "You were not the biddable old spinster Justin had imagined, you were . . . yourself, and he was clearly enamored. I was reluctant to join you on your wedding trip, but Justin insisted. He told me that you would understand, that you had been brought up in France and had a more pragmatic view of marriage and adultery."

When Harry hesitated, Marguerite nodded to encourage him to go on. She didn't want to disrupt his story by telling him that she'd dreamed of a handsome man sweeping her off her feet, of true love, or happily ever after, thought she'd found it in Justin. She'd been a fool wanting that, wanting to be normal, to be loved.

"Anyway, the more time I spent in your company, the more I liked you, and the less comfortable I felt with our deception. I told Justin he should tell you the truth—let you decide for yourself, but he was reluctant to disturb the apparent harmony between us all."

"And then I found you in bed together one afternoon when I was supposed to be on a sightseeing tour."

Harry nodded. "And you were shocked, and rightly so. Justin, of course, hated being caught in the wrong and handled everything very badly. If it wasn't for your good sense, things might have turned ugly." He leaned forward in his seat. "You were magnificent."

Marguerite shrugged. "I merely told Justin that I understood his needs. There is nothing particularly heroic about that."

"I beg to disagree, my lady," Anthony said. "But please continue, Sir Harry."

Harry's gaze flicked between Marguerite and Anthony. "Well, she allowed Justin and me to be together, she even stayed and watched, which Justin adored." He licked his lips. "In truth, I found it difficult to enjoy myself in those circumstances, when I knew I was interfering in a marriage. When we reached Dover, I told Justin I was no longer comfortable being his lover and that I intended to return to London.

"I tried to explain to him that I respected Marguerite too

much to want to come between them. Justin lost his temper and accused me of coveting his wife, accused her of allowing my attentions. Nothing was his fault, nothing ever was." His smile was full of anguish. "So I returned to London and set about requesting a transfer to India, to get me as far away from the Lockwoods as possible."

Harry got up and walked to the small window, aimlessly peered outside and then sat down again. "Of course, Justin followed me to London and found me at my club. He accused me of sleeping with you in front of everyone and demanded satisfaction." He buried his face in his hands. "God knows, I tried to persuade him to back down, promised him anything, even that I'd fuck him again if he'd only stop the duel."

"I always wondered where that rumor came from. I didn't realize it was Justin who said I was an adulterer." Marguerite stared down at her hands, gripping them tightly together until her nails dug into her skin. "How could he do that to me?"

"Because he was jealous?" Anthony asked. "Because he had finally realized his true nature and knew how much Harry meant to him? Perhaps he couldn't bear the thought of Harry going away?"

"But I told him I didn't mind, that he could bed Harry as much as he wanted."

"And did you really mean that?" Anthony said quietly.

"I thought I did. I was willing to accept anything if it meant he stayed with me." She met Anthony's compassionate gaze. "But I was a fool, wasn't I? Trying to save something that didn't even exist."

"With all due respect, Marguerite, Justin did love you; he told me so." Harry swallowed hard. "And if we are being honest, he also knew I was attracted to you, that if we'd stayed together, I would've wanted to make love to you myself. He didn't want that. Didn't want to share either of us with the other."

Marguerite stared into Harry's eyes, feeling Anthony stiffen and shift forward on the bed. "If you had stayed, I would probably have let you."

"Did you tell Justin that?"

"I tried. On our last night together in London, when I was still trying to work out exactly why you had left so abruptly and why Justin was so angry."

Silence fell between them until Marguerite lowered her gaze. Now Anthony knew the truth she'd held so close to her heart, her impure thoughts, her responsibility for the tragedy. She'd been prepared to promise anything, to do anything, simply to keep her sham of a marriage alive. He believed he was a coward, but she was far worse.

"I thought it would help bring you back, not result in Justin's death."

Harry sighed, "Marguerite, Justin made his own choices that night. I gave him every opportunity to stand down. He chose not to, and we can't blame ourselves for that."

"So how did he end up dead and not you?" Marguerite's sharp question made Harry visibly wince.

"I told Justin I would delope, that I would never shoot at him, that he could kill me if he wanted to. On the morning of the duel, his pistol misfired. I brought my gun down to my side to indicate I wouldn't take a shot, but he kept coming at me, tried to grab my pistol, tried to kill me with my own gun, said if he couldn't have me, no one would. In the struggle the pistol went off, and he was hit in the chest."

Sir Harry stared at the floor. "If there had been another loaded gun there, I would've killed myself and covered his body with my own. But I was dragged away by my seconds and taken across the channel before I even knew if he was dead or not."

He raised his head, and tears glinted in the corners of his brown eyes. "I loved him, Marguerite, for all his selfishness and arrogance, I loved him, and I'll never forgive myself for what happened until the day I die."

Marguerite felt answering tears slide down her cheeks. She tried to make sense of what she'd heard, felt every word twisting and turning in her mind until she wanted to scream. Despite everything she'd done, Justin had loved Harry more than he'd loved her, had been prepared to kill him rather than lose him. Whatever she did, she'd always be blamed for the duel because Justin had used her to get what he wanted. Yet again she was irrelevant, second best, pushed out . . .

"I'm sorry, Harry."

"For what? I'm the one who is apologizing; I'm the one who killed your husband."

"If I hadn't married Justin, none of this would've happened, so I am just as guilty."

"Marguerite . . ."

She ignored Anthony's attempt to intervene, fixing her attention on Harry. "Will you give me your address in France? I would like to write to you."

"Why?"

"Because I think Justin would've wanted to know that you were safe."

Harry scrubbed at his face. "As I said, I'm going to India. That's why I came back to England. A relative of mine has found me an obscure post with one of the trading companies where I can work hard to redeem myself."

"Then write to me when you are settled. Please." Marguerite hesitated. "I want to forgive you, but I need to think about what I've heard. Do you understand?"

"Perfectly, my lady." Harry stood up and bowed. "It's taken me two years to get to a point where I can accept my responsibility for this tragedy and also accept that Justin wasn't blameless. I hope you can do the same. I will write to you."

Marguerite rose as well and curtsied. "I hope your sea voyage is safe and that your new life is everything you want it to be."

Harry walked across the room and went down on one knee before her, took her hand and kissed it. "I'm sorrier than I can say about Justin. I've gone over what happened a thousand times, and I still can't decide what I could've done to change the outcome."

She patted his shoulder. "I understand, and I know you loved him. I'll pray for you."

He looked up, the pain in his face almost unbearable to see. "Thank you."

Marguerite went toward the door, and Christian opened it for her. She barely noticed Anthony fall in behind her. They reached the ground floor, and the noise of the tavern was even more startling after the quietness of upstairs. A chorus of boos and jeers went up as they headed for the door and didn't join in the festivities. Marguerite almost smiled. How ludicrous life sometimes was, the blaze of color and laughter down here compared to the stark story of the destruction of a man's life she'd just heard upstairs.

She gulped in the slightly fresher air, forcing herself to walk to the wall that protected the river down below.

"Are you all right, Marguerite?"

She suddenly became aware of Christian's calm voice in her ear and Anthony's firm grasp of her upper arm as the whole river vista swayed and dipped before her eyes.

"Yes, I want to go home."

"I can take her, Delornay."

"*Non.*" Marguerite removed herself from Anthony's possessive grasp. "I want to go *home*, to my mother."

Anthony stepped back and bowed, his face impassive. "Then I'll come and see you in the pleasure house tomorrow, after you have rested. Good night, my lady, Mr. Delornay."

She watched him leave, vault on his horse and disappear into the night. She'd have to talk to him at some point, but why did it have to be tomorrow?

"Are you ready to go now, Marguerite?" Christian leaned against the stone wall beside her, arms folded as if he were happy to wait on her all night. She shivered and drew her cloak tighter.

"Yes, and thank you for coming with me."

He straightened and buttoned up his coat, shoved one hand in his pocket and offered her the other. "Thank you for helping me understand what happened."

She glanced up at him as he led her back toward the carriage. "Do you still love me?"

He stopped and put both hands on her shoulders. "Sometimes, Marguerite, you ask the most ridiculous questions. You married the wrong man. He made a fool of himself. Why wouldn't I still love you?" He shook her gently. "It was not your fault or poor Sir Harry's. You must try to remember that."

She bit her lip. If it were only that easy. Perhaps it was for Christian, who had never been in love. She nodded and managed a smile.

"It's freezing out here. Let's go home."

24

"*Maman*, I don't want to see him!"

"Marguerite, you have to."

Marguerite swung around to glare at her mother, who had invaded her bedroom at the break of dawn complete with a breakfast tray and a lecture.

"Why must I see him?"

"Because you owe him an explanation?"

"He got an explanation. Thanks to your interference, he was there last night! I'm sure he heard everything he needed to hear about my transgressions."

"There is no need to be rude." Helene settled her skirts around her knees. "Obviously he's not satisfied if he insisted on meeting you again this morning."

"He probably just wants to tell me he never wants to see me again."

"Why would he do that?"

"Because he knows what I did, he knows everything."

"He knows that your marriage was full of problems and that your husband caused most of them."

Marguerite rounded on her mother, fists clenched at her sides. "Why are you being so nice to me? Why isn't anyone blaming me?"

"For what? You married Justin in good faith, *oui*? You didn't know that after a few days of marriage he would suddenly produce a male lover?"

"Of course I didn't know that, but I didn't stop him, did I? I let him believe that it was all right, that I understood, that . . ." She ran out of words and stared helplessly at her mother. "God, I was prepared to do anything to keep him. I wanted a family of my own so desperately."

Helene sighed and held out her hand. "Marguerite, you always had me and the twins; why do you make it sound as if you were alone?"

"I felt alone, *Maman*. I always tried to be a mother to the twins, but I knew they would be leaving the nunnery soon and coming to you. I knew they would no longer need me. When I met Justin, he seemed the answer to my prayers."

Helene's hand dropped onto her lap. "I'm sorry, Marguerite. I'm so sorry for giving you that burden. I should never have abandoned you like that."

Marguerite went to kneel at her mother's feet. "It's all right. I know why you did it, *Maman*. I understand. Please do not feel guilty."

Helene sighed. "I knew something was wrong when I came to meet you in Dover just after your marriage. I should've acted on my instincts and questioned you more closely."

Marguerite took her mother's hand and squeezed it hard. "And I would have continued to lie to you. I'd already made my decision to marry Justin, and I was prepared to live with that choice."

"And now? You will destroy your chance at happiness with Anthony Sokorvsky by living in the past forever?"

"I thought you didn't approve of my liaison with Anthony."

Helene smiled slightly. "I've changed my mind. I think he has the potential to become an extraordinary man. You haven't answered my question. Are you going to allow your guilt about Justin to sour your future with Anthony?"

"But how can I tell, *Maman*? How can I know if he is the right man for me? I haven't chosen very well so far."

"Anthony told me that Lord Minshom shared all his secrets with you, and that you didn't turn away from him. Is that true?"

"Why would I?"

Helene's face softened. "Most women would, my dear. Do you think he would have told you himself if Minshom hadn't forced the issue?"

Marguerite met her mother's searching gaze. "Yes, I think so; in truth, I *know* he would."

"And were you intending to tell him about your complicated relationship with Justin?"

"Yes, I was."

Helene smiled. "Then what is the problem? Lord Minshom saved you both a lot of trouble, didn't he?"

Marguerite thought about that. Lord Minshom in the unlikely role of matchmaker felt decidedly odd, yet he had helped her connect with Sir Harry at the end, and had walked away from Anthony . . .

"I don't know if Anthony wants me, *Maman*. I know he values our friendship, but he has never spoken of love."

Helene patted Marguerite's hand and released it, then got to her feet in a rustle of blue silk. "Both of you have good reasons not to want to fall in love. Both of you fear being vulnerable again. I suggest you see Anthony, tell him how you feel and see what he says in return."

"You make it sound so easy, *Maman*."

"Hardly that." Helene hugged Marguerite. "It took me almost nineteen years to understand that I loved Philip. I couldn't believe that anyone would find me remotely lovable, but I was wrong. Don't waste your life like I did, Marguerite; be honest with yourself, forget the past and find happiness."

Marguerite looked into her mother's face and nodded. "I'll try, *Maman.*"

"I'm so glad you agreed to speak to me."

Anthony bowed as Marguerite hesitated at the door. Despite the current surroundings, he tried to look as nonthreatening as possible. He'd stripped off his coat and waistcoat and could feel the chill of the as yet unheated upper floor of the pleasure house in his bones. At ten in the morning, the place looked almost harmless—a stark contrast to the excesses that normally played out on this stage of extreme sexual pleasure.

Marguerite wore a simple brown dress, her long hair caught back in a bow at the nape of her neck. She looked far too pale for his liking, but after the series of shocks she had suffered over the past few days, he could hardly blame her. Her hands clasped the ends of a thick cream shawl over her breasts.

"I didn't want to see you. My mother made me."

He smiled. Her honesty always touched him. "But you are here, and I am grateful."

"I think I know you well enough to understand that if I don't deal with you now, you'll follow me around until I do."

Anthony shrugged. "What can I say? I've become very tenacious of late. I've realized I can't allow others to dictate the pace of my life or make my decisions for me."

Marguerite walked into the center of the room, her blue eyes fixed on his. "That is good. I am pleased for you."

Silence fell as he contemplated his next move. So much hinged on her reactions that he was unsure of where to begin. His gaze fell on the farthest corner of the room, and he reached for Marguerite's hand. She let him lead her toward his darkest moments, to the place he still had nightmares about.

"I used to strip naked and have myself chained up here." He pointed at the bare floorboards, the manacles draped over a nearby stand containing whips of every type and length. "In the punishment corner, a man no longer has the right to say no, or to deny anyone the chance to fuck him or hurt him."

Marguerite didn't speak, but she didn't pull away from him either. He gathered his courage. "Sometimes I even enjoyed it, giving up the responsibility of my sexual needs to others; sometimes I craved that pain. At first I did it to blot out the nightmares about Aliabad, the man who raped me. In my naiveté, I decided that if I had to experience such sexual torment every night, I'd prefer to make it real. I soon learned that was a mistake and that I had no control over the new nightmares either."

He let go of Marguerite's hand and crouched down to stroke the cold metal of the manacles. "And of course by then I was addicted to the sexual thrill of it all, thought I deserved it, thought Aliabad and Minshom had it right, that I was born to be submissive and crave pain.

"And then one morning I woke up here alone, covered in bruises and Minshom's cum and realized I couldn't take it anymore." He looked up at her. "I know that sounds ridiculous, but that's how it was. I realized that I'd allowed others to dictate my sexuality to me for far too long and that I deserved the chance to find out what I wanted for myself."

He sighed. "And then Christian introduced me to you. And I felt such a connection to you from the first . . . You fascinated me. I tried to tell myself that it was simply because you were the first woman I'd ever tried to be honest with, that the attraction was all on my part. But it wasn't, was it?"

Marguerite shook her head but didn't speak, so Anthony plowed on.

"Despite what you know of my sexual preferences, I've had plenty of opportunities to bed women, even up here, and I never felt the urge to do it until I met you."

"Anthony, are you saying I was the first woman you made love to?"

He tried to smile. "If you overlook the lady Peter introduced me to at the pleasure house who showed me how to give a woman pleasure with my mouth and fingers, then yes."

"I'm honored."

Anthony let the manacles fall to the floor and stood up. "Honored that you were my first woman? I thought you'd laugh at me."

She stared at him, her expression serious. "Why would I laugh? It took a lot of courage for you to try something different, to break away from what you were used to."

He held her gaze, keen to come to the crux of the matter, to lay himself open for her, to pray for understanding. "But it doesn't change everything. I still enjoy the unusual in my sex life. I think I always will."

"Do you want to go back to Minshom?"

He shuddered. "Not at all."

"Then what do you want?" She gestured at the racks of whips, the masks, the chains hung on the red-and-black-painted walls. "What here would make you sexually happy?"

"I don't know. I'm not trying to be coy; I really don't know quite what I, Anthony Sokorvsky, would actually enjoy."

Marguerite picked up one of the riding crops from the stand nearest her and studied it. Despite himself, Anthony's pulse quickened.

"You enjoy being tied up, don't you?"

"Yes, and as you saw, David Gray is an expert in that."

She came toward him, the tip of the crop stroking her palm. He couldn't take his eyes off it.

"But how much pain is enough, Anthony? How is your lover supposed to know when to stop if you don't?"

He looked away from her. "I don't know."

"I don't think I could hurt you."

He exhaled and slowly forced a smile. "It's all right, I appreciate your honesty . . . I understand." He turned toward the door, his heart felt like a lead weight in his chest. "I just wanted to explain, to tell you the truth, to . . ."

She barred his way with the crop, pushing it against his chest.

"Don't walk away from me. You asked to see me, insisted on it."

"Because I had some stupid idea that you cared about me, that you might want to help me discover myself sexually. But I understand now that it would be too distasteful for you."

"That's not what I said." Marguerite sighed. "Why me? I'm not the woman you thought I was. Wouldn't you prefer a young debutante who would be too ignorant to understand your preferences and probably oblivious to your partaking of them, if you were careful?"

"And I would be living my life as a lie? Unable to share my true self with the woman I'd chosen to marry?" He hesitated, making himself meet her gaze. "I'd much rather live with a woman who knew the worst of me and loved me despite myself. Wouldn't you prefer a relationship like that?"

"It's not the same, is it? A man can stray sexually, and no one thinks anything of it. If a married woman is unfaithful, she becomes an object of scorn, of ridicule."

"Marguerite, do you really think I find you an object of scorn?"

"No, you prefer to pretend I was wholly innocent of anything that happened in my marriage, and that isn't true. Didn't you hear me say I would've slept with Harry if it had meant Justin stayed with me? I was so fixated on hiding my past, on becoming socially acceptable, that I was prepared to do almost anything."

"So what? I know you, Marguerite. You are incredibly loyal,

and I can understand that you would've done anything to save your marriage."

"It's not that simple." She struggled to meet his gaze. "I was intrigued by the idea of sleeping with two men—aroused!"

Anthony smiled. "Do you think that shocks me? I saw the way you reacted to David when he was tying me up. I know you enjoyed it."

"So you'd be quite comfortable with me fucking any man I want?"

He grabbed the tip of the whip, drew her hard against his body. "If you were mine, you wouldn't need to fuck any other man."

"Because you'd be fucking them for me?"

He stared down at her face, absorbed her pain and his own, allowed the emotions inside him to solidify and condense, and sent them outward to her. "Marguerite, I love you, don't you understand that yet?"

"You are infuriating!" She tried to kick his shin, but he pulled her even closer.

"I would only fuck another person if you ordered me to. In truth, I would probably like it if you did. And only men. I wouldn't want another woman besides you." He kissed the top of her head. "And you're right. I mustn't be selfish. If you asked nicely, I'd let you join in." He hesitated. "And, of course, if you asked me not to touch anyone else but you, I'd try to do that as well."

"You mean that after all you've just said, you'd be prepared to give up all your sexual interests for me?"

He sighed. "I'd certainly try. I don't know what I want. I don't know what I crave and what I can do without." She tried to move away from him, but he held on. "I'm trying to be honest here, Marguerite; can you at least give me credit for that?"

"Then what do you want me to do?"

"Help me? Explore all the possibilities with me?"

She looked up at him, her lower lip caught between her teeth. He bent his head, licking the spot she'd gnawed on, tasting her blood. She moaned as his tongue slid into her mouth, took possession of it and dueled with hers. She pulled back, her breathing as short as his.

"Why would I do that?"

"Because you want to? Because you care about me?"

"Anthony, I'm not sure I am the right woman for you. Perhaps you need to experiment more before you make any decisions."

"Because I've only made love to you?" He released her and took two steps back, let her see his already tented breeches. "Perhaps I am a man who finally knows what he wants."

"But you just told me you didn't know."

"What I *know*, Marguerite, is that you are being a coward." He pointed at the door. "You'd rather I went out there and spent the next six months trying everything the pleasure house has to offer. Then I suppose you'd like me to run back to you with a list, so that you could make up your mind if you could bear to love me?"

"You don't understand; I can't risk another mistake. I can't . . ."

"Can't risk loving me." Anthony bowed. "I have to go and speak to my father now. I've decided to take up his offer and become his land manager for at least the next six months. It might not work out, but at least it will be valuable experience if I decide to branch out on my own again."

He picked up his coat and waistcoat and headed for the door, his mouth uncomfortably dry as he swallowed down his agony. "Good-bye, Marguerite. Let me know if you change your mind."

"Anthony . . ."

He heard the riding crop clatter to the floor, but he couldn't turn back. He'd risked all and he'd lost, but he'd also learned something. Despite his heartbreak, he wasn't going back to the life he'd led before. He grimaced into the darkness of the stairwell. Perhaps he should follow his own advice and start on a career of true debauchery. As long as he fucked women, his father wouldn't mind.

He came to an abrupt stop on the first landing. But he didn't want to do that. He didn't want any other woman but Marguerite. Briefly, he closed his eyes. A morning spent with his father was the perfect cure to any emotional display he might be tempted to make. But it wouldn't cure his heartache; he doubted anything ever would.

Marguerite stared at the bare floorboards until the sound of Anthony's retreating footsteps disappeared completely. She'd lost her nerve, frightened herself, doubted herself and finally succeeded in pushing Anthony away. She swallowed hard. He loved her? She drew her shawl closer around her body.

God, she needed to think. Could she bear never seeing him again, never touching him, never waking up with him moving over her? She shivered just at the thought of it. Had she just made a colossal blunder? Was Anthony right? Was she a coward?

She made her way back to the door and crept out into the deserted hallway beyond. This had all happened too fast. She'd known him only a few short weeks. After the disaster of her first marriage, she was right to be cautious, wasn't she? She stared out of the window. Anthony would be halfway to his father's house now, ready to start his new life—without her. Oh God, what had she done?

25

Marguerite knocked hard on the door to Captain David Gray's lodgings and tried to look more confident than she felt. She hoped he was home but knew from experience that naval officers were at the mercy of the tide and the winds and sometimes had to leave far too promptly.

"Lady Justin?"

She fixed a smile on her face.

"Captain Gray, may I come in?"

"Of course, my lady."

To her relief, he managed to conceal his understandable surprise behind a mask of calm courtesy she could only envy. She walked into his sitting room, noticing again how clean it was and how empty of personal belongings.

"How may I help you?"

Marguerite sat down. She'd spent the last three days trying to decide what to do about Anthony and had finally found the courage to act. It was time to forget her notions of ever being conventional and of fitting in. Her family might be unusual, but at least they loved and supported her. The least she could do was to be proud of them and embrace her unusual heritage. She could only hope Captain Gray would be amenable to her remarkable request.

She cleared her throat. "I need your advice about Anthony Sokorvsky."

"Mine? I'm not sure if I'm the best person to ask." He relaxed back in his chair, one leg crossed over the other. "Have you spoken to his brother or Mr. Peter Howard? They know him far better than I do."

"I need a very *particular* kind of advice, the kind that you are an expert in."

His eyebrows rose. "I'm not quite sure I understand you."

"May I be honest with you, sir?"

"Of course, and please, call me David."

"I'm trying to understand Anthony's sexual needs."

"Ah."

"He says he doesn't know what he likes, that his tastes have been formed for him and that he needs to experiment to find out his own desires."

David nodded. "I can see how he might feel like that. Minshom tried to control him, and as far as I am aware, it wasn't until quite recently that Anthony realized there were other ways to gain sexual release without subjecting himself to pain, humiliation and complete domination."

"He wanted me to help him."

"But you are afraid you won't be able to provide what he needs?"

"I'm afraid to let him down, to prove unworthy of him." *And why hadn't she said that to Anthony's face instead of appearing to simply give up on him?*

David studied her, his expression considering. "And how can I help you with this dilemma? Are you also afraid that he will hurt you or make you hurt him?"

"Yes." Marguerite bowed her head. "He called me a coward, and he might just be right."

"I don't think you are a coward. You have a right to protect yourself and him." He leaned forward, his large capable hands clasped together. "But if it helps, I don't believe Anthony will miss the extremes Lord Minshom put him through." He shivered. "I've met men who need to be dominated, and Anthony isn't one of them. He wouldn't inflict pain on you either; it's just not in his nature."

Marguerite nodded as relief shuddered through her. She already knew in her heart that Anthony would never harm her, but it didn't hurt to have her thoughts confirmed.

"Do you think it would help if I experienced some of the things he likes? He asked me if I would do that for him."

"Well, you certainly might understand him better. Is that why you came to me?" David smiled. "I did offer to teach you how to tie Anthony up, and I'm more than happy to do that."

"Actually, I was hoping you might tie us both up."

David's smile was slow and full of respect. "You, as well?"

"Do you think Anthony would like that? I want to help him, I really want to try, and I trust you. My mother said you were the perfect man to help me."

"She would know. What is it with the Delornay family needing my services?" David stood up and grinned at her. "Thank you, my lady, I'll strive to be worthy of your expectations. And I think Anthony will be in heaven."

Anthony took off his hat and knocked on the door of David's lodgings, trying to shake off the slight sensation of a headache lodged deep in his temples. He hadn't realized what managing a complex estate required and was still struggling to keep up with his father's immense knowledge. In the last few days, his respect for his father had increased tenfold. He could only hope he hadn't displayed his lamentable ignorance too often.

"Anthony, come in." David welcomed him inside with a bow and a friendly pat on his shoulder. Anthony took off his hat and gloves then slowed as he saw a familiar bonnet and cloak draped over the same chair.

"You invited me over, didn't you, David?"

"I did."

David was in his shirtsleeves and breeches, his hair tied neatly back from his face, as usual. Anthony gestured at the bonnet.

"But you already have company."

"I know."

Anthony gave his friend a quizzical look. "Is this some kind of game? Am I missing something?"

"It's not so much of a game as the beginnings of your tuition. Why don't you come into the bedroom, get undressed and then we can start?"

Anthony followed David down the narrow hallway to the bedroom. "I don't know what you are talking about, and I'm not in the mood for riddles. Perhaps I should go."

He abruptly stopped speaking as he saw Marguerite sitting on the side of David's bed. She wore her muslin shift, and her hair hung down her back in a single braid.

"What is going on?" He stared at Marguerite and tried to disguise his shock behind a dismissive smile. "Have you decided to take David as a lover?"

"No, she hasn't. Now get undressed so that I can begin."

Anthony remained in the doorway, one hand braced on the door frame. "I'm not doing anything until Marguerite tells me what is going on."

"But *I* told her not to speak unless I allowed it."

"You told her?" Anthony swung around to look at David, who was taking something out of the tallboy drawer. "What in damnation are you talking about?"

David straightened up, two sets of *shibari* ropes in his hands.

"A lesson, a shared experience—if you would shut up and take your clothes off."

Anthony stopped talking and obediently started to strip, his mind a tumult of chaotic emotions. He still wasn't quite clear what was going on, but he wasn't a complete fool. And if Marguerite was willing to try this for his sake, he was not going to disappoint her.

David gestured at the bed. "Anthony, go and sit on the bed, cross-legged, your back against the headboard."

Anthony walked over to Marguerite, climbed on the bed and took up his position in the center of the bed. His cock was already erect, his body humming with anticipation. David brought the red *shibari* rope over and trailed it over Anthony's shoulder and chest allowing it to pool on his stomach.

"We'll start with you, Anthony. Lean forward."

David anchored the rope through the back of the headboard and brought it over Anthony's shoulders and around his torso. Marguerite watched intently, her hands gripped together in her lap, her nipples already showing through the delicate muslin of her shift. Anthony exhaled as David crossed the rope over his chest in an X and brought the ends around his waist.

"Put your hands behind your back."

Anthony tensed as David looped the rope around his wrists. He flexed his fingers as they were drawn inexorably into the small of his back. The rope reappeared in front of him again, this time anchoring his hips. His cock jerked as David slid the rope beneath it.

"As you can see, Marguerite," David said, "The rope isn't very tight yet. The skill comes later, in determining how tightly to bind a person, how much they can stand, how much they enjoy being restrained."

David crossed the thin red linen below Anthony's balls and under his thighs, crossed it again and brought both strands up between the valley of his arse cheeks before separating them again at his hips.

"We'll wrap his cock up later, but I want you to tighten the ropes now, and see how Anthony reacts." David brought Marguerite to sit in front of Anthony and transferred the ends of the rope into her two hands. She bit her lip and stared into his eyes. He held her gaze and nodded slowly.

"Do it, Marguerite. Tie me up as tightly as you want, make me beg."

He tried to brace himself for the inexorable constriction but was still unprepared to have his whole body from arse to neck gradually slammed back against the headboard, impaled there, held immobile like a butterfly pinned to a wall. His breathing shortened and the blood pumping through his cock increased. He could no longer look down, but he knew he was dripping with pre-cum from the wetness on his stomach.

Would Marguerite see the possibilities? Enjoy having him there at her mercy?

David murmured, "Tighten the ropes a bit more."

Marguerite obliged, and Anthony moaned her name as the bonds around his wrist tightened and his knuckles drove into his spine, shoving his groin forward. David tied off the ropes on the corner of the headboard.

"God, Marguerite." Anthony's chest was so constricted he could hardly get the words out. "Suck my cock. Own me."

David frowned. "If you can't speak, Marguerite, I hardly think it is fair for Anthony to order you around, do you?"

Marguerite shook her head, her gaze fixed on the swell of Anthony's cock, making him even harder and hornier.

"I'll gag him, then."

Anthony could do nothing to stop David placing a black silk scarf over his mouth and fastening it tightly at the back of his head. He swallowed hard, his mind already anticipating the next thing, the next onslaught on his sensually beleaguered body.

"Would you like to do anything to him before I tie you up as well, Marguerite?"

Anthony tensed as Marguerite considered him and then dropped her head and used her tongue to follow the path of the red linen around his hips and under his cock. There was no give in the ropes, nowhere for his hips to go, but he still tried, still craved her mouth on him, all over him.

He made a stifled sound as her tongue stroked over the crown of his cock, lazily lapping at the wetness, creating even more. She licked his balls, bit the linen beneath them as if testing its ability to keep him confined. When she finally sat up, his whole body was shaking with need and straining against his bonds.

"It's your turn now, Marguerite. Take off your shift and kneel up in front of Anthony."

Anthony tried to look at David, heard nothing in his voice but amusement and sexual satisfaction, knew he'd kill his friend if he had appeared to want Marguerite for himself. Marguerite took off her shift, and Anthony wanted to howl with lust. Her breasts were flushed, her nipples erect and the scent of her arousal already perfumed the room.

Marguerite took a deep breath as David knelt behind her and placed the black *shibari* rope around her neck so that the long ends hung forward over the curves of her breasts and pooled on the white bed cover. She'd enjoyed seeing Anthony tied up; how would it feel to be tied up herself?

She trembled as David took control of the rope, crossed the ends under her breasts and drew them behind her back, crossed them again and brought them around her hips. Soon the thin linen circled her wrists keeping her arms imprisoned behind her. David was so close that she could feel the pulse of his arousal against her buttocks, but his hands were as impersonal and efficient as a servant's.

She studied the rope, felt a gentle tug at the back of her neck when David wound the ropes around her thighs down to the knees and back up again, leaving her mound uncovered and suddenly exposed. She watched his fingers fly over the rope, saw the intricate patterns he made and wondered what Anthony made of it, whether he liked it as much as she had.

As if he'd heard her thought, David paused and looked at Anthony. "Do you like her, like this? Do you want her bound to you?"

Anthony's slight nod was enough to make David urge her closer to Anthony. It was difficult to move with her body restrained and on display. She gasped when David lifted her to kneel in the cramped space between Anthony's crossed legs. Her bound breasts brushed his chest, and his cock pressed against her stomach, making her shiver.

David braced himself behind her.

"I'm going to tighten the rope, Marguerite, are you ready?"

Before she could even nod, she felt a quickening sensation that started at her shoulders and gradually moved down to her knees, as if she were slowly being hugged, being controlled, being captured. She started to pant and rock forward, seeking Anthony's strength to rub herself against to relieve the ache building inside her.

When David finally stopped, she was shivering uncontrollably, her body on fire, Anthony's wet pulsing cock pressed hard up against her belly, his lust-filled eyes almost level with her own.

"As I'm in control of you both, I really think you should fuck." David laughed. "Well, you are going to fuck, because you have no choice, and I want to see it."

Marguerite moaned as he effortlessly picked her up and slowly lowered her over Anthony's cock.

"Don't come yet. There's more." David drew the black *shibari* ropes back over Marguerite's shoulders and slid them under the red ropes that secured Anthony's shoulders to the headboard. "Now I pull both sets."

David deftly removed Anthony's gag and set about joining them even more tightly together. Anthony groaned and shoved his tongue in her mouth as the pressure increased, as they both struggled to draw breath into their lungs. Marguerite hovered on the brink of losing consciousness, and they climaxed together in a frenzy of white heat and the frustrated passion of shared, long-repressed need.

"God . . ." Anthony's cock still pulsed inside her even though he'd come. "That was the best fuck I've ever had."

Shyly, Marguerite looked up at him. "The best fuck?"

His smile was breathtaking. "I meant the best love I've ever made."

Marguerite swallowed hard. "I'm trying, Anthony. I'll try for your sake, but I can't hide from my true nature any more than you can."

"I'll try too. If you are willing to explore our sexual opportunities together, I'm sure we'll find our own particular level of pleasure." He kissed her forehead, sighing as David eased their bonds a fraction.

"I love you, Marguerite. You might not believe me yet, but I'll prove it to you. You'll never be second in my life. You'll always come first for me."

Marguerite wanted to cry at the sincerity in his eyes, the certainty of hope for his future that she had helped him discover. She had to tell him the truth, had to stop being a coward and follow his lead.

"I love you too, Anthony."

He went still. "You don't have to say that yet, Marguerite. I'm more than willing to wait."

She smiled up at him through her advancing tears. "Well,

I'm not. My entire family has told me I would be a fool to lose you, and for once I agree with them." She hesitated, casting him a provocative look from under her eyelashes. "It's not as if you're asking me to marry you and settle down or anything."

His expression turned thunderous. "I bloody well am."

"But what about all the time we need to explore the possibilities of the pleasure house?"

He glared at her—actually glared at her. "We can have our wedding trip there, if you want. It would be cheaper and safer than going abroad anyway."

David cleared his throat. "If you are making wedding plans, perhaps I ought to wish you happiness and untie you?"

Marguerite gasped as Anthony's cock jerked inside her and filled out again.

"In a minute, David," Anthony said. "I still have to convince my intended to marry me."

David sighed and climbed up onto the bed. "I really can't leave you like this. I'll untie you both from the headboard and leave it at that. What you choose to do with the ropes afterward is entirely up to you."

"That suits me perfectly," Anthony growled, his gaze still fixed on Marguerite. "I'm sure I can persuade Marguerite to agree with me. She'll hardly want to be tied up like a parcel and taken to Gretna Green to be married. I'm sure I can make her to change her mind and consider a long engagement."

Marguerite didn't even hear David leave as Anthony bore her down onto the mattress, settled himself between her thighs and started pounding into her as if he'd never stop. Perhaps she should consider marrying him one of these days after all . . .

Want more of Kate Pearce's House of Pleasure series?
Then please turn the page for an exciting sneak peek of
Lord Minshom's story,
SIMPLY INSATIABLE
coming in May 2010!

1

He'd made a fool of himself.

Over a man.

Lord Minshom raised the bottle at his elbow, drank deeply, then carefully set it down again. He licked the brandy from his lips and tasted his own defeat and humiliation at the hands of that upstart, Lord Anthony Sokorvsky. A man who'd had the nerve to walk away from him—from *him*!

All of London was whispering about how his former sex slave had forsaken him for a woman. Minshom smiled bitterly in the direction of the fire and exhaled, feeling the tug of recently healed bone. At their last meeting, Sokorvsky had punched him so hard he'd ended up unconscious at the bottom of the stairs with two cracked ribs. Luckily, Robert had been there to drag him away before Sokorvsky and his nauseating lady love had descended the stairs to gloat over him.

Minshom picked up the bottle again and drank until there was nothing left. And it wasn't even as if he was "in love" with Sokorvsky. He didn't love anyone, didn't believe he was capable of it anymore. All his sexual encounters were exercises in power, opportunities to show that he was still at his peak and able to subdue or seduce anyone he wanted.

Yet Sokorvsky had found the balls to walk away from him. And for the first time in his life, despite his threats, Minshom had given up the pursuit and allowed his former lover to follow his heart. He grimaced at his own saccharine choice of words. Was he slipping? Was he losing his touch?

"My lord?"

He turned his head toward the door of the oak-paneled study, blinked at the blurred outline of his valet, Robert Brown.

"What?"

Robert came farther into the room, his dark red hair glinting in the meager candlelight, the only spot of color against his pale skin and somber black attire.

"Would you like to retire for the night, sir?"

Minshom held out the brandy bottle. "Get me another one of these."

Unlike most of his staff, Robert held his ground and didn't even hesitate.

"I'll get you more brandy if you take it up to bed with you, how's that?"

"Go to hell."

"I'm already there, sir; I've lived with you for far too long. You'll have to think of something else to threaten me with."

Minshom raised an eyebrow and threw the bottle toward the marble fireplace where it shattered into a million glittering fragments and almost put the fire out. "Get me my brandy, damn you."

Robert sighed. "I'll go and get someone to clean that up, sir; wouldn't want you cutting yourself."

"Leave it."

Robert hesitated, his gray eyes fixed on Minshom's. He was in his early thirties, had come to Minshom Hall as a stable boy and had stayed with his master ever since.

"Sir . . ."

"Come here and kneel down." Minshom pointed to the rug in front of him.

"Are you sure you don't want to go upstairs? Anyone could come in."

"And see you sucking my cock? I'm sure they've all seen that before."

Robert looked resigned, but he did as he was told and came to kneel in front of Minshom. He eyed Minshom's groin.

"After the amount you've had to drink, I'm not sure I'll be able to get a rise out of you, sir."

"You'd better try hard then, hadn't you?"

Robert sighed again and undid the buttons of Minshom's placket, pushed aside his underclothes to reveal his half-erect cock. Minshom reached forward to slide his hand into Robert's thick pelt of auburn hair.

"Make it fast and hard; make me come."

He closed his eyes as Robert's warm mouth closed over his shaft and began to suck and pump his flesh. He hadn't been back to the pleasure house since his injury. The discovery that Sokorvsky's woman was Madame Helene's daughter hadn't helped either. Would he ever go back there? Was it time to move on?

Coward.

He could almost hear his father saying it, the way his lip would curl, the sting of the beating he would no doubt get for his impudence in begging for the punishment to end. He dug his fingers deeper into Robert's hair, heard his valet draw in a hurried breath and suck faster. Perhaps he hadn't completely lost his ability to make men sexually serve him after all. But then he and Robert had always been simpatico.

A slight commotion in the hallway below registered through his drunken arousal. He wasn't expecting guests and had told his damned butler to deny anyone who inquired. He had no desire to see the glee in his so-called friends' eyes as they recounted yet more gossip about Sokorvsky and his new love. To be fair, he'd liked Marguerite Lockwood, had felt an unexpected stir of interest in his loins despite his refusal to fuck women. She'd reminded him of someone . . .

The disturbance was getting louder, rising up the stairs, coming closer. The agitated sound of his butler's voice and the clearer high tones of a woman. What in damnation was going on? Robert stopped sucking and tried to raise his head. Minshom shoved him back down again.

"I didn't tell you to stop."

He didn't bother to turn his head as the door flew open and his butler started apologizing.

"I'm sorry, sir, she refused to leave and . . ."

And sure enough, his vision was filled with an apparition from the darkest recesses of his personal hell.

"Good evening, Robert, good evening, Minshom."

Minshom kept one restraining hand on Robert's head. He used the other to wave the butler away and waited until the door shut behind him before addressing his visitor.

"What the hell are you doing here?"

"Visiting you?"

"I didn't give you permission to do that."

She raised her eyebrows and took off her bonnet, holding it at her side by its wide blue ribbons. Her brown hair was neatly parted in the center and drawn back into two coiled braids over her ears. At first glance, she still looked far too young to be anyone's wife, let alone his.

"I don't believe I need your permission to visit my own house."

"It's my house. Don't you remember? When you married me, everything you brought with you became mine."

"How could I forget? You've always been very good at making me feel like a possession."

He met her clear gray eyes and smiled. "And yet, here you are. Where you are not wanted."

She sighed. "Can we stop this? I need to talk to you."

He glanced down at Robert. "I'm busy. Make an appointment with my secretary and get out of my house."

She regarded him for another long moment and then turned on her heel. "Fine, I'm going to bed, I'll see you in the morning when you are sober."

He closed his eyes as the door slammed behind her; waited for the front door to slam as well and heard nothing. Dammit, where was the woman going? He sat forward and hissed as his now-flaccid cock caught on Robert's teeth.

"Sir . . ."

"What?"

He glared down at his valet, who was busy wiping his hand over his mouth.

"Was that her ladyship, sir?"

"Yes."

"Did you finally send for her?"

"Of course not!"

Minshom shoved his seat back and stood up, waited for the room to readjust itself to his unbalanced drunken gaze. Where the hell had Jane gone? Surely she hadn't had the audacity to stay and bed down here for the night? He'd made it quite clear he wanted her off his property. Minshom started for the door, almost tripping over Robert in his haste.

The marble stairway was dark, and Minshom paused to listen. A door closed upstairs and he set off again, following the faint trail of lavender soap Jane always left behind her. He was aware of Robert tracking him, but at least he had the sense not to speak.

Minshom passed the door into his own suite and kept going down the hall. A faint light gleamed under the door of the room next to his. He entered without knocking and found his wife kneeling in front of the fireplace encouraging a wisp of smoke to ignite the kindling.

"I told you to get out."

She rose slowly to her feet and faced him, her expression as mulish as he suspected his was.

"I am not going anywhere."

"Despite your age, you haven't put on that much weight." He allowed his lascivious gaze to flow over her, let her see it, resent it, waited for her to blush. "I wager I could still pick you up and toss you out myself."

"I'm sure you could, if you wanted to cause yet more scandal."

"You think I'm afraid of scandal?" He smiled. "My whole life is a scandal."

"I know. I might live in the countryside, but I do read the London newspapers and the gossip columns." She unbuttoned her pelisse and laid it over the back of a chair, meeting his gaze unflinchingly. "And I don't think you have done anything to be particularly proud of."

"And you think I care about your opinion?"

"Probably not, but there it is, all the same."

He moved toward the chair, picked up her discarded coat and held it out to her. "Put this back on. I wouldn't want you to catch a chill on your journey back to Minshom Abbey."

She ignored him and continued to unpack her small valise, taking out a long white nightgown and her hairbrush. He stared at the back of her head and realized that Robert had slipped into the room behind him. Jane was right. Did he really want more scandal? He was already out of favor with the *ton*. Throwing his wife out into the street would certainly make matters worse.

But then, if he was already convicted, why not add to his infamy? He took a step toward Jane, hesitated as she started to take down her long hair. God, he remembered watching her do this a thousand times, the anticipation building in his loins as she readied herself for bed, for him . . .

"Stop doing that."

She looked over her shoulder at him, her hands still busy in her hair.

"I can hardly sleep with all these pins sticking in me, can I?"

He throttled down his frustration and the unexpected surge of interest from his cock, knew he couldn't bear to watch her disrobe. He'd forgotten how clever she could be. Was this battle worth fighting while he was drunk and still incapacitated from his cracked ribs? In truth, he was in no state to follow through on his threats. Perhaps he should make a strategic retreat and face her on the morrow.

"Are you sure I can't convince you to leave?"

"No." She walked toward him, and he tensed until she presented him with her back. "Can you undo my buttons and loosen my laces, please, Blaize?"

He recoiled from her as if she was a raddled old whore. When was the last time someone had called him by his given name? Dammit, he couldn't remember, never allowed anyone to get that close to him anymore, even Robert.

"I'm no serving maid. Do it yourself."

"But I can't reach."

"I don't care." He set his jaw and snapped his fingers at Robert. "Come here and help my wife, not that she deserves it."

He walked around to face her, received the benefit of the warm smile she meant for Robert, and headed for the door.

"I'll bid you good night, then."

She opened her eyes wide. "You're leaving?"

"What did you expect? Did you imagine I'd be so delighted to see you that I'd drag you straight into bed and fuck you?"

Her expression stilled. "No, hardly that. Good night, then."

He inclined his head a glacial inch and walked out, heard her start to chat to Robert and Robert's warm laughter in return. They'd always gotten along well, and he'd been selfishly glad of it in the early years of his marriage. It was only a few feet back to his bedchamber, but it felt like a mile. He glanced back at Jane's door and scowled. Robert had better be quick about unlacing her, or he would feel the edge of his master's temper. How dare she turn up and act as if she had a right to be here?

He flung open his door, steadied himself against the frame and stared at his large four-poster bed. But, devil take it, she did have a right. She was, after all, his legally wedded wife.

"Are you all right, my lady?"

As her stays and gown were loosened, Jane gripped the front of her bodice to stop it falling down and turned to Robert.

"Yes, thank you for your help."

His smile was warm, his slight Welsh accent as soft as butter. Despite knowing he was Blaize's lover, they'd always had a good relationship.

"You're welcome." He hesitated, one eye on the door her husband had just slammed behind him. "Is there anything else I can do for you?"

"Not tonight, although I would appreciate it if you could arrange for one of the maids to help me get dressed in the morning. The rest of my baggage is still in the hall, so I'll have to make do with this gown until I can unpack properly. I wouldn't want to face Lord Minshom in my nightgown."

"Neither would I." Robert bowed. "If it helps, I'm glad you are here. The master has gotten himself into a devilishly difficult situation."

"I gathered that from your letters." She sighed. "I doubt he'll let me help him, though."

"He probably won't, my lady, but we can hope. Give me your gown and I'll have it pressed and freshened for you. I'll also arrange for a maid to attend you in the morning." He hesitated by the door. "Sleep well, and I pray I'll see you tomorrow."

"Why? Are you worried I might not survive the night?"

Robert grinned. "I don't think his lordship has quite sunk to those depths, ma'am, but maybe you should lock the door into his suite, just in case."

Jane waited until he left and sank down into the nearest chair. Her knees were still shaking, her breathing as ragged as her thoughts. Blaize's study had stunk of brandy, and glass had littered the fireplace. Was that how he lived now? In a permanent drunken stupor, not caring if anyone saw him use Robert to satisfy his unnatural sexual appetite?

But perhaps having caught him at such a disadvantage had worked in her favor. He'd backed down and allowed her to stay at least for one night. When she'd first seen the cool detached rage in his pale blue eyes, she'd wanted to run away, wanted to forget her stupid notion of making peace with him.

But that was never the best way to deal with her husband. He pounced on any show of weakness with the speed and ferocity of a starving cat. It was her lack of fear that had first won his interest and brought about their marriage ten years previously. Jane bit her lip. Not that that had proved to be much of a success . . .

On the long journey to London from Cheshire, she'd spent many hours wondering how Blaize would look, if the depravities of his lifestyle would be reflected on his countenance. To her dismay, he was as fascinating as ever. His gaze colder, perhaps, the pure line of his jaw and high cheekbones more sharply defined, but hardly the debauched drunkard portrayed in the satirical cartoons in the newspapers.

She got up and hurried to check that the door between the two suites was indeed locked. The thought of waking up with Blaize's hands around her throat wasn't pleasant. She returned to the fire, made sure it wasn't smoking and stepped out of her gown and stays. Her suite of rooms didn't look as neglected and unused as she'd assumed. They'd even been redecorated in soft shades of blue and lavender, her favorite colors. But then knowing Blaize's sexual appetite, they probably hadn't remained empty for long . . .

Her nightgown felt cold against her skin, and she crouched down beside the fire to warm her hands. There was no water to wash in and nothing to slake her thirst. She certainly wasn't prepared to draw attention to her presence in the house by requesting anything. She was here, and she was not going to leave until she and Blaize had explored what needed to be said.

She shivered despite the building heat. Knowing her cynical, malicious, enthralling husband, she didn't expect her task to be quick or easy at all.